Wicked Scars

JANE BLYTHE

Cover designed by RBA Designs

❀ Created with Vellum

Acknowledgments

I'd like to thank everyone who played a part in bringing this story to life. Particularly my mom who is always there to share her thoughts and opinions with me. My wonderful cover designer Letitia who did an amazing job with this stunning cover. My fabulous editor Lisa for all the hard work she puts into polishing my work. My awesome team, Sophie, Robyn, and Clayr, without your help I'd never be able to run my street team. And my fantastic street team members who help share my books with every share, comment, and like!

And of course a big thank you to all of you, my readers! Without you I wouldn't be living my dreams of sharing the stories in my head with the world!

CHAPTER One

March 27th
 11:10 P.M.

Was he dead?

Because it certainly felt like he had to be.

Pain, unlike anything he had ever experienced before, raged inside his skull.

Axel "Axe" Lindon was not a novice when it came to pain. The physical or the emotional kind. He'd had concussions before, been shot and stabbed, and even suffered some burns to his back in a Delta Force mission gone wrong.

But none of it compared to this.

The only thing worse than the agony tearing apart his brain was the pain that came from knowing the woman he loved no longer loved him back.

With that thought, awareness seeped back in. He wasn't dead, but he had been blown up in an explosion.

The key found at the bottom of the ocean amongst the broken remains of a yacht that had almost exploded with him and his team on board, had led them here. To a warehouse just three hours from the secluded compound where Axe lived with his friends, the other members of Prey Security's Bravo Team.

A place he lived with his wife.

All except those eight hellishly long months she had been missing.

Whatever had happened to her during those months had caused her brain to completely wipe itself blank. Beth no longer knew who she was or who he was, but worst of all, she no longer remembered the love they had shared.

Desperate for answers, any answers, anything that provided him with a bridge to reach the wife he loved and had failed, they had jumped on the key without taking the time to properly research the area, the building, or the owners.

Now, he was paying the price for that rash decision.

As was his team.

Somehow, worry for the men he considered his brothers gave him the strength he needed to stagger to his feet.

It was raining if the moisture dripping into his eyes was anything to go by. When he lifted a shaking hand to brush the water out of his eyes, his hand came away sticky.

Not water.

Blood.

His blood.

And from the way it was gushing down his face, he knew it wasn't good.

Shoving the pain into a box, Axe did his best to compartmentalize it as he did a mental check of his body. Since he was standing, he didn't think he had spinal injuries, and while he ached and throbbed all over, there was nothing other than his head that stood out as a major concern. Bumps and bruises he could work with, the head injury might be a different story, but he was conscious, aware, and could move, so it couldn't be all that bad.

Stumbling as he walked, he checked to see if his comms were still in place. Somehow, despite being thrown what had to be close to ten feet from the door he'd been entering when he set off the explosion, Axe found that it was.

"Guys, report," he said into the device, praying he got five responses. These five men meant the world to him. Next to Beth, there was nobody he loved more than the men who had served under him on their Delta Force team before targets were painted on their backs by notorious Russian oligarch and human trafficker wanted across the globe, Leonid Baranov. They were so close that after their Delta careers were tanked, they came together to work for the world-renowned Prey Security.

If any of them had died because of his impatience, he would never forgive himself.

"I'm with Scorpion, his arm is trapped beneath debris but he's conscious," Gabriel "Tank" Dawson's voice came through the comms.

Relief that two of his men were alive was only minimal.

That still left three to go.

"You injured?" he asked Tank.

"Cuts and bruises. Nothing serious," Tank replied.

"Stay with Scorpion," he ordered. Just because it appeared that the warehouse had been unoccupied didn't mean that someone wasn't waiting nearby to take them out if they survived the explosion. Mason "Scorpion" Markson had only just learned that his girlfriend was pregnant with his baby. It would break Jessica's heart if anything happened to the man she loved and would leave her once again alone to handle the responsibilities life piled onto her.

No other voices echoed down the comms line, so staggering as he went, Axe turned to his right—since Tank and Scorpion had been on his left—and began walking. Fire danced from the remains of the building, rubble and debris were everywhere, and if they hadn't already, it was only a matter of time before the local fire department would be notified.

He made it around the corner where he saw Sebastian "Rock" Rockman leaning over a prone body. It had to be either Patrick "Trick" Kramer or Rafe "Panther" Neal because they were the only two who he hadn't had an update on.

His gait was unsteady as he staggered toward the two and dropped onto his knees. Rock was kneeling beside Panther, and the man had a piece of debris embedded in his side. Panther's eyes were closed, and in the eerie red glow from the fire, he looked far too pale.

"You good?" he asked Rock. Just because the man was giving first aid didn't mean it could be assumed that he wasn't injured himself.

"Yeah, man. Cuts and bumps, nothing serious," Rock replied.

"Panther?" Whatever Rock was using to press against Panther's wounds to slow the bleeding was already soaked.

"Other than this, I couldn't see any other wounds. He's losing a lot of blood, but as long as help gets here soon, he should be fine."

Help.

Right.

He'd thought of the fire department but hadn't called this in.

They couldn't rely on someone seeing the fire.

Not when the lives of his teammates were on the line.

"You okay, Axe?"

Rock's voice suddenly seemed very far away, and the pain in his head was getting worse, not better.

But he didn't have time to not be okay.

Four of his friends were accounted for, but that still left Trick.

"Trick, got to find him," he mumbled as he shoved onto his feet, very nearly losing his balance and falling right back down again.

"You should sit down, Axe. You don't look good, man," Rock called out.

No doubt his friend was right, but he had to find Trick.

Couldn't live with himself if one of his men died because he'd come rushing in to check out this potential lead without doing his due diligence.

Should have waited.

Should have followed procedure.

It was all his fault.

Now they wouldn't find any answers in the warehouse because anything in there was destroyed, and he might have lost one of his friends.

Failed Beth.

Failed his team.

Failed.

Failure.

The words tumbled restlessly inside his head as he somehow managed to circle around the building, but there was no sign of Trick.

Had he been inside the warehouse when it blew?

Surely, if his friend had, there was no way he could have survived.

But if Trick was in there, he had to at least attempt to get him out.

"Axe, don't," Rock yelled as he stumbled toward the building.

Ignoring his friend, he went through the door closest to where Trick would have entered. The fire wasn't quite as bad back here. It was on the opposite side from where Axe had entered and set off the explosives.

Still, there was smoke and flames, and his head was hurting so badly he could barely function.

Spotting what looked like a shoe partially buried under what used to be a wall, Axe somehow managed to get over to it.

Trick.

It didn't matter if the man was already dead or still alive, either way, he had to get him out. Grabbing hold of Trick under the armpits, he began to pull him toward the door.

These men all had families. Tank was engaged to Tillie, they were getting married in just a few weeks. Rock and Ariel were getting married in the summer. Scorpion and Jessica planned to marry before their baby arrived. Trick and Stephanie were still healing from their ordeal earlier in the year and were very much in love. Panther had an eight-year-old son and had literally just found out he was having a baby with Elle, adding child number three to their soon-to-be blended family.

Whatever happened, their loved ones needed to get them back.

He might have been the first member of their team to fall in love, but now he was the only one who was alone.

Beth didn't remember loving him and didn't seem to want to try to get back to where they had been before.

Living with his wife under his roof, but not really there was hell.

It had been almost a year since she returned with no memories, and yet she hadn't made an ounce of progress getting them back.

Hopeless.

That's how the whole thing felt.

Like the best thing to do for her was to just walk away, give her a divorce, set her up anywhere in the world she wanted to be, and give her a chance at starting her life over.

When you loved someone, sometimes you had to do what was best for them even if it killed you.

And it just might kill him to let her go.

Fresh air suddenly filled his lungs.

Voices shouted.

Sirens shrieked much too loudly for his throbbing head.

The flash of red and blue lights seemed to cut right through his eyes, and then his vision just seemed to go black.

Axe knew he was falling but didn't have the energy to remain on his feet.

Blackness descended and swept him away.

March 27th
    11:27 P.M.

Was it really too much to ask for one good night of sleep?

Just because Beth Lindon didn't remember herself or her past, she didn't need to in order to know that sleep had always been something she was lacking. It was written into her body's DNA, the way it seemed to know exactly how to adjust to living on little to no sleep.

Throwing back the covers, she sat up and massaged her temples, willing her memories to return to her.

She was pretty sure everyone here on the compound believed she didn't *want* to get her memories back, but they couldn't be more wrong.

It was what she craved.

Knowing that mixed with the good would be a whole lot of bad made it a terrifying prospect, but that didn't mean she didn't want it.

One thing she knew was that she was no coward.

It was weird because, while she literally had no memories beyond arriving at the compound almost a year ago, she *felt* certain things about herself and knew them to be true even though she had no proof. It was almost like some things weren't memories, they were feelings, and her body still had access to them.

The most important being her love for Axel.

Just because she didn't remember him or the life they had shared, he was, in essence, a stranger, even if she had lived under his roof for the last eleven months, her love for him was ingrained into her.

Not that Axel would believe that.

He thought the distance between them was because she didn't know who he was and didn't want to. He hadn't said anything, but she knew he blamed himself for her being kidnapped.

But the reason she kept her distance wasn't that she didn't want to be with him, it was because she knew she was too damaged inside to be able to give him what he deserved. Eleven months without so much as a glimmer of a memory of the time before she ran back onto the compound last April was proof of that.

She kept her distance *because* she loved him.

Because she wanted what was best for him.

And what was best for him wasn't her.

Climbing out of bed, she rubbed at her chest above her heart as she wandered out of the guest bedroom in Axel's cabin. It hurt so badly to know that she wasn't what was best for the man she loved. But she loved him enough to let him go and find happiness with someone who could be there for him in the ways he needed. Watching the members of Axel's team—men she knew loved her like a baby sister even though she didn't remember them—falling in love had just proved that to her over and over again.

She saw the way Tillie loved Tank, the way Ariel loved Rock, the way Jessica loved Scorpion, the way Stephanie loved Trick, and the way Elle loved Panther. She saw it all and knew she was no longer capable of loving Axel that same way. She was a failure as a wife, a failure as a friend, and a failure as a person.

So, she had to keep her distance, and sooner or later, Axel would be forced to acknowledge what she already knew.

After Axel divorced her, Beth wasn't quite sure what would happen to her. He was a good man and would probably allow her to stay, but how could she live there and watch him fall in love and marry someone else? Watch him have children someday?

Finding herself in Axel's bedroom, Beth stared at the neatly made bed. Unlike the guest bedroom, which she had moved into when she showed up there a year ago, it was dark. The dark scared her, and she didn't have to remember exactly what had happened to her to know why. Whatever it was, was bad enough that her brain decided wiping out her entire memory was the preferable option rather than attempting to deal with it.

After switching on the light, she crept over to the bed.

Beth wasn't really sure why she was creeping. She was alone in the cabin, and it was close to midnight. Everyone else would be in their beds, and the other cabins were nowhere close to Axel's.

Still, she felt the need to creep, maybe because this space didn't feel like hers. The nightstand was obviously the way she had left it the day she'd been abducted. A book she must have been reading was there, and there was a framed photo of her and Axel on what was obviously their wedding day. A teddy bear was also sitting there, and a little angel figurine.

The photo of the two of them wasn't the only one in the room. There was one on the other nightstand, and a large canvas picture of the two of them on the wall above the bed. It was obvious that Axel hadn't moved or changed anything in the months she'd been missing, but why hadn't he changed them in the months she'd been back?

Didn't he realize she was already lost to him?

Didn't he know she just wanted him to be happy, which was why she was doing everything she could to show him she was no good for him?

Why was he so determined to stand by her?

By now, he should have gotten frustrated with her and told her that he wanted to divorce her and kicked her off the compound. At the least, he should have gotten angry with her and screamed at her in frustration, but he didn't do that either.

He was just always … there.

This was why when Axel was away with his team, she usually found herself in his bedroom, slipping beneath the covers and curling up surrounded by Axel's scent. While her mind had no memory of him, knew only what she had been told or managed to put together from things people had said, her body felt differently.

When Axel was nearby, she was filled with a longing to reach out to him, lay her head on his firm chest, and have those muscled arms of his wrap around her. He would offer her his strength and take her burdens so she didn't have to carry them, Beth knew that without a shadow of a doubt, but how selfish would it be of her to make him?

He had everything to offer her, but she had nothing to offer him.

Nothing was going to change that.

Unlike usual, tonight she didn't get the same sense of peace as she lay in Axel's bed. No matter how hard she tried to reach for it, it remained tantalizingly out of reach. Axel's scent was there like it always was, but for some reason, he felt so far away from her.

With a disappointed sigh, Beth climbed out of the bed, stripping off the sheets and carrying them to the laundry room. Every time she crept into his bed while he was away, she washed the sheets after. The last thing she wanted to do was leave behind the scent of her shampoo or body wash and let on that she found comfort in his bed. Leading Axel on was the last thing she wanted to do. Hurting him wasn't her goal, in fact, she was doing everything she could to minimize the damage she was inflicting.

After putting clean sheets on the bed, she threw the old sheets and all the towels into the washing machine so Axel wouldn't wonder why she was washing just the sheets from his bed, and turned it on.

Then feeling lost and so very alone, Beth walked outside onto the deck. Despite no memories, and despite knowing not only had she been kidnapped but she was still in danger, she felt completely safe out there on the compound. The woods the buildings were nestled in filled her with peace. She loved the wildlife, loved the fresh air, loved the snow, and the sunshine. A river ambled through the woods, and when the weather had been warm, she would go out there and swim or lie on the dock and soak up the sun's rays. As soon as summer returned, she was going to get back out there, drink up as much nature as she could, and figure out the rest of her life.

Because one thing had become clear to her over the last few months, watching the men of Bravo Team fall hard and fast, was that she couldn't remain there indefinitely.

Yes, this place made her feel safe, and no, she had no idea what she would do when she left. She'd never been to school and had no high school diploma, let alone a college degree. She didn't know what she was good at or how she would support herself, but being there was starting to feel wrong.

She couldn't be the woman Axel and the others wanted her to be.

That woman had died a year ago.

There was no going back, her past was gone, lost to her forever, it was time to stop hiding, time to stop waiting for something to happen. It was time for Beth to take control of her future, and unfortunately, that meant leaving the compound and Axel.

CHAPTER *Two*

March 27th
11:59 P.M.

Everything felt so far away.

Axe felt lost.

Like he was floating.

Trapped in the darkness and unable to find his way out.

Through the crushing pain, one thought kept screaming for his attention.

Beth.

She needed him, and yet he felt like he was being dragged away from her.

It didn't matter that this last year he had been unable to help her remember who she was and her life before she was taken. That he hadn't been able to crack through the wall she had erected around herself to keep everyone else at a distance. Every time he looked at her, it felt like losing her all over again.

All that mattered was that he knew deep down that she needed him.

Knew it.

In a way he couldn't express.

Beth was *his*.

That he knew.

The only family she'd had kept her locked up and abused her. Sexually, physically, emotionally, and psychologically. You name it, and it had been done to Beth from the time she was born. She'd never attended school, taken a dance class, or played a soccer game. Had no friends outside a couple of female cousins who lived the same horrific life she did.

From bad to worse, when she reached her teens, her parents grew tired of her and sold her to Leonid Baranov, a well-known buyer of trafficking victims, which was where he and his team had rescued her from six years ago.

As soon as he had laid eyes on her he knew.

She was his.

A part of him.

The other half of his heart.

His soulmate.

At the time, Axe hadn't even believed such things existed. In the world of money he had been raised in, marriage was about forming strategic partnerships that advanced both families' wealth and prestige. It had little to do with love. His parents hadn't loved one another, and they hadn't loved him. He was an heir to carry on the family name, and when he had abandoned the family real estate empire to join the military, he had been all but disowned.

His team had become his family, and he considered them all brothers, but Beth wasn't just his wife, she was a part of him.

It's why he could never leave her and had to fight now.

"Axe, come on, man, stay with us."

The voice was familiar, and he knew he should be able to place it, but he was too overcome with fear for Beth.

What would she do without him?

His team loved her like a little sister, they would take care of her, but she'd still be on her own.

Always on her own.

Sudden crushing pain in his chest stole his breath.

Stole his ability to think.

"Damn it," a voice muttered. "We're going to lose him."

Unfortunately, that was probably true.

It was weird, but he could feel his life slipping away, although he tried to cling to it for Beth's sake.

He'd never known you could feel your life like this. It always just was. But now it felt like a thing inside him, almost like he was a bottle of water someone had poked a hole in, and now that water was draining out. Only it wasn't water it was his life.

Something pressed against his chest, and the searing pain had him grunting, his eyes flying open as he tried to jerk up, dislodge whatever had caused him the pain.

The light was too bright for his eyes, and even if it wasn't blinding him, he found his vision blurry at best.

Hands grabbed at him, pressed at him, pushed him down, and held him there when he tried to fight them off.

He had to get Beth.

Had to tell her he was sorry.

Had to beg her to remember him because he didn't want to die a stranger to the woman he loved more than anything else in this world.

"Stop fighting us, man," the voice from before urged.

Rock.

The voice belonged to Rock.

And when Axe blinked his eyes and willed them to clear, he could see his friend leaning over him.

"You with me?" Rock asked.

A single nod was all the answer he could manage.

"You must have cracked some ribs when the explosion went off, and you were thrown backward. Pulling Trick out of the building must have snapped one of them and it has punctured your lung. You're in an ambulance and we put in a chest tube to help you breathe. You'll be at the hospital soon," Rock told him.

"Trick?" he asked. He'd had no idea whether his friend was dead or alive when he found him inside partially buried beneath debris.

"Concussion and some smoke inhalation, but he's going to be okay, he's on his way to the hospital in another ambulance," Rock answered.

Rock was here, so his friend seemed to be okay, but when he searched his memories, he remembered that Tank had been with Scorpion who was trapped with his arm pinned, and Rock had been tending to Panther who had something embedded in his side.

"Panther?" he asked, one-word sentences seemed to be all he could manage through the pain.

"Lost a bit of blood, he's being rushed to the hospital as well. He'll need emergency surgery to remove the piece of wood that impaled his side, but he should make a full recovery," Rock told him.

"Scorpion?"

"He's still at the scene. They're working on unpinning his arm, but it sounds like he was lucky. He's trapped, but the pressure is mostly on the debris piled around his arm, it's kind of in a bubble, he can't get it out, but it doesn't look like the damage will be too severe," Rock assured him.

His men were alive. At least his impulsiveness hadn't gotten anyone killed.

Yet.

Two of his guys were on the way to the hospital and a third would be following. Just because Rock and Tank didn't appear to have serious injuries didn't mean shock wasn't masking something.

All of this was on him.

If he had just waited, let Panther do his thing and dig up as much intel as he could on the warehouse, they wouldn't be in this position.

This was precisely why he had stepped down as Bravo Team leader when Beth was first taken. He'd known he couldn't devote the mental energy it took to successfully lead a team and keep everyone alive while his wife was missing and in danger. But after she'd come home, and as the distance between them seemed to grow, he'd slowly taken the role back over from Tank, although the two of them worked closely together.

"Sorry," he croaked through his dry throat, dry mouth, hell, even his skin felt dry.

"Not your fault," Rock assured him.

They both knew it was a lie.

Just because his team hadn't called him out on rushing in to check the warehouse out as soon as they linked it to the key didn't mean they all didn't know it had been a mistake.

A mistake that had almost cost them their lives.

A mistake that would have left the women they loved all alone and their children to grow up fatherless.

His mistake.

His fault.

"Sorry," he repeated. He wanted to say so much more, but he could still feel his life dripping away. He didn't have a lot of time and he needed his friends to know he hadn't intended to put their lives in danger.

"It's okay, Axe. We all wanted answers for Beth, we all wanted to go rushing in there. It's on all of us."

It wasn't, but he didn't have the energy or the time to argue the point.

He needed to say one more thing before he let the inevitable happen and his life slip through his fingers.

"Beth," he said.

"As soon as we get you to the hospital, we'll call her, Ariel, and the others to let them know what happened."

Axe shook his head. He wasn't going to make it that long. "Tell her ... I love her ..." he gasped out, the pressure in his chest increased at the same rate as the pain in his head. Already the edges of his vision were starting to go black.

"You'll tell her yourself when she gets to the hospital," Rock said firmly.

Another shake of his head. He wanted to see her one last time, make sure she knew she was the center of his world whether she remembered him or not, but he wasn't delusional. Dying, yes, but crazy, no. He could feel what was happening to his body, he just couldn't stop it.

"Take care of her," he said, managing to lift one of his hands, which felt like it was encased in concrete, and grabbing Rock's, squeezing it with every ounce of energy he had left.

Rock's gray eyes filled with empathy. "If the worst happens, man, you know we all have Beth's back. We'll take care of her and make sure she never feels alone, but you have to fight for her, Axe. She fought like hell to get home to you, you can't give up. She needs you."

He knew that.

Knew his wife was a fighter, that she would survive this like she had survived all the rest of the hell life had thrown at her.

But that was just it, he didn't want his girl to have to fight anymore.

All he'd ever wanted to do was give her the safe place she'd always lacked, the love she had been forced to live without for the first eighteen years of her life.

He'd failed.

And now he was going to fail her again.

Beth hadn't felt safe enough to let her memories return, and now he was going to die and leave her all alone.

The blackness grew, the sounds around him faded, and although he clawed to hang onto life, it was too late.

It had already drained away.

~

March 28th
  12:34 A.M.

Usually, the moonlight, the cool air, the soft sounds of the night, the rustle of trees in the gentle breeze, and the hoot of an owl all served to reassure her. Calm her.

But not tonight.

Tonight, Beth's anxiety seemed to be continually ramping up.

It made no sense.

This wasn't something new. Every night she couldn't sleep. If Axel was away, she would sneak into his room and get a couple of hours of sleep in his bed. If he was home, she would bake in the kitchen or come outside to stroll the grounds. Sometimes, she would paint. She wasn't all that good at it, but it was a technique her therapist had taught her, and most times painting her feelings helped.

Nothing was helping tonight though.

Not even sitting at the edge of the pier with her bare feet dangling in the cold water. Like always, the water was cold on her skin, but she liked the chill, it usually distracted her from the worries that fought constantly inside her.

It was exhausting.

Although her doctor told her not to, it was hard not to try to force her memories to return. Hours had been spent out there, sitting surrounded by nature that shared its beauty with her and didn't push any expectations on her, trying to will her memory back into existence.

The harder she tried to force it, the further away it seemed to go.

And the way that every person there who had known her before looked at her, so expectantly, like at any second she might suddenly remember all of them, just made it worse.

She was failing everyone.

Maybe it would be better for all of them, not just Axel, if she wasn't there.

Then they could be free to move on with their lives without worrying about her. She didn't want their concern. Okay, that was kind of a lie. It *did* help to know she wasn't completely alone, but being surrounded by people on the outside didn't help the loneliness on the inside.

The loneliness was slowly smothering her. Beth didn't need her memories to know it was a feeling she was intimately acquainted with.

Over the last eleven months, she'd picked up bits and pieces of her life, even though her doctor had said nobody should push her to remember but allow her memories to come back on their own when her subconscious felt safe enough to do so. She knew that she had no family, that her family had hurt her, then eventually, she had wound up the prisoner of the notorious human trafficker Leonid Baranov. That was how she'd met Axel and Bravo Team. They'd saved her life, and because she had nowhere else to go had also taken her under their wing.

Which they were still doing six years later.

Still looking after her like she was a broken little bird who couldn't fly on her own.

The more they thought it, the more she believed it.

And honestly, they weren't even wrong.

She had no memory, no skills, no education, and no way to support herself, she was a broken bird and no amount of wishing on any of their parts could change that.

Helplessness washed over her, and because she was alone out there, Beth allowed herself the freedom to shed a few tears. For the woman she could have been if life didn't seem so determined to break her. For the woman who had been lost along the way and might never return. For the woman she was now who was so scared, so alone, and so terrified she was broken beyond repair that a future of any sort seemed next to impossible.

"Beth?"

Startled, she quickly scrubbed at her wet cheeks and scrambled to her feet, almost slipping and losing her balance as water sloshed on the smooth wooden planks of the pier.

Who was out here calling her name at this time of the morning?

"Beth, are you there?" It was Tillie's voice, and it sounded scared.

Fear echoed inside her at the other woman's tone, and she hurried down the pier. "I'm here. What's wrong?"

So many things could be wrong, starting with Axel and the guys being off on a mission. He hadn't told her where he was going when he left, but she assumed it had something to do with her and what had happened to her while she was missing. Two children lived on the compound, either of which could have gotten sick or hurt. There were also two pregnant women, Beth prayed it was nothing to do with Jessica or Elle's unborn babies.

And, of course, there was a chance that one of Bravo Team's enemies had found them and were attacking the compound right this very second.

"Are you okay?" Tillie asked her when they met at the end of the pier. The light from the flashlight on Tillie's phone showed how worried her friend looked, but was it just because she was wondering why Beth was out here after midnight or because something was very wrong?

The sour feeling in her gut said that it was the latter.

"What's wrong?" she asked. This wasn't about her, not everything was about her, and she hated how everyone was always trying to prioritize her needs even when other people were going through trials of their own.

She wasn't so weak and pathetic she didn't know how to be there for the people she loved and cared about. And whether she remembered them or not, she loved each of the men on Bravo Team and the women they had fallen for. They were her big brothers, and she would support them any way she could if they just gave her a chance.

While she could admit she was fragile, she wasn't going to shatter into a million pieces because someone else needed care and attention.

"Tank called and said to gather everyone together," Tillie told her.

So at least it wasn't anything to do with the kids or the pregnancies. "What for?"

Fear was etched into every one of Tillie's features, evident even in the thin light of the phone and the moon. "He didn't say."

Wanting to soothe away that fear but not knowing what to say, Beth just reached out and grabbed Tillie's hand, squeezing it tightly. "At least you know he's okay, right? I mean, you talked to him so he can't be hurt or captured or anything."

How would she face these women who had come to mean a lot to her, even if they probably didn't realize it, if their men died because of her? Because they were chasing down a lead about who had taken her. They thought she needed answers to move on, and in some ways they were right, but what she needed more than that was to be a person, not just the poor young woman with amnesia.

She needed to be Beth.

Just Beth.

"Yeah, at least we know Tank is okay," Tillie mumbled, and what her friend meant clicked into place.

They knew *Tank* was okay. But what about the others?

What about Axel?

Fear pummeled her at the thought of anything happening to him. He had to be okay. He had to. There was simply no other option.

Now in a hurry to get to the others, both she and Tillie began to run as they headed for the main building that housed some offices, conference rooms, and the guys' hangout space. Everyone else was already there, including the kids who had been bundled up and were asleep on the couch while everyone else sat around the table.

"They're here," Ariel said into the phone at her ear, and Beth took that to mean that Rock was okay as well.

Two guys accounted for, but what about the other four?

What about her Axel?

Ariel nodded at whatever Rock said to her, and a moment later, she turned the phone around and they could all see Rock standing in what was clearly a hospital.

Beth felt her knees wobble.

It was bad news.

She knew that.

Had felt it all night.

Something was very wrong with Axel.

"The warehouse we went to tonight was rigged to explode," Rock told them. His face was dusty and smeared with blood, and his clothes were torn in places and likewise dirty and bloody.

Whose blood?

Rock's own, or one of the others?

"Tank and I are okay, minor injuries. Scorpion was trapped by his arm beneath some rubble, but I heard they almost have him free and the damage is minimal," Rock told them.

Jessica's hands flew to her face, and she choked on a sob, tears streaming down her cheeks as one of her hands moved to caress her stomach where her and Scorpion's baby was growing.

"Trick has a concussion, and Panther was impaled by a piece of debris, he's already been taken into surgery. They're both serious but stable," Rock continued.

Relief covered Stephanie and Elle's features, and both women began to cry, Elle looking over to the two sleeping children while rubbing her pregnant belly just as Jessica had done.

It wasn't until five sets of eyes—six if you counted Rock's—turned to stare at her that she realized she was taking short, sharp, panting breaths, bordering on hyperventilating. Rock was giving the news out from best to worst.

Axel was the worst.

But how bad was he?

Was he dead?

Dying even at this very second?

Her stomach churned with nausea and a headache began to pulse between her temples.

"Say it," she whispered, needing to hear whatever it was.

"Axe punctured a lung, and he has a serious head injury," Rock said gently. "His condition is listed as critical."

Critical.

She knew what that meant.

It meant she was about to lose him.

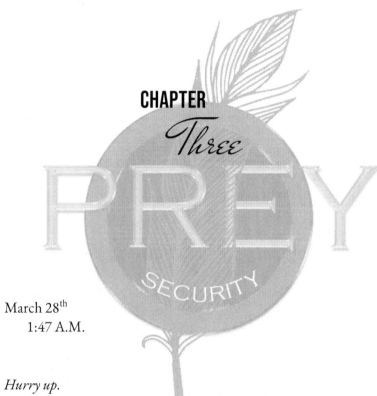

CHAPTER
Three

March 28th
 1:47 A.M.

Hurry up.

Beth silently urged Ariel to drive faster. This was the first time since she returned to the compound that she hadn't remembered was her home that she wished she knew how to drive.

Maybe she did. Who knows. She didn't know much about herself, and nobody wanted to tell her anything because the doctor's orders said she should be left so her memories could return on their own.

Even if she didn't know how to drive, it didn't look all that hard, stomp on the gas and steer with the wheel. Surely, even she could manage to do that. And if she was driving, they'd be going a whole lot faster than Ariel was currently driving.

They'd left the countryside behind them twenty minutes ago, and the more they drove the more lights, buildings, and other vehicles began to surround them. They had to be close to the hospital by now, didn't they?

Since turning back up at the compound, she hadn't left it ... until now.

Because she was a coward.

A coward who would rather hide than face the complete and utter mess her life was in. Shambles. It was really the only way to describe it. The problem was she didn't know how to go about fixing it.

How did you fix something that seemed like it was beyond repair?

If only Beth could find an answer to that question, then maybe she could finally stop being the broken bird everyone saw her as. After all, so far, she hadn't done anything to contradict their notion even if she hated it.

"Almost there," Elle soothed, and Beth realized that she had been twisting her hands together so tightly her knuckles had gone white.

Here she was freaking out like she was the only one who was scared. Elle and Panther were having a baby, she had a daughter, and he had a son, they were already a family, and Beth could only guess how terrified the other woman must be to think she might have to raise their little family alone.

But at least Panther and Trick were both stable.

Unlike Axel.

She might have amnesia, but that didn't make her stupid, she knew critical meant he could die at any moment.

What if he was already dead?

After Rock's call, they'd all thrown on clothes, waited until Mrs. Pfeffer had arrived to watch eight-year-old Andy and seven-year-old Ruthie, and jumped into Ariel's vehicle since it was the only one big enough to fit all six of them. They hadn't called Rock back, and he hadn't contacted them again, so there was every chance that by the time they arrived at the hospital, Axel would have already passed away.

Tears were rolling in a nearly continuous stream down her cheeks since Rock had broken the news about the guys, and Beth didn't have the energy to do anything about them. All her energy was focused on not falling apart.

Hysterics weren't going to help right now.

If Axel was still alive, he was going to need her.

When was the last time someone had ever needed her?

Had anyone ever needed her?

As in needed her for her, not just because she was a warm body who could be used and abused.

For eleven months she'd felt useless, like a burden. No one ever asked anything of her, and even though she helped when and how she could, it always felt like people thought they were somehow taking advantage of her by letting her help. Like she was some poor, pathetic, fragile little girl who had to be protected above all else.

Beth hated it.

No one wanted to feel like a burden, yet that's how Axel and the others made her feel. This, in turn, made her feel bad about herself because not only was she a burden, but she was resentful of them pointing it out to her even though she knew they meant well and were only trying to protect her because they loved her.

When Elle held out a hand to her, Beth didn't hesitate to grab it and hold on.

At least whatever happened she wasn't alone.

Axel's friends were her family, and that made their women her family, too. Just because she had no family of her own didn't make her all alone in the world.

If the worst happened, that would be what she had to cling to.

But no matter how many times she reminded herself of that, and even knew it to be true, a voice in her head whispered that Axel had once been her everything. She might not remember it, but she still knew it to be true. Without him, she *would* be all alone even if surrounded by people.

Finally, they pulled into the hospital parking lot. It was the middle of the night, which thankfully meant there were parking spaces in the lot. As soon as Ariel had parked, they all jumped out of the car and ran for the emergency room doors.

The second they stepped inside, they spotted Rock and Tank.

The men had obviously been watching the door because as soon as the six of them ran through it they were crossing the busy room.

There was no hesitation on either of the men, or either of the women's parts. They just launched themselves at one another. Tank caught Tillie as she jumped into his arms, and Rock dragged Ariel up against him, both couples hugging, kissing, and crying.

More tears stung her eyes as she watched them.

Even if Axel hadn't been so badly hurt, she wouldn't have jumped into his arms like that. She would have felt awkward and distant, every bit the stranger she was. Axel wouldn't have grabbed and kissed her like Tank and Rock had done, he would have been too worried about upsetting her. He was so focused on doing everything the doctor told him he should do to think about finding out what she needed him to do.

And she was too cowardly to tell him what she needed.

They were stuck in a stupid circle, and one that felt incredibly immature in this moment. It was plain to see that Axel loved her, and she knew she must have loved him deeply, too. If they both stopped pretending, maybe they could find that love again or build a new love, different but still special.

But it seemed neither of them were prepared to make the first move.

And now it might be too late.

As though he just remembered the rest of them, Rock turned to them, keeping Ariel tucked close against his side. "Scorpion arrived here not long after I got off the phone. He was lucky, the break in his arm is a clean one and doesn't need surgery, just a cast for a few weeks. He's waiting in an exam room to get it put on. Trick is in there, too. He's still groggy, but he's been in and out of consciousness."

Jessica and Stephanie hugged one another, both women crying tears of relief to know the men they loved were relatively unharmed.

"Panther is in surgery," Rock continued, "but I spoke with the surgeon and he expects everything to go smoothly. Ariel and I will take you up to the surgical waiting room," he said to Elle.

Again, that left everyone else accounted for except her Axel.

Beth knew it wasn't by accident that Rock had left mentioning him until last. It was because he was either dead and nothing could be done for him, or he was close to death and he was worried about telling her that.

Slowly, Rock's gray eyes shifted to meet hers.

She felt his pain, his reluctance to tell her anything.

He wanted to wrap her up in cotton wool and put her in a bubble wrap covered room.

But he couldn't.

Reality was reality, and they all had to face it.

This wasn't something anyone could protect her from.

Tentatively, she took a step closer, facing her demons head-on for once rather than trying to run from them. "Axel?"

"He's in a trauma room, sweetie. They're doing everything they can for him." Keeping one arm around Ariel, he reached out with his other to grab her hand, tugging her closer so he could hug her.

"So, he's still alive?" It sounded like he was, but honestly, she needed to hear it be said aloud before she could allow herself to believe it.

"Yeah, sweetie, he's still alive," Rock assured her.

Relief had her knees wobbling but she locked them. She wasn't going to be weak anymore. Wasn't going to keep acting like a scared little girl who needed to be protected. If she wanted the others to stop treating her like an injured baby bird, she had to stop herself from acting like one.

"Can I see him?" Beth asked.

"I don't think he'd want you to see him like that, sweetie," Rock told her, using the big brother voice she simultaneously loved and hated. "Why don't you go with Tank and the others to Trick and Scorpion's room? I'll make sure the doctor knows Axe's wife is here and that they are to keep you updated as often as they can."

"No." From everyone's startles, Beth knew she had surprised them with her strong tone and clear objection. Honestly, she had surprised herself. She never said no, always did what others wanted, and was meek and mild, but no more.

If their positions were reversed, Axel would stay by her side.

Nothing would make him leave.

Nothing *had* made him leave these last eleven months when she had been pushing him away out of fear that she could never give him what he deserved.

He had been there every day, giving her space when what she really wanted was for him to break through her walls, but still always there.

Always.

She owed him the same.

~

March 30th
4:12 P.M.

More than forty-eight hours had passed since Beth had been escorted into Axel's room at the hospital.

Back then it hadn't been a real room, just a trauma bay in the emergency room where so many doctors and nurses had been buzzing about Axel that it had been completely overwhelming. He'd been hooked up to machines, there was blood all over his body, and he'd looked so vulnerable that it had shocked her.

Axel wasn't the vulnerable one in their relationship, she was.

They both knew it, everyone knew it.

But seeing him like that, so still and quiet, so exposed with his body mostly naked and no way to protect himself, had stirred up something inside her.

A protective instinct that she hadn't even known she possessed.

Whether she remembered him or not, this was her husband and she had chosen to marry him because she'd fallen in love with him. Having watched him for almost a year now, it wasn't hard to see why she had fallen. He was steady and dependable, strong and brave. He fought for the innocent to make the world a safer place, he loved his teammates, he was sweet and attentive, and he was everything anyone could ever want.

Now he needed her, and she was going to be there for him.

Hours after arriving at the hospital, he had finally been upgraded from critical to stable but serious, and Beth had naively thought the worst was over.

How stupid she had been.

The quiet room in intensive care that Axel had been moved to seemed peaceful enough, even with the hiss and beeps from machines and the nurses constantly in and out. It was a step up from the emergency room and she'd believed that everything was going to be okay.

But it wasn't.

Not even close.

Slowly, Axel's punctured lung was healing, but the injury to his head didn't seem to be. Axel just laid there, still, quiet, unconscious, trapped inside his own head, and she was beginning to get an inkling of how he must have felt all these months.

She wanted him to wake up.

She wanted him to open his eyes.

She wanted him to come back to her.

But wanting it didn't change anything, didn't make it happen.

No matter how much she prayed, how much she begged, or how many hours she sat beside his bedside holding his hand, Axel didn't wake up.

Scared to go to sleep because she wanted to be the first thing he saw when he woke, Beth had barely gotten more than snatched minutes of sleep here and there when she could no longer hold her eyes open long enough to remain awake. Luckily, lack of sleep was nothing new to her, so she was hanging in there.

All she wanted was for Axel to wake up.

She had to tell him she was sorry for keeping him at a distance these past eleven months.

How badly she wanted to go back in time and do it all differently.

If she could, she would have grabbed onto Axel, demanding that he tell her every single thing about the woman she was so she could be that person. It was the worst feeling in the world to be floundering with no stable ground to find footing on. Her doctor had been wrong, it didn't help to get your memories back on their own if those memories never actually returned. Maybe if she knew more about herself and her life, she could have gotten those memories back.

Regardless, she never should have pushed Axel away.

At the time, it seemed like the right thing to do. She couldn't be the Beth he had known and fallen in love with, that woman was probably lost forever, there was no guarantee he would want whatever woman she became shaped by this newest trauma. It was better to force distance even when you craved comfort than to be rejected.

Because deep down inside that was what she feared most of all.

The rejection of Axel's love.

Without it, she was nothing.

There was no family to fall back on, no job or life outside him and his life. Even their friends were all really his friends who had only adopted her as a little sister because of her connection to Axel.

For months she had refused to allow herself to acknowledge that the only place she wanted to be was in his arms. If she allowed herself to fall into his embrace and then he got tired of the fact that in a year from now, or two years, or five years, she still had no memory and still couldn't be the woman he knew, and he left her, it would shatter her.

Whining about being treated like she was weak while simultaneously being weak was stupid. She should have voiced her fears, her concerns, her needs to the man who had steadfastly stood beside her, silently offering her his unwavering support.

What she wouldn't give to tell him that.

If he never woke up from the coma he had slipped into, how would she ever forgive herself?

He'd die without ever knowing that while her memories hadn't returned, her love for him was still there. Still inside her. If they had just been open with one another without tiptoeing around, maybe they wouldn't have had to live the last eleven months feeling miserable.

"Hey, sweetie, how you doing?"

At the sound of the voice, she turned to find Scorpion and Jessica standing in the doorway to Axel's room. The cast on Scorpion's arm was covered in drawings from all their Bravo family, she'd even written her name on it. It was funny, when he'd held out a handful of colored markers, she had immediately chosen the pink one. Obviously, it was her favorite color, she knew it without knowing it because she always chose pink. Beth was locked inside her head somewhere she just had to find the key to let her out.

"Axel hasn't woken up," she replied. The guys all made sure to come by regularly, it was rare for her to spend more than an hour or two at a time alone with Axel. Trick had been discharged later that same day they were brought to the hospital, and Panther was discharged yesterday. Everyone was back home now except Axel, and as long as he was there, she was there.

She wasn't leaving him alone for anything.

"Asked how *you* were doing, sweetie," Scorpion said as he came up behind the chair she was sitting in and wrapped his good arm around her chest pulling her back against him in a tight hug.

Brushing off his concern, she nodded. "Fine. I'm fine. I wasn't the one who was blown up. How's your arm?"

"Fine. I'm fine," Scorpion teased her, and she relaxed a little. If anything, this ordeal had forced her to dig deep and find her strength. No more hiding. No more cowering. It was time to fight for herself, the man she loved, and her future.

She was getting her memories back.

She wanted them, needed them because they might wind up being all she had of Axel.

If he never woke up, she didn't want all she knew of him to be this last year when everything was so messed up.

"Why don't you let us take you home so you can shower and get some proper sleep?" Jessica said, coming up beside Beth and taking her hand.

"I'm not leaving Axel." Were they crazy? If he was there, she was there. Like any one of them would leave their significant other alone in a hospital bed. What if Axel woke up and she wasn't there? What if he needed her and she was hiding at home?

What if he woke up and had amnesia like she did?

He needed her right now, she knew that, felt it. She wasn't going anywhere.

"There's nothing you can do for him right now," Scorpion reminded her gently. "And he wouldn't want you to wear yourself out. You haven't left this room since you got here."

"And I won't leave it until he does," she said firmly. It felt good to stand up for herself, to not cower. Just because she didn't know who she was didn't mean she couldn't be strong and say what she wanted. If she had been stronger all along, Axel wouldn't have been so desperate to rush off to get her answers and he wouldn't have gotten hurt. Wouldn't be lying in a hospital bed in a coma right now.

No more being weak.

No more being pathetic.

This new Beth was going to be stronger than the old one, she was going to fight. She wasn't a quitter, she didn't give up, she'd survived a lot in her life, and she wasn't going to let it break her.

"At least come to the cafeteria and get something to eat, stretch your legs," Jessica cajoled.

"No," she said firmly.

Scorpion sighed, but she could have sworn she saw a hint of pride in his gaze. Maybe this was the attitude she should have adopted early on. Okay, so those first few weeks she was in shock, hysterical, terrified, confused, and hurting, but once the shock had worn off she should have reached down deep inside and done what she always did—find a way to survive.

It had taken Axel almost dying for her to realize she had a second chance at life. She had escaped something horrific, she didn't need to remember it to know it had been awful, her body was literally littered with scars as proof. It had taken strength to do that. That strength was still inside her, she just had to find it.

She *would* find it because Axel needed her to.

Nothing else was acceptable.

She wasn't going to let him down, not ever again.

CHAPTER *Four*

April 3rd
8:32 A.M.

Don't go to sleep.
Don't go to sleep.
Don't go to sleep.

Despite Beth's best efforts, exhaustion weighed heavily upon her, and against her will, her eyes began to drift closed.

She had no idea how many hours straight she'd been awake, time had blurred into nothingness here in the hospital. Sitting beside Axel, waiting for him to wake up, whispering words she had been afraid to tell him when he was awake. Eating only when someone brought her food and forced her to consume it. She hadn't showered in the six days Axel had been in the hospital because she didn't want to be away from him for the time it would take. She left his side only to use the toilet, nothing else.

So, it was no wonder that exhaustion had finally pulled her deep enough under for her to dream.

Weird snippets of images.

A little girl who couldn't be more than three or four, with blonde pigtails and brown eyes much too serious for her age, running.

Not playing.

Running.

Like the devil was chasing her.

When her small legs finally gave out, the child collapsed onto the ground and began to cry.

Helplessness emanated from her.

But when a tall figure stalked through the trees, the tiny girl wiped away her tears, leaving dirty smudges behind on her otherwise pale cheeks, and stood, bravely facing the man with a strength that belied her young age.

"Ya know ot happen to lil girls oo run, Beth," the man snickered.

Beth?

The little girl was … her?

Although she could feel the child's fear, the little girl didn't say anything, didn't cower.

She accepted the hand life had dealt her like she wasn't a mere preschooler.

When the man grabbed the child, snatching her off the ground and holding her in a grip that hurt, she got a good look at his face.

He looked … familiar.

Her father?

No.

Her father had a large scar running across his face from just below his left eye to the corner of his mouth.

This man was her uncle.

His pockmarked face was forever burned into her memory.

Her father hurt her. Her grandfather, too. There were another two uncles and six much older cousins who all joined in abusing her. But this uncle? He was the one little Beth feared the most.

Even at four, she knew why.

The others were always drunk but not this uncle. He didn't drink which meant he wasn't impaired in any way when he assaulted her. He did it because he wanted to. Because he was pure evil.

The image faded as the man carried the little girl through the woods, back to the secluded, dilapidated house they all called home.

Her breathing was harsh, and part of Beth wanted to find a way to wake herself up. These were dreams, but they were also memories of her life as a child. She was terrified to learn more of what she had endured at the hands of her own family, and didn't want to see anything else, didn't want to remember.

But another part of her knew she had to face this.

Had to face everything.

Had to learn who she was so she could have a future.

That little abused girl had eventually found freedom, love, and safety, and adult Beth wanted to hold onto that. She wanted to have a future where she was more than just the woman who had been abused all throughout her life and who pain and sorrow constantly followed.

Fighting the urge to attempt to wake herself, she faced the next image to shimmer into her mind. This time it was a slightly older version of the little girl—of herself—who stood in a filthy kitchen attempting to wash off an equally filthy plate.

Instead of watching like an outsider like she had when she watched the little girl run through the woods, this time around she felt closer. Not quite an active participant, but she could feel rather than just see what the girl was going through. Maybe nine or ten, the young girl's stomach was growling, aching with hunger, despite having just eaten dinner.

Sitting at her feet was a younger cousin, maybe three years old, and young Beth was trying to figure out how she was going to keep the little girl quiet for the rest of the evening. A screaming child would draw attention she didn't want for herself or the toddler. Attention meant pain and she was so very tired of pain.

As she set the plate on top of the pile in the cupboard, closing the door that was mostly broken, she eyed the blistered burns on her arms. Courtesy of an older cousin who smoked constantly and had taken to putting out his cigarettes on her thin arms.

Tears wanted to fall, but she had long since learned crying didn't solve anything.

Nothing would solve her problems.

This was her life. She was trapped there on her family's property. She didn't go to school, didn't have friends, and never left the land that had been in her family for generations. When she got older—*if* she got older—she would be married off to one of her father's or uncle's friends.

Before the girl could dwell on the rough hand life had dealt her, she heard drunken voices from outside. Panic filled her, accepting your life didn't mean that it wasn't terrifying.

The back door was thrown open so hard it banged into the wall, causing another dent in the already battered paint. Her eyes grew wide when she saw it wasn't just her uncles and cousins, but a whole bunch of drunk men. Since she didn't know how to count, she had no idea how many there were, but it was a lot.

"Time you learn how to take care of a group of men, girl," one of her uncles said as he reached for her.

Terrified if she screamed or fought that this group of predators would turn on the helpless little girl sitting beside her, Beth forced herself to remain still as hands grabbed at her. They ripped at her clothes, they held her down, they hit, they hurt, they ripped into her small body and shattered another part of her battered soul.

Beth wasn't sure if there were real tears on her cheeks or if she was simply feeling the echo of the tears of her much younger self.

As badly as she wanted to reach back through the passage of time and save that poor little girl that nobody even knew existed, there was nothing she could do.

This was too much.

How had she spent the last eleven months praying to regain her memory?

She didn't want this, she didn't want to remember, she never wanted to know the horrors she had lived through.

How had she survived this?

No wonder her mind had just locked itself away. Why would it ever want her to know just how bad life had been for her?

But she was powerless to stop another image from forcing its way into her vulnerable mind.

She was older again in this memory, maybe sixteen or seventeen, the blonde had turned into brown with the same lingering natural blonde highlights that remained to this day. More scars and fresher wounds littered the exposed skin on her arms and the lower half of her legs. The brown eyes she saw on the teenager were one step away from dead.

Small, much too thin, and dirty, this girl had been forced to fight for her life every second since she had been born. No wonder she looked like she was more of a functioning zombie than a human being.

"Okay, girl, get out here," her uncle called, and the teenager wrapped her arms around her waist as she crept across the floor and out onto the sagging porch. Beside her uncle was a man who stood out in his crisp black suit and clean, slicked-back hair. Even without seeing the huge wad of cash in her uncle's hand, she knew this man was money.

What she didn't know was what that had to do with her.

"Come," the suited man ordered in a voice that sounded nothing like the ones she was used to hearing.

Confused, she looked to her uncle. She was supposed to go with this man? Why? She'd never been anywhere off the property, why was she going now?

"You stupid, girl?" her uncle demanded. "You go with him. You're not our problem no more."

More confused than ever, Beth had no idea what that meant, but it didn't matter, the suited man grabbed her roughly around the elbow and dragged her to a shiny black car sitting in the driveway.

When she was shoved inside, she found another man in there.

Evil.

It crashed into her the moment she was in his presence.

No idea if it was teenage Beth or Beth now, but a scream filled the air.

"Beth. Beth! Wake up, sweetie. Now. Wake up, Beth."

She was shaken roughly, and her eyes snapped open. White walls. A bed with a body in it. Light streaming through the windows. The hiss and beep of machines.

The hospital.

The evil man was gone, but the images she'd seen, the memories she had relived, remained in her mind.

"Bethie, you okay, sweetie? Were you having nightmares?" Tank asked. He was crouched in front of the chair she'd fallen asleep in, his hands on her shoulders, and concern written all over his face.

It was on the tip of her tongue to say it hadn't been dreams but memories that had her screaming, but for some reason, she held back. She had just taken the first step in finding the woman she'd been, but it was a painful step and the only one she wanted to share it with was the man lying unconscious in the hospital bed.

Come back to me, Axel. I need you.

What would happen to her if she lost Axel but gained herself? How was she supposed to survive reliving the hell that had been her life without the man who had become her whole world, the only safety she'd ever had, the only love she'd ever experienced?

～

April 8th
2:06 P.M.

As much as she didn't want to, it was time for Beth to accept that this might be her reality from here on out.

Eleven days had passed since Axel was hurt and rushed to the hospital. While his lung was healing well, and he was breathing independently, he hadn't woken up. Hadn't so much as stirred a teeny, tiny little bit, and she was beginning to give up hope that he would ever wake up.

How had Axel survived eleven *months* with her all but lost to him?

It had only been days and she was about to lose her mind.

She wanted him so badly to come back to her, but there was nothing she could say or do to make it happen. The feelings of helplessness were crushing. Literally, that was what it felt like. There was a pressure in her chest she had no idea how to relieve because what she needed was for Axel to wake up, tell her he loved her, and that everything was going to be okay.

Was everything going to be okay?

With him?

With her?

With the threat that still lingered over them and all of Bravo Team?

"Is he going to be okay here?" she asked, for what had to be the hundredth time in the last hour.

To their credit, no one complained, and no one got frustrated with her, not the guys and not the nurse who would be working the day shifts. It hadn't been her decision to bring Axel home from the hospital. But everyone else had agreed that he would rather be there, surrounded by his things, in the home he shared with his wife. They believed it would give him a better chance at waking up from the coma his brain had trapped him in.

Beth, on the other hand, was worried.

What if something went wrong?

Eagle Oswald—billionaire former SEAL and founder and CEO of Prey Security—had hired two nurses who would be at the compound around the clock to monitor Axel and be there if anything happened. But in the hospital, there was a whole lot more than one nurse around if something went wrong. There were doctors there, too, and medical equipment.

Okay, a glance around Axel's room at his cabin showed even more equipment than had been in his room at the hospital. But still, she would have felt better if a whole hospital was there if the worst happened.

"He's going to be fine, sweetie," Rock assured her. The medic had more training than the rest of them, but was it enough to keep Axel alive until they could get him back to the hospital if his condition worsened?

How badly she wished someone could guarantee that.

Guarantee that Axel would be okay and that everything was going to work out.

"If this is too much for you, we can take him back to the hospital," Rock said, wrapping his arms around her in a brotherly hug.

While she had continued to have memory flashes whenever she was exhausted enough to fall into a sleep deep enough for dreams, she had yet to share that with anyone. As far as they all knew, she was still suffering from complete amnesia. But because her returning memories were only of her childhood years trapped on her family's land deep in the Appalachian Mountains, she still didn't remember her life with Axel.

What would he want right now?

It killed her that she knew that while she might be his wife, Rock knew more about what Axel would want.

"Is ... would ... what would Axel want?" she asked softly, unable to meet Rock's gaze as shame washed over her. What kind of wife was she that she didn't even know what choices her husband would make?

Amnesia had stolen her identity from her without her permission, but Beth herself had allowed it to steal her life. Now that she was remembering bits and pieces of her childhood, she finally understood why her therapist hadn't wanted her to be overwhelmed learning about her past and whatever had happened to her with Leonid Baranov all at once. Still, it would have been nice to be able to sit with her husband's arms around her as she felt like she died inside each time another snippet of memory reappeared.

"Axe would want to be here. With you," Rock told her. There was absolutely no shred of doubt in his voice. He believed what he was saying, and since she had no evidence to the contrary, she had to believe it, too.

"Then I want him to be here. This isn't about me, it's about Axel and whatever he needs to get better," she said.

Rock's arms tightened around her in another fierce hug. "I'm proud of you, kiddo. You're doing amazing. You've found your voice, that fight we all knew you had inside you. You are the very definition of a survivor, Bethie. Don't give up on Axe and don't give up on yourself. I know you don't remember it, but what you two had was the truest, purist form of love I've ever seen. Love like that doesn't die. Not ever."

His lips touched the top of her head, and then he released her and took a step back. Usually, when one of the guys tried to talk to her about her and Axel's relationship it made her uncomfortable. None of them would tell her anything substantial so it just made her feel like a failure. That she wasn't trying hard enough to get her memories back, but at the same time, frustrated because how did people expect her to get her memory back if they wouldn't help?

"Nurse will be in the living room, you call out if you need her,"

Rock told her. "I'm going to go spend some time with Ariel, but if you need anything at all you call. Any of us. All of us. Whatever you need, okay? We are all here for you. All of us. You are not alone."

Although she nodded at his words, Beth didn't believe them.

How could she?

She had been alone as a child, suffering unspeakable horrors. She had been alone when she was sold to Leonid Baranov even if she didn't remember what had happened to her there. She had been alone when she was kidnapped and held captive for eight months, even though again, she had no memory of her time during those months.

The only time she hadn't been alone was when she had Axel's love and she had stupidly let that slip through her fingers.

Was it too late to get it back?

Alone now with her husband, Beth went into the bathroom adjoined to the bedroom, and filled a bowl with warm water. Grabbing a washcloth, she returned to the bedroom and sat beside Axel on the side of the mattress.

"Can't you wake up, Axel? For me?" she asked softly as she dunked the cloth in the warm water and then squeezed out the excess. There was no answer, not that she had expected one,

Carefully, she cleaned every inch of his bare chest and arms. There were bruises there and mostly healed cuts from the explosion. Even the gash on his head from where he'd hit it was healing nicely. The doctors kept saying there were no signs of permanent brain damage, and nothing was stopping Axel from waking up.

So why didn't he?

It was selfish to think that his subconscious was in some way punishing her for shutting him out, and yet it was hard to think up another reason why his brain needed to take a metaphorical time out. It needed a break. From her. That was the only thing that made sense, and it hurt so badly to know she had hurt the man she knew deep down she loved with all her very being.

Axel thought she no longer loved him, and that was completely her fault.

"I love you, Axel," she whispered, touching her lips to his cheek. "I want you to come back. I *need* you to come back. I don't think either of us has handled things the way we should have this last year. I know I can't really be mad at you for not knowing what I needed when I didn't tell you, but I wish you had just asked me what I wanted rather than listening to that doctor. I get where she was coming from now," she admitted as she smoothed the damp cloth over her husband's face.

She had told her comatose husband that she'd been having memory flashes, hoping he might hear her and wake up. The doctors kept saying that coma patients had been known to hear what was going on around them, so Beth hadn't held back in telling Axel how badly she needed him.

But it never made a difference.

There were so many fears fighting for control inside her that Beth didn't even know how to untangle them all. She knew the biggest fear though. And that was that even if Axel woke up, and even if she told him how sorry she was for shutting him out, it was already too late to salvage their marriage.

And once again she would be left all alone.

CHAPTER *Five*

April 10th
    10:49 P.M.

The sound of a voice prodded him from outside the blackness that engulfed him.

There were no words, it was simply the distant hum of a sound that Axe knew unequivocally belonged to the woman he loved.

He didn't need to know what was wrong with him, where he was, or what she was saying to know that it was her.

She was ingrained in him, Axe would know Beth anywhere.

Focusing only on her voice, he allowed it to draw him slowly out of the darkness.

Over time, it grew louder and closer, no longer did it seem like an entire ocean was between them. As he became more aware, he realized someone was touching him. Stroking a hand over his hair. The repetitive motion soothed something inside him.

Beth.

Beth was with him.

Talking to him.

Touching him.

His Beth, his wife, the woman who had been afraid to come anywhere near him ever since he got her back, ruining what should have been a happy ending for their love story. She was here with him now, and the more he focused on the feel of her hand and the sound of her voice, the more he could make out her words.

"I wish I knew if you could hear me," Beth's voice whispered. It was so full of pain that he longed to do whatever it took to take that pain away.

How long had it been since he had seen her smile?

Not since the morning of the day she was taken from him.

Axe still remembered that day like it was yesterday. Remembered waking Beth up with slow, lazy kisses, making love to her like he had all the time in the world. He'd made her waffles for breakfast, they were Beth's favorite, and given the horrific life she had lived, he found he wanted to spoil her as often as he could. She'd taken a shower while he was in the kitchen cooking, and when she'd come downstairs in a pastel pink sundress, it had taken every ounce of his willpower not to strip it off her and make love to her all over again.

Instead, they'd laughed and talked as they sat at the kitchen table eating waffles, fresh berries from Beth's garden, and homemade ice cream. Everything in that moment had been perfect, and if he'd known when he kissed her before she climbed into the car to drive into town to do some shopping that it would be the last time he saw her in eight long, hellish months, he would never have let her go.

It wasn't until lunchtime he realized she'd never called or sent a single text.

Given the threat from Leonid Baranov, he always asked Beth to check in regularly if she was going to go out on her own, which wasn't often.

When he'd called, there had been no answer, and that's when the panic had really set in.

This was Beth they were talking about. She wasn't reckless, she'd twice lived through a hell no one could ever understand. She checked in because it helped her as much as it helped him. There was no way she wouldn't answer his calls.

No way.

So, when he'd driven into town and found her car sitting in a parking lot with no signs of Beth, he'd known.

She was gone.

And it wasn't until eight months later, when Tank's words had come over the comms unit announcing the intruder on the estate was none other than Beth, that he'd taken a full breath again. Only he hadn't known then that his nightmare was nowhere close to being over.

But now Beth was here, talking to him, touching him, and he wanted to savor every second of it.

"Even if you can't hear me, I'm going to keep talking to you," Beth continued. "Maybe if I do, eventually you *will* hear me and then you'll know how much I need you to come back to me."

Beth *needed* him?

For the last year, it had seemed like what she needed the most was for him to keep his distance.

"I messed everything up, Axel." There was so much misery in her voice that he did everything he could to fight through the blackness weighing him down.

He had to get to her.

Soothe her.

That was his job.

From the moment they had found Beth chained up with a rusty metal collar around her neck, attached with a metal chain to the door of the metal cage she was locked up in, he had known she was his. It was weird because, at the time, Beth had been so vulnerable, so traumatized that a future should have seemed impossible.

But it wasn't.

She was his, and he was hers. That knowledge had been unshakeable inside him as soon as he broke the lock on her cage and gently eased her out and into his arms.

That was why the last year, with her having amnesia, had been such a hellish journey. He knew she needed him, but with the distance between them, he didn't know how to be there for her.

"I wish I could go back and do it over. I just ... got annoyed with you I guess. Scared too. You wouldn't tell me anything, and I needed to know. I understand now why Dr. Jager didn't want you to tell me, but she was still wrong, and I guess part of me resented you putting her orders above me, above what I needed."

Fresh pain crashed down upon him.

All this time he'd known the doctor was wrong. *He* knew Beth, she didn't. Beth would need to know. She processed information in a logical way that completely belied the horrors she'd been through. It was *because* of those horrors that she'd found a way to shut down her emotions when processing a problem.

If he'd trusted his instincts, maybe eleven months of torment for them both could have been avoided.

Aching to touch and hold his wife, he focused every bit of his energy on moving just the hand closest to where he could feel her body.

"I wasn't just mad with you," Beth continued, oblivious to the fact that he was listening to her every word. "I was mad at me, too. I knew I had to tell you, but I was so afraid I couldn't make my memories come back, and without them, you would fall out of love with me and then I'd have no one."

Oh, baby.

While he was hungry to hear it, every word she spoke broke his heart a little more. There was absolutely nothing she could ever say or do that would make him stop loving her. She was amazing, so strong, so brave, and although damaged inside, she still looked for moments of joy, still saw beauty in the world, and still had a good and caring heart.

Axe could have sworn his fingers twitched, but Beth didn't seem to notice.

"I'm sorry I didn't trust you like I should have. I'm sorry I didn't trust us and our love like I should have. I should have known you would never leave me. Not ever. Not for anything. I need you to come back now, Axel."

I'm trying, wisp.

I'm trying to come back to you.

"I ... I've been having memory flashes," Beth confessed softly like she was afraid of being overheard.

Beth was getting her memories back?

Knowing what he knew about her childhood and her time as

Leonid Baranov's captive, Axe knew he had no choice but to force his body's cooperation.

There was no way the wife he loved was going through that alone while he lay uselessly in a bed. He hadn't been able to find her in the eight months she had been missing. If she hadn't escaped and found her way home, he would never have found her. He hadn't been any help to her while she had no memory of who she was or her life.

Failing her again was not an option.

Forcing his fingers to move, he reached for the hand that continued to stroke his hair, using it as a lighthouse to guide him through the darkness.

"They're only when I'm sleeping. Just flashes of moments in time from when I was a ch—" Beth broke off as his fingers brushed against her hand. "Axel? Can you hear me?" He felt her move and wanted to beg her to come back. "Axel, answer me right now." Her voice was becoming shrill, and he could hear the hope and fear warring inside it. "Please."

It was the whispered plea that was the final tug he needed to pull him out.

His eyes opened slowly, and he saw Beth perched on the side of a bed. Their bed, in their room, a bed he knew she crept into when he was away even though she thought she was hiding it.

One look at the dark circles under her eyes, the paleness of her face, the weight she'd lost, and he remembered everything. The warehouse, his impatience, the explosion, thinking he was going to die.

How long had he been unconscious?

Long enough for him to be brought back home.

Long enough to terrify Beth enough to bring her back to his side.

"I love you, wisp," he murmured, hating how weak his voice sounded and the effort it took to say the words.

With a sob, she carefully pressed her face into his neck, her tears wetting his skin, her breath warm as it puffed onto his collarbone. Then she spoke the words he had feared he would never hear again. "Oh, Axel, I love you, too."

~

April 11th
    8:06 P.M.

"Hey, you shouldn't be doing that," Beth said as she walked through the door of Axel's room to see him trying to sit up and reach for the glass of water on the nightstand. "You know you're supposed to call me if you need anything."

Not even twenty-four hours had passed since Axel first opened his eyes, yet it felt like it had been a hundred years or more.

To say she was exhausted would be the understatement of the century.

Although he was awake, Axel's body was weak and he kept passing out again, only able to remain conscious for short periods of time. Of course, in those brief periods, everyone wanted to come and see him to confirm for themselves that he was okay.

It wasn't that Beth begrudged them that at all. She loved that Bravo Team and Prey as a whole were such a close-knit family, it was just that she had so many people to care for. She was so busy ensuring the coffee pot was always filled, and a selection of other drinks and food were available. Then there was keeping the kids busy when various Prey people stopped by, washing dishes and tidying up. There were talks with the doctor and the nurse, trying to get a couple of minutes alone with Axel to make sure he wasn't overdoing things, and she was spent.

Completely spent.

There had been no time for her to sleep, and she'd barely eaten anything, but she was grateful that Axel was awake and he was going to be okay.

Frustration was rolling off him now though, she knew how annoyed he was with his body and his lack of control over it. He wanted to just jump out of bed and go back to the way things had been, but he had been in a coma for two weeks and it had taken a toll. It wasn't like it was going to take months to get his strength back, probably not even weeks, but it was going to take a few days at least.

"I don't like you running yourself ragged like this," he growled as she hurried over to get the glass and pass it to him.

That's what he was upset about?

She would have sworn it was his own inability to just jump out of bed and do things for himself.

Despite their exchanged I love yous, things were kind of awkward between them. It was because she had no idea what he'd heard her say while he was in a coma, if anything at all, and she wasn't sure how to broach the topic of what she needed. Right now, her focus had to be on him, on taking care of her husband and helping him rebuild his strength. Everything else they could sort out later.

"I don't mind taking care of you," Beth said honestly as she helped Axel steady the glass and hold it to his lips so he could drink.

"You at least need to sleep, and have you had anything to eat today?" Axel grumbled.

"Like you didn't miss sleep yourself when I first came home." The words burst out of her without conscious thought. It had taken months for her to feel comfortable enough—safe enough—in Axel's company to just say what she was thinking without fear of being punished for it.

But the last few months that fear had been back.

The distance had been back.

They'd felt like strangers instead of husband and wife, in many ways, they still did. Just because she remembered that she loved him didn't mean any of her memories of their lives had returned.

A small smile curled Axel's lips. "I at least took the time to sleep."

"Liar," she muttered. "You stayed up watching over me every night."

Axel blinked in surprise. "You knew I was there?"

"I *always* know when you're there. And when you're not. That night you were hurt, I felt this ... distance from you. Different than the normal distance, this time it felt like you were too far away for me to reach. I didn't like it," she whispered as tears blurred her vision.

"Oh, wisp, come here." When he opened his arms, a clear invitation for her to curl up in them, Beth resisted the urge.

"Can't, I don't want to hurt you." Axel might be awake and talking to her, might be healing from his injuries, but he had still been almost killed and she wasn't going to do a single other thing to cause him pain. Not after everything she had put him through this last year.

The coma was her fault.

The head injury had contributed to it, sure. But the doctors themselves had told her that Axel wasn't waking up because his body had reached its limit and needed the time to rest and heal.

She was the reason Axel had reached his limit.

Her and her amnesia and inability to let him help her.

"Beth Lindon, you get yourself on this bed and into my arms this instance," Axel ordered, every bit the alpha male he was inside.

With a small sigh, she climbed onto the bed and very carefully stretched out so she was beside Axel but not really on him.

Apparently, that wasn't good enough for him. His arm curled around her waist, and he managed with one arm to move her so she was draped across his front.

Her protest died on her lips because the sigh that rolled through Axel's body was one of deep contentment. The arms that held her were like steel bands around her, and his face buried in her hair, and she felt him breathe in her scent. Beth would have sworn she felt teardrops drip onto the top of her head, but she had never seen her big, strong, tough, alpha husband cry before.

"Thought I was never going to get to hold you again," Axel whispered, his voice broken as he touched kiss after kiss to her head.

Guilt surged through her. "I'm sorry."

Axel stilled for a moment, then touched another kiss to her crown. "What are you sorry for, wisp?"

"For shutting you out." Although she hated that she'd done it, it felt good to say the words aloud. Freeing somehow. No more secrets, at least on her end, she just had to pray that Axel would believe her when she told him, hard as it was, that she needed to hear the truth about her past and who she was. Without it, she felt like a balloon floating into space with nothing to tether it and no way to come back down to earth.

Saying the last thing she expected, Axel asked, "Do you remember why I call you wisp?"

"No," she admitted, wishing that she did. She needed things to help her connect to her husband, otherwise, they would forever feel like strangers.

The arms around her tightened protectively. "The day I found you in Leonid Baranov's House of Horrors, you were this tiny, pale little thing trapped in a cage. At first, I almost thought I imagined you, you were so still and the room was so dark. You were like a little wisp of smoke, there one minute, gone the next. I knew in that second, I didn't ever want to let you be gone. You were mine. I knew it. Felt it. Prayed that maybe one day you would know it, too. But even if you were never ready for a romantic relationship, I would be there as your friend, your protector, whatever you needed me to be. I'm sorry I failed you, wisp."

Tears filled her eyes, and she didn't stop them from rolling down her cheeks. "You heard."

"Not everything you said while I was unconscious, just those last few minutes before I woke up. It's why I knew I had to come back to you. I failed you once and I wasn't going to fail you again. Not ever. Not for anything. I love you, wisp. More than anything on the face of this earth."

Turning her head a little, Beth placed a kiss on Axel's chest, right above his heart. A heart she knew brimmed with love for her. "I know, Axel. I never doubted that. I *felt* your love for me even if I didn't remember it."

His body relaxed, but his arms only tightened around her. "Good. I was afraid that you had lost our love along with your memories."

"Never. I don't even think that's possible. Our love exists whether or not we consciously remember it."

"And you don't remember it." The pain was still there in his voice, but there was no judgment.

"Not *yet*. But I will. I believe that." Especially now if Axel was willing to share their life with her rather than waiting for her to remember everything on her own.

"Have you had any more memory flashes?"

Beth shook her head. "I only get them when I'm asleep. Deep enough sleep to dream, and I haven't really taken more than a quick catnap since you woke up."

"You're exhausted, wisp." There was a small reprimand in his voice.

"Maybe, but here by your side, that's the only place I want to be."

"Visited me every day in the hospital, huh?" he teased.

But she straightened and frowned down at him. "I didn't *visit*, Axel. I stayed with you."

"You stayed the whole time?"

"Of course I did. You're my husband, and you would have stayed with me no matter what. I wasn't leaving until you left."

A huge smile broke out on Axel's handsome face. "You didn't leave me. Even when you had no memories and were angry with me for not giving you what you needed, you stayed with me."

"I love you," she said as a way of explanation. The problem was that their love might be enough to reclaim their marriage, but it wasn't enough to eliminate the threat that still hovered over them and Bravo Team.

Leonid Baranov was still out there, he'd taken her from her husband once already, and Beth was terrified that if he took her again, there would be no third chance for her and Axel.

CHAPTER *Six*

April 13th
6:53 A.M.

Axe had never been so glad for a headache in his life.

He strongly suspected that if it hadn't been for the explosion giving Beth the scare she needed to finally speak up and admit what she needed, he would have lost her forever.

Over the last few weeks, he'd felt her slipping further and further away from him.

Every time he looked at her, he could tell she was near her breaking point, and once she reached it she was going to ask to leave, get Eagle to set her up somewhere else, and make sure he didn't know where.

So many times it had been on the tip of his tongue to tell her everything. Her horrific childhood, how her uncle had sold her to notorious Russian trafficker Leonid Baranov, that the man had treated her like a pet, keeping her locked in a cage when he wasn't playing with her. The man had been intrigued by his inability to break Beth, who was already well-trained in surviving abuse since it had been her life since birth.

To tell her everything about their time together, how they'd been friends first and then she'd fallen in love with him. How he'd loved her from the beginning but given her what she needed at the time. About their wedding there on the grounds one magical Christmas Eve night, the fairy lights the guys had strung up around the trees, the way the moon had been shining brightly amidst a myriad of stars while they said their vows, but then after soft snowflakes had begun to tumble down.

The only reason he'd hung back was the doctor's orders that it would be too much for Beth to handle to learn everything about her tragic life in one go.

Although, if Axe was being honest, the only person he had to blame was himself.

He knew Beth, not some doctor. He should have known that she was strong enough to survive it. Strong enough to survive anything.

It had been his own fear of losing her once she learned how he had promised to always keep her safe and failed so spectacularly.

Now he'd lost almost a year with his beloved and adored wife, and if it hadn't been for his head injury—the headache now more an annoying background ache than anything else—he would have lost her forever.

"I'm sorry, wisp," he whispered as he leaned down and touched a kiss to his sleeping wife's forehead.

Feeling strong enough for the first time since he'd woken up a few days ago to get out of bed on his own, Axe carefully maneuvered out from under the covers, doing his best not to disturb Beth.

Learning that she had stayed by his side the entire time he was in a coma had surprised him at first. With the way things had been between them, the tension and distance, he wouldn't have blamed her for seeing his accident as a way out.

Instead, it had drawn her back to him.

Still a little unsteady on his feet, he headed down the stairs and into the kitchen. His wife had spent the last two weeks doing nothing but worry about him and be there beside him, taking care of his every need. From the weight she had lost and the dark smudges under her eyes, it was plain to see she hadn't been taking care of herself, and when he was feeling better, he was going to have a talk with his team. If he couldn't be there for his wife, he needed to know that someone else was doing the job. Doing it the same way he would. Things had changed, and his friends all had partners now, but he still needed to know that Beth would be okay if anything happened to him. That she wouldn't be alone. That his team would have her back.

And having her back meant forcing her to take care of herself if she wouldn't do it herself.

Finding the ingredients for waffles, he went to work making them. He'd just set the last of the batter into the waffle maker when he heard shuffled footsteps behind him.

"You shouldn't be up by yourself," Beth said, voice husky from sleep. The first real sleep she'd gotten in … months … since before she'd been kidnapped, and even then she never slept a lot, usually not more than a couple of hours a night.

"You were sleeping peacefully for the first time in far too long, I wasn't going to wake you."

Beth's harrumph sounded so much like the woman he had known before she was taken from him and returned with amnesia, that he spun around to look at her. Drinking in the sight of her, all sleep-rumpled, brown locks with natural gold highlights all tangled and messy around her face, her cheeks were perfectly pinked, and she looked far too good dressed in nothing but one of his old T-shirts.

Instinct had him walking toward her, and it wasn't until he'd hooked an arm around her waist and pulled her up against him, her hands lifting to rest against his pecs, that he realized what he was doing.

But when he looked down at Beth, ready to offer apologies for acting without thinking, he found hunger in her eyes as she looked up at him.

Desire.

More than that, love.

Knowing she wasn't ready for more than a soft kiss, he dipped his head and whispered his lips across hers. Something inside him settled at the contact, brief though it had been, and when Beth sighed and snuggled against him, Axe knew everything was going to work itself out.

"Distracting me with kisses won't work. You shouldn't be up by yourself," Beth said, her warm breath tickling his bare skin.

"What about distracting you with waffles?"

"Waffles?" Her head lifted, and interest filled her brown eyes. Eyes he finally saw his Beth in again. She wasn't all back yet, but she was within his grasp, and he was going to reach out to her, grab hold, and pull her back.

"Your favorite," he said, unsure if she remembered that or not. Not that it mattered, he was done holding back. It wasn't like he was going to sit her down and tell her every detail of the horrors she had survived, but she wanted to learn about herself, and he wasn't going to deny her.

Never again.

When she opened her mouth, he cut off whatever she was going to say with a kiss. "You better not tell me again I shouldn't be up on my own. I'm fine. Perfectly capable of walking downstairs and cooking breakfast for my wife." Damn, it felt good to call Beth his wife again and actually feel like it meant something.

Nudging her toward the table, Axe went to the fridge, grabbed some strawberries and cut them up, then grabbed the ice cream and carried everything over to the table where Beth was watching him, a thoughtful expression on her face.

Setting everything down, he took the seat beside her. "Ask me anything."

"Huh?" Beth put two waffles on her plate, added a few pieces of strawberry and a scoop of ice cream, and took a bite. Her eyes closed, and a moan of delight fell from her lips. "Mmm, so good."

Smiling, he reached over and caught a drip of ice cream rolling down her chin. "Whatever you want to know, ask me and I'll tell you."

Her thoughtful expression returned, and she took another bite as though thinking about what she wanted to ask. Given she knew nothing more than little flashes of her childhood, there must have been a million things running through her head.

"How did you find out waffles were my favorite? I don't have a lot of memories, but from what I know of my family, I can't imagine we sat around on a Sunday morning and had waffles for breakfast."

"When I first brought you home you were so tiny, so thin, nothing more than skin and bones. I wanted to get some meat on you, so I started making a list of every single thing I could think of making for you." That list included everything from mashed potatoes to lobster, macaroni and cheese, and cookies. With each thing he tried, he noted whether she liked, disliked, or loved it. He made sure to cook everything she loved for her as often as possible, anything to coax out her barely existent appetite.

"How many things were on your list?"

"Had to be a couple of hundred."

Her eyes widened. "A couple of hundred? Must have taken you forever to work through that list."

Reaching out, he covered one of her hands with his. "I didn't care. I loved taking care of you, knew you'd never had that, and it was my honor to look after you and make sure you were okay. As soon as I learned how much you loved waffles, I made them for you as often as I could."

Beth's smile was shy, but there was no hesitation in it. "You took good care of me. The best. I don't have to remember to know that. I'm … lucky to have you, Axel. I'm sorry—"

Touching a finger to her lips, he cut off her apology. "You handled a horrific situation the best way you could. I'm the one who should be sorry, I'm the one who—"

A small finger touched his lips, and he smiled against it. "If I can't apologize, you can't either," Beth told him.

Pressing a kiss to the pad of her finger, he took her hand and laced their fingers together. "We can't go back and do it over, but from now on out we're open and honest with one another. No secrets, no hiding, we're a couple, we handle this mess together."

"Together," Beth echoed. Her gaze grew troubled. "Axel, I'm scared. You were almost killed, Leonid Baranov is still a threat to us."

Fear—no, blinding terror—filled him, and he grabbed her and dragged her over into his lap. "I will not let him touch you again."

"But you can't—"

"I can and I will make you that promise. No one is ever taking you from me again."

Whatever it took, he was protecting his wife. Losing her again was not an option.

April 15th
   12:13 P.M.

Everything felt so perfect.

That kind of perfect you got right before a storm hit.

Beth was no longer afraid that Axel was going to die or be lost to her forever. Although she hadn't had any more memory flashes since he woke up, she had learned so much about herself and her relationship with her husband that she didn't care that she hadn't experienced them herself. Learning about who she was and the kind of marriage they had shared from Axel's point of view was almost better than seeing it from her own.

It gave her insight that she could never otherwise have gotten, and it cemented in her mind just how much she was loved.

How could she ever have doubted this man who was standing in his kitchen—*their* kitchen—making lunch for the two of them? It was so obvious that he loved her more than anything. It was in each gentle touch, each soft look, the way he couldn't wait to get back on his feet for no other reason than he wanted to take care of her because no one else in her life ever had.

He was perfect.

No other way to describe her husband.

Despite every horrific thing she had lived through, Beth knew she was lucky to have come out the other side and found love, peace, stability, and a future with Axel.

So easily her life could have ended any number of ways. Her family could have taken things too far with their abuse and killed her, or they could have gotten tired of her and decided to end her life rather than sell her. Only four people had survived Leonid Baranov and his many houses of horror. If Axel and his team hadn't found her, she knew she wouldn't have either, but that they had arrived while she was still alive and gotten her out was a miracle in itself.

Lucky.

Call her crazy—as she was sure many would given what had happened to her in her twenty-four years—but she felt lucky. Lucky to be alive, lucky to have fallen in love, lucky to be able to live her life any way she chose.

But how long could that luck last?

Each special moment here with her husband, amazing as they were, was tarnished by the knowledge that neither she nor Axel nor anyone else on Bravo Team was truly safe.

Leonid Baranov didn't like to lose.

Already he had killed one of the other four survivors, and killed the daughter of another, seemingly abducting her as well. And he'd tried to get Beth back once and almost killed Axel and his team at that warehouse.

They weren't safe, none of them were, not until Baranov was dead.

Pushing away the darkness before it could curl around her, Beth got up from the table where Axel had insisted she sit while he made them both lunch.

"I'll grab the drinks," she announced.

"I can get them," Axel said, looking over his shoulder from where he was making two bowls of nachos.

"I know you can, but I can, too. And tonight, I'm cooking dinner for you." She huffed.

Sweet as her husband's desire to take care of her was, and happy as she was that he was recovering well and had already regained a lot of his strength, she wasn't a baby who needed someone to do everything for her, and she wasn't sure how much longer she could sit back and let Axel treat her as such. It was only because she knew it was helping him to feel like he could finally take care of her again that she'd acquiesced this long.

After choosing apple juice for both of them, she poured two glasses, set them on the table, and then stared at the carton.

True to his word, Axel had answered honestly every single question she had asked over the last few days. Mostly they were things about her, and about their lives together. Beth wasn't quite ready yet to confront her time as Baranov's prisoner and what Axel knew about it. She'd get there, but just from the evil she sensed when her younger self had been bought and put into that limo, she knew she wasn't ready for it yet.

"How did I learn to read?" she asked as she set the apple juice carton back into the fridge. "I know my family didn't send me to school. I was there to cook, clean, do the laundry, be the punching bag, and a toy for when the men were bored. Yet even though I don't remember anything after I was sold, I know how to read. Did you teach me?" That had been her best guess, although she had wondered if it had been Andy's nanny and former teacher, Mrs. Pfeffer, who had taught her.

"When you first came here you were traumatized, withdrawn. You didn't get hysterical very often, but you would just pull away from everyone and lock yourself inside your head. I knew it was your coping mechanism. Back then, I didn't know much about your past, only that you told me you had no one for me and my team to call and that your family had sold you to Baranov. It was enough to know that where you came from was just as bad as where I'd rescued you. I wanted to help, I didn't like you being locked away inside your head because it was the only safe place. I was selfish. *I* wanted to be your safe place. So, I started reading to you. Everything. Alice in Wonderland, Winnie the Pooh, Lord of the Rings. It didn't matter, I just wanted to give you something else to think about."

Warmth flushed through her. This man never ceased to amaze her. On the outside, he was every bit the alpha protector, but inside he was so sweet and tender that it made her eyes sting and her heart swell.

"You weren't selfish." Walking over, she pressed herself against him and wrapped her arms around his waist, relishing the comfort his presence gave her. "You were everything I needed. Everything I will ever need."

Lips touched the top of her head. "I think it was about a month after we brought you home that you told me you didn't know how to read but wanted to learn. Once I knew you'd never been to school, I wanted to teach you everything, not just reading. So, when my team wasn't out somewhere, we did our own school together. Reading, writing, math, science, geography, and history. We learned it all and you just soaked it up."

Nuzzling closer, she touched a kiss to his neck, then tilted her head up so she could brush her lips against his jaw. "See? Not selfish. The most amazing man. My man."

The smile he beamed down on her was pure love. "My woman."

"My heart."

Something flashed through his eyes, and she wondered if she'd said something they used to say to one another. "My life," he whispered.

"I love you, Axel. I know I don't remember anything, but I swear I remember how much I love you and how much you love me."

"No apologies, remember," he teased, eyes soft. "Those memories will come, wisp. I believe it, keep believing it, too."

Withdrawing from the security of his embrace, she let him stick the first bowl of nachos into the microwave to heat while she picked up the bag of cheese to return it to the fridge. "I do believe it, Axel. I'm just scared. Not of remembering you and our lives together, I want those memories back so bad. But the rest ... that's terrifying."

"Of course it is. What happened to you was horrific. It's completely normal, it would be weird if you *weren't* worried about it. Honey, *I'm* terrified for you to get those memories back."

Startled, Beth turned just as she opened the fridge door. "You are?"

Whatever answer he gave was lost when the cheese missed the shelf and tumbled to the floor. As it landed the bag opened, and pieces of shredded cheese spilled across the wooden floorboards.

Along with them came a memory.

Beth shrunk back into the metal cage she was locked into as the door to the basement was thrown open.

It was him.

It was always him.

No one else came down here.

She ate only if he decided to visit her that day.

With a metal collar around her neck, attached with a metal chain to the door of her cage, there wasn't really anywhere for her to go.

His footsteps sounded harsh on the cold concrete floor, fitting since the man was cold and harsh.

Violent.

Terrifying.

Worse even than her family had been.

He stopped in front of her cage, a handful of scraps in his hand. Beth hated that her mouth salivated at the sight, and against her will, her starving body edged closer to the food.

Grinning at her, he threw the food onto the floor, some landing inside her cage, the rest outside it where he would taunt her with doing things she didn't want to do to get to eat it.

With hunger too strong to ignore, she moved forward, scrambling to scoop up whatever he'd thrown down, not caring what it was, not caring she ate it off the floor with her hands like an animal.

In this place she was an animal.

"You keep surviving," the man said in pleasant surprise as though he liked the idea that he hadn't broken her yet, that she was a challenge. It wasn't the first time he'd said it to her, and she never knew what he wanted her to say in return.

Survival had been her entire life.

Of course she knew how to do it.

If she didn't, she would have been dead a long time ago.

When he reached down to unlock her cage and open the door, there was nowhere for her to go. The rusty collar dug into the bloody wounds circling her neck as she was pulled forward by the chain.

"Present," he ordered.

Weeks or months or years or however long she'd been here of training had her shuffling on her knees to turn so she was facing away from him. Lowering her head, she rested her forearms and forehead on the unforgiving concrete and left her bottom up in the air.

His hands gripped her hips painfully tight, and as he shoved his way inside her he leaned in to whisper in her ear. "One day I'll break you."

CHAPTER *Seven*

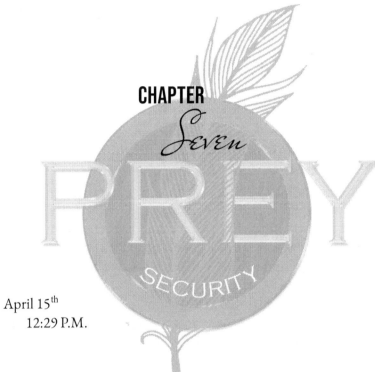

All the color drained from her face.

Even before Beth's knees began to buckle, Axe was closing the distance between them and wrapping an arm around her waist, yanking her up against his body when she would have collapsed.

"Beth?"

There was no answer to his panicked call, the woman in his arms may as well be a rag doll. Her eyes were open, but it was more than obvious they were staring at nothing, the blank, glassy look was utterly terrifying. Her mouth was moving but no sound came out, and fine tremors rippled through her otherwise limp and pliant body.

What was going on?

The change in her had been instantaneous.

One moment she had been bantering with him, asking more questions about herself and their lives together. There had been a second there when he thought all her memories had returned because she'd said words they always used to say to one another.

My man.
My woman.
My heart.
My life.

How many times had they whispered those same words? Every night when he was home, every morning he was lucky enough to wake up with her body draped across his. Any time he left on an op because they both knew there was a chance he wouldn't be coming home to her.

Those words were locked inside her head, Beth knew them even if she didn't know she knew them.

But then he'd admitted he was afraid of her memories returning, afraid of how he would deal with watching her being forced to relive all the horrors she'd been through. She hadn't heard what he'd said to her after asking him if he was really afraid of her memories coming back.

Like a switch had been flipped, she'd gone into a trance.

Was it something he had said?

Done?

No, couldn't be. They had agreed to be honest with one another, no secrets, no holding back.

Was she having memory flashes?

So far, she hadn't had any while she was awake, and she hadn't had a single one since he had woken from his coma. Part of him had believed she wasn't going to have anymore. That they had been a way for her subconscious to work through her fears of losing him and now that she knew he wasn't going anywhere, he wouldn't have been surprised if her subconscious shut that down again.

"Beth? Wisp? Come back to me, honey. Do you know where you are? You're here, in our home, in the kitchen making lunch. You're safe here, wisp. Perfectly safe. No one can hurt you here. I won't let them. Whatever is going on inside your mind can't hurt you. It's all in the past. No one is ever going to hurt you again."

Axe prayed that was a vow he could keep.

But even as he knew he would do anything to keep her safe, Leonid Baranov was still out there, and as long as the man remained free, Beth would always be in danger.

Gathering her into his arms, he ignored the microwave's insistent beeping—fear a knot of nausea sitting heavily in his stomach made him have zero interest in lunch—and sat at the table, cradling his wife in his lap.

"It's okay, wisp, everything is okay. Come back to me, honey. Please. It's Axel. Your husband, the man who loves you more than anything else on the planet. The man who would do anything for you. Right now, I need you to do something for me. I need you to look at me, Beth. I need you to tell me if you're okay, I need you to tell me what you need from me."

There was no response and his fear and anxiety ramped up several notches.

Unsure what he should do, how to coax Beth out of her trance and back to him, he pulled his cell phone from his back pocket.

Speed dialing Rock, he disposed of pleasantries and got straight to the point. "I need you here. Now. Something's wrong with Beth."

In the background, he could hear his friend moving about. "What's wrong with her? Is she sick? Did she fall and hurt herself?"

"We were making lunch, and she just ... checked out." Axe wasn't sure how else to explain it.

"Checked out how?"

"I'm not sure, but I think she's having memory flashes."

"What?" The surprise in Rock's voice reminded him that no one but him knew that Beth had gotten any of her memories back.

"She's been having them since I was in a coma," he explained. "Only flashes of her childhood, although she remembers being sold and getting into a car with Leonid Baranov. Nothing after that. She's been asking me questions, and I've been telling her things about our time together after we found her. We were talking, and then suddenly, she just froze."

Tightening his grip on his wife, Axe pressed a kiss to her temple, concerned about how cold her skin felt.

"Froze, how? Is she talking? Interacting with you in any way?" Rock asked, and he could hear the rev of an engine that told him his friend was on his way.

"No. Her eyes are blank, and her lips are moving, but she's not saying anything. She's cold, trembling, and completely limp. She's like a doll, Rock. I'm talking to her, trying to get her to answer, but she's not hearing me. She's locked inside her head, and I'm terrified about what she's reliving."

That was why he was afraid of those memories returning.

All he wanted to do was protect her from fear and pain, and yet he was forced to sit here, completely uselessly, holding his wife, doing nothing meaningful to help her while she relived the hell she had lived through.

"I'm on my way, I'll text the others. If she's having memory flashes, she'll likely wake up on her own when she's ready. If she doesn't, we'll take her to the hospital," Rock told him. "For now, just keep talking to her, keep doing what you're doing."

As he set the phone back on the table, Axe began to rock his wife on his lap, so very aware of how impotent he was in this moment.

Since there was nothing else to do but sit there and wait it out, he rocked Beth, whispered to her, touched kisses all over her face, her cheeks, her forehead, and her temple, whispering his lips against the corners of her mouth, praying every second that she would come back to him.

Minutes or hours might have passed when he heard the door to his cabin swing open, and the sounds of several sets of footsteps. Rock appeared in the kitchen doorway, the others standing behind him.

With his team there his confidence grew a little. Beth wasn't lost to him this time, she was still here, safe in his arms. While he couldn't protect her from the memories assaulting her mind, he could hold her, make sure she felt his presence, be there for her when she snapped out of it.

"How's she doing?" Rock asked as he knelt beside the chair and picked up Beth's wrist to check her pulse.

Hating how her hand hung so limply in the medic's hold, Axe forced himself not to focus on it. Beth was breathing, her heart was beating, she would be okay. "Still the same. I don't know how to snap her out of it."

"Maybe you shouldn't try," Trick suggested. "Just let it run its course. If her mind has decided it's time for her memories to start returning, then it knows she's ready to handle it."

"I agree," Panther said. "Beth is tough. Tougher than any single one of us. She can handle this. You just need to make sure you can."

There was no choice.

He *had* to handle it.

Beth was his number one priority, and he would give her everything she needed. More. He'd give her everything he had to give.

"Here, tuck this around her," Tank said, holding out a blanket.

Taking it, he wrapped it around Beth, then stood, carrying her through to the living room, he sunk down onto the couch. A couch where they had spent many an evening together, curled up reading or watching TV. There had been more of those shared moments the last few days since he woke up from his coma, and he'd been able to feel his wife slowly moving closer to him again. Beth hadn't felt so far away anymore, that distance was almost gone.

Just as he sat down and curled his wife into his lap, he finally felt her stir.

"Axel?" Beth's weak voice murmured his name, and relief hit him hard.

"Right here, wisp. I'm right here," he assured her, touching a kiss to her temple and tightening his hold so she could feel him around her.

Tears began to flood down her cheeks and she buried her face against his neck as she began to sob. Still her words when she spoke were clear enough for all of them to hear. "I remember everything Leonid Baranov did to me."

~

April 15th
    1:01 P.M.

Pain burned every nerve ending.

It didn't matter that it was nothing more than echoes of pain from newly recovered memories, right now, Beth was feeling every single thing she had felt in those months she had been Leonid Baranov's prisoner.

This hadn't been how she'd expected her memories to return.

What she'd thought would happen was more flashes appearing in her dreams. Dreaming had afforded her a measure of distance from those memories. More like she was watching them play out rather than experiencing them herself even as she knew she was seeing things that had actually happened to her younger self.

But this had been like she was picked up, transported back through time, and set down right in the middle of that hell she had lived through.

There had been no distance.

None.

At all.

She had felt each burning sting as the whip connected with her back, each hit as the man who had bought her ordered his men to strike her. She'd felt the gnawing pain in her stomach from being starved, she'd felt the pain and humiliation as he forced his way inside her body. She'd felt the terror as he covered her mouth until she passed out, then revived her and did it all over again, and the terror when he did the same thing shoving her head in a bucket of water. The agony as he burned the soles of her feet, dragged the tip of his knife over her nipples, and peeled off layers of skin on her backside, then made her sit on it for hours.

Every horrific second played out in her mind and she was powerless to stop it.

Even now, the lingering pain had her shaking and crying, the only thing stopping her from completely falling apart was Axel's arms, warm and steady around her.

Axel was here. That meant she was okay. It meant she was safe.

Beth knew that down to her bones even as the pain and terror refused to release their hold on her mind and body.

"Shh, wisp, it's okay, I've got you," Axel's voice murmured against the top of her head. The warm puff of air and the steady beating of his heart helped to reassure her that she was safe. She had been rescued, and Leonid Baranov would never touch her again.

Of course, she had seen the scars littering her body, there was no way she could not have. The only thing she had been told when she turned up there with amnesia was that there was a bad man who had hurt her in the past and who had taken her again. They had only told her that much because they needed to see if they could get her to remember where she had been held so they could hopefully get a lead on Baranov.

But knowing she had been hurt and experiencing that pain were two completely different things.

"You're not alone, Beth. Not anymore. Not ever again," Axel's voice continued to speak. She wasn't sure it had ever stopped, she remembered it even as she'd been trapped in reliving her trauma. "It's not just me here. All the guys are here, too. We all love you. You're not just my wife, you're family to all of us. None of us will stop until he's caught, until he's dead and you can believe he will never hurt you again."

Slowly strength began to ebb into her, quieting the panic.

While she still had no memories of the months she had disappeared before returning with amnesia, she did know that she had escaped.

No one would have set her free, if they had, they wouldn't have just dumped her and let her run through the woods to find her way home.

That meant she had strength inside her.

Strength she needed to summon.

Because if Axel and the others were going to have any chance at finding and stopping Leonid Baranov, they needed her help to do it.

Carefully, she eased herself off Axel's chest. While she wasn't ready to leave the security of his hold, she needed to face this head-on.

Abysmal as her childhood had been, it had taught her to be a fighter from the earliest of ages. Survival meant fighting, for a scrap of food, to ignore the pain, and to not give in to the voice whispering in her head that it would be easier to be dead than to keep enduring.

But dead wasn't better.

Dead meant giving up, and never once in her life had she given up.

If it hadn't been for the lessons she had learned as a small child, she wouldn't have survived Baranov. That much she now knew without a shadow of a doubt. Baranov had kept her alive so long because he was yet to break her. That intrigued him, that a person could be immune to his sadistic torture. Well, not immune exactly, but Beth had already suffered so much that while intense, he wasn't dishing out anything she hadn't already endured.

The moment she gave in she was dead.

That was Baranov's game. Play with his toys until they broke, and then get a new one. His near-limitless finances meant he would always have the money to buy another person. It made him almost unstoppable because he also had the money to keep moving to remain hidden. You couldn't catch what you couldn't find.

Grasping her chin between his thumb and forefinger, Axel tilted her face so he could study it. "You okay, wisp?"

Yes.

No.

Had to be.

Giving a shaky nod, she crushed her mouth to his, Beth infused every ounce of love she felt for this man into that kiss. He hadn't just saved her life when he and his team rescued her from Baranov, he'd saved her soul. Without him, she would never have experienced love, peace, and belonging. While she might have been alive she wouldn't have *lived*. Not like this, not the way Axel had taught her.

"I'll be okay," she whispered against his lips. "I have you."

His dark eyes were serious as he stared back at her. "Always."

"Then I can do this." Drawing strength from her husband, Beth faced the others. "I don't remember when I was missing, I'm sorry. I've been having memory flashes since Axel was in a coma, well *while* he was in a coma, but they were just of my childhood. Today something triggered my memories of when I was sold to Leonid Baranov. I remember ... everything ... from while I was there."

When Axel's arms tightened convulsively around her, Beth rested a hand on his forearm and began to stroke, soothing him, knowing how hard this was for the both of them.

"We don't have to do this now, Bethie," Scorpion told her.

"You can rest now, and we can talk about it tomorrow ... or another time," Tank added.

Okay, so it wasn't just hard for her and Axel but all of them.

Since she couldn't sit on all of these men's laps and stroke their arms to soothe them, she offered what she could, a reassuring smile.

"I can do this. I have all of you, I'm not alone, I'm okay." The words were for their benefit and her own. "I think two other women were rescued with me, right?"

"Two others," Panther confirmed. With a glance at Axel, when her husband nodded, Panther continued, "One of the women committed suicide shortly after being rescued. Her name was Veronica."

"Veronica," she murmured to herself, forcing her brain to focus so she could sift through those newly returned memories. "I ... remember her. She was new. Had only been there a few days. He hadn't broken her yet."

"Broken her?" Trick asked.

Her memories of after she was rescued hadn't returned yet, so Beth wasn't sure what she had told them the first time around. "Baranov only liked to play with his toys until he broke them. Then he killed them. It's why I was there for so long, he hadn't broken me yet."

"He would *never* have broken you," Axel said fiercely, and Beth found herself smiling despite the lingering pain and fear still rolling through her body.

Pressing a kiss to his jaw, she continued, "Veronica wasn't broken because there wasn't time, but I remember the other woman. Sarah?"

"Sarah," Rock confirmed.

"She had been there longer than me, but ... I don't think that makes sense," she said, unsure if her memories were reliable.

"What do you mean, sweetie?" Tank asked.

"Baranov told me on more than one occasion that I was intriguing to him because I was the only toy he'd had who had lasted that long without breaking. It was exciting to him, he was curious about why I was able to withstand his torture better than all the others. So, if I was the only one who lasted that long without breaking, why was Sarah still alive? If he considered her to be broken, why wasn't she already dead by the time you guys found us?"

CHAPTER Eight

April 15th
11:52 P.M.

She was the picture of angelic perfection.

Sweet, beautiful, and peaceful.

Axe couldn't take his eyes off his sleeping wife.

He never ceased to be amazed by Beth's strength. Growing up in a home where she had been abused basically twenty-four-seven. Never allowed to go to school, she had no friends, was rarely fed, was dirty, and given only ripped and filthy used clothes to wear. Forced to cook and clean before she was old enough to do those chores, and abused physically, sexually, emotionally, psychologically, and verbally.

Her life had been hell on Earth.

Yet she survived it, got up each morning, kept putting one foot before the other as though a part of her knew one day, if she could make it through all the bad, there would be so much good waiting for her on the other side.

Then she was sold, endured an even worse hell, and yet again, somehow, she managed to endure it all with a strength that was rarely seen and possessed by few.

Now as he held her, lying in their bed, her cheek pillowed on his chest, her hair a tangled mess of golden brown, her dark lashes fanned out against her pale cheeks, he realized how very lucky he was to have her at all. So many times he could have lost her. All it would have taken was for one of her family members or Baranov to take things one step too far and he would have lost her before he even had her.

As much as he hated her childhood, he had to admit that it was the only thing that had kept her alive until he found her.

This sweet, beautiful, strong woman had been through so much, and all he wanted to do was make sure she never suffered so much as a stubbed toe ever again.

But he couldn't.

Because Baranov was still out there.

Still a threat.

With his money, Baranov had the means to stay off the grid possibly for the rest of his life.

Love for his wife and fury for the trafficker flooded his system.

No.

Baranov didn't get to get away with his crimes.

Prey was owned and run by a billionaire family, and although Beth didn't remember it yet, Axe himself came from a very wealthy family. While he had given up a lot of that money when he refused to go into the family real estate business and instead joined the military, he had a trust fund worth several hundred million. A chunk of that money had been spent buying this property and building all the cabins, the main building, and the training courses. The rest would be spent tracking down Baranov and spoiling the woman he loved.

Shifting slightly in her sleep, Beth nuzzled closer. Unsure if she was having bad dreams or more memories, Axe smoothed his hand up and down her spine.

He was so damn proud of her.

Like the trooper that she was, she had pulled herself together to relive the horror she had survived and told them what she remembered. When she'd first been debriefed after being rescued, their focus had been on what she knew about where Baranov might have gone. Did she know of any other properties? Did he speak to her about his plans? Did he talk about interests that might help them narrow down a location?

No one had thought to focus on the whys of what Baranov did what he did.

He was a sadistic psychopath. He bought and tortured people because he had the money to do so, and it brought him pleasure.

While her comments that she was alive only because Baranov had yet to break her were in her original statements, none of them had thought to wonder why Sarah Sanders was still alive if Baranov already considered her to be broken.

After telling them what she knew, Beth had been exhausted. He had taken her upstairs, run her a hot bath, and once she was settled, he'd gone back down to check in with his team. They were going through Sarah's statements from when she had first been rescued, seeing if there were any clues to indicate why she hadn't been killed like all the other toys Baranov had broken and discarded.

There were none.

But given that they knew someone had gone after Sarah even after she should have been safe with her new identity, had killed her daughter, and since she was nowhere to be found likely taken her, too, they had a theory.

Tomas Butcher, Baranov's second in command.

They had spotted him with a woman a few months back. After tracking him to a yacht, they'd arrived moments before the man climbed onto a helicopter and the yacht exploded. The woman with him could have been Sarah Sanders.

Was Butcher obsessed with the woman?

Had she been given to him as some sort of reward for his loyalty to Baranov?

From what they could gather, Butcher served as Baranov's personal bodyguard, as his head of security, and as the man who organized their constant travel to remain off the radar of various country's law enforcement departments. It was completely plausible that Butcher had taken a liking to Sarah and asked if he could have her.

It seemed to be the only logical explanation as to both why Sarah's life had been spared and why she had disappeared.

Whatever the reasons, Axe was trusting his team to handle it. His priority had to be his wife. Beth had been through so much, and there were still painful memories that she would have to relive. She now remembered her life up until he and his team rescued her, and while there were the wonderful memories of her time with him and the life they had been building for her to unlock, there were also the memories of whatever happened to cause her to have amnesia in the first place.

Baranov's house of horrors hadn't done that.

Her family hadn't done that.

It terrified him to know what had happened to her in the eight months she had been missing that had been so horrific her mind had completely shut down.

Axe was unable to shake the feeling that something bad was coming.

Baranov was still out there, had taken Beth once already, might have Sarah Sanders back in his clutches, and had almost killed Bravo Team in the warehouse explosion. If Baranov really was cleaning house, then he needed Beth, Axe, and the rest of Bravo Team dead. They'd gotten close to him once already and they could do it again.

They wouldn't stop until they had done it again.

Until Leonid Baranov was dead.

That was the end game as far as Axe was concerned. He didn't want Baranov living in a prison, he wanted the man dead. That was the only thing that could really give Beth peace.

"Axel?" Beth's sleepy voice called his name and she lifted her head, blinking up at him.

"Go back to sleep, honey," he urged. It had taken a lot out of her getting so many traumatic memories back at the one time. What she needed was rest and reassurance, which he was happy to give her and had been trying to give her all afternoon before they climbed into bed early.

Instead of putting her head back down, she smiled at him. "I was dreaming about you, about us."

His entire body went still. Was she saying what he thought she was saying? Not wanting to get his hopes up too high, he asked, "Memories?"

"All of them. I remember how gentle you were with me when you first found me. I remember you sitting by my bed holding my hand so I could fall asleep every night those first few months. I remember you making my first Christmas the most amazing one ever with so many decorations there was practically no inch of the cabin left bare. I remember you giving me my first birthday party, my first cake, and so many more presents than anyone needed. I remember you proposing to me on a hot summer night when we were sitting on the pier with the moon shining down and the stars twinkling and fireflies dancing about. I remember the first time you made love to me. It was so special, so amazing, that we both cried and held each other afterward."

Tears burned the backs of his eyes.

Every single thing she'd said was true.

All beautiful memories he had treasured over the last year when his wife had no idea who he was, and he didn't know if she ever would.

"My man," Beth whispered.

"My woman."

"My heart."

"My life."

Without this woman, he didn't want to go on. She was the beating of his heart, the oxygen in his lungs, she was his purpose for living. She was his everything.

"I love you so much, my sweet wisp."

Tears trickled down her cheeks. "I love you just as much. More than anything. More now that I remember everything, and I know how much you must have been hurting this last year. I've survived so much, but the one thing I couldn't survive is losing you. I love you, Axel, and I don't ever want to be apart from you again. Make love to me."

∾

April 16th
   12:22 A.M.

. . .

Shock passed over Axel's face as she asked him to make love to her.

"Are you sure?" he asked.

There was the man she loved, always worried he might be taking advantage of her. Now that she had gotten her memories back of their lives together, she remembered that it had taken months to convince him she was ready the first time they made love. He'd been so concerned that he might have unintentionally pressured her. Or she felt it was something she had to do rather than wanted to do. Or she was convinced she would be kicked off the compound if she didn't.

None of those things had been true.

She'd just been ready for a sexual relationship with Axel.

Ready to embrace her future rather than her past.

Just like she was ready now.

"I'm sure," she told him.

"Because I'll wait as long as you need."

"I know."

"Just because you've gotten more memories back doesn't mean I expect sex."

"I know."

"We've spent the last year living as virtual strangers, that distance will fade on its own, we don't need to jump right into this."

Exasperated but also filled with affection, she pressed her mouth to his. It took all of half a second for him to respond. His arms came around her and he shifted her so she was draped across his front, chest to chest, his hands on her hips as he ravished her mouth.

"I'm sure, Axel. I love you, I remember everything, there's no barrier between us anymore. Nothing between us at all. Just us, our love, our commitment to one another. Do you know how much it means to me that you never gave up on me? I was so worried I couldn't be your Beth anymore, the woman you remembered, that you fell in love with. I knew I was hurting you, I didn't feel like I deserved everyone's constant reassurance. I was hurting you and that hurt me."

"Nobody blamed you for having amnesia, wisp. Nobody expected you to jump back into being the Beth we all knew. Nobody was angry with you or disappointed in you. We all just loved you and wanted you to know you weren't alone."

"Never alone," she whispered, knowing with a certainty deep down inside that she would never be alone again, had never been alone since Axel came into her life.

"Never alone," he agreed.

"Make love to your wife, Axel," she murmured, framing his face between her hands and feathering kisses across his lips. Her body was burning for her husband's touch, she was already wet for him, aching for him. Not that she would force Axel. If he wasn't ready yet, she would wait, wait patiently like he had been for her for months.

"I can't resist you, wisp."

"I don't want you to because there is no way I could resist you."

Flipping them over in one smooth motion so she was spread out against the mattress beneath him, Beth looked up at this man who had saved her in so many ways and thanked her lucky stars that she was there now. The worst was behind them, it had to be. From here on out, she and Axel were going to get the happy ending they deserved.

"Clothes have to go," Axel said, gripping the hem of his old T-shirt that she was wearing to sleep in and stripped it up and off, tossing it aside. Once he had shoved off his pajama pants, leaving him gloriously naked, he climbed back onto the bed, stretching out above her.

So many wonderful memories flooded her mind. How soft and gentle Axel's touch was, how he paid close attention to what she liked, what made her feel good, how he lavished attention on every single part of her body.

This man was a gift from God.

No other way to describe it.

"Do you know how amazing you are?" Axel asked before his lips touched a soft kiss to a pale scar on her neck just below her right ear.

To her, it didn't matter if she was amazing or not, it only mattered that Axel thought she was. She had survived, but Axel had taught her how to live, and she would forever be grateful to him for that.

A swipe of his tongue along the sensitive spot behind her ear made her shiver in delightful anticipation, and then his tongue swept down her neck and Axel paused to press a kiss to where her pulse was fluttering in the hollow of her neck.

They had quickly learned that while his fingers touching her could sometimes spike panic, tossing her mind back in time to the abuse she had suffered, Axel's tongue didn't do the same. Probably because nobody in her family had ever taken the time to make love to her with their mouth, they had just thrown her down, shoved inside her, and used her to get themselves off. Leonid Baranov was the same, he used her as a toy who was there for his own needs.

The feel of Axel's mouth on her body always kept her locked in the moment.

Like it was doing right now.

Trailing a line down one of her breasts, Axel drew her already pebbled nipple between his lips and began to suckle on it. The sensations were so familiar that tears sprang to her eyes. How had she not been able to remember this?

How had she forgotten the man she loved for even a second let alone almost a year?

When he released her nipple Axel blew a breath against the wet skin, making delightful little shivers rocket through her. Moving on to her other breast, he circled it with his tongue, repeating the circular motion as he inched closer to her needy nipple. By the time he finally drew it into the heat of his mouth, Beth was about ready to grab his hair and force him to lavish the same attention he'd shown her other breast on this one.

Allowing herself to get lost in the moment, to feel and not think, Beth focused on absorbing the featherlight caresses Axel's fingers made as he moved down her body. He was always careful to make sure his weight was never too heavy against her because he didn't want to trigger any bad memories of being held down.

"You are the most perfect thing God ever created," Axel whispered as he settled between her spread legs.

While she absolutely didn't believe that to be true, Beth loved that her husband thought it. And it was exactly the same thing she thought about him. Even if she had a genie in a bottle and three wishes to go with it, there wasn't a single thing about Axel that she would change.

He was just perfect.

Perfect for her. Everything she needed. He was more than she could have dreamed of.

It might have been twenty months since they last made love, but when Axel's tongue swiped across her center it felt like no time had passed at all.

There was no hesitation on his part, he knew what she liked, and he didn't make her whimper and beg for it. Covering his fingers with the evidence of her desire, he slipped one inside her, slowly pumping it in and out, preparing her for him to add a second. While he did so, his mouth found her throbbing bundle of nerves and began to suck on it, flicking it with the tip of his tongue.

Once he added a second finger, he spread her open so his tongue could delve inside. Keeping her stretched open, he alternated between burying his tongue inside her, and suckling on her bud until her body began to writhe as pleasure built.

So long had passed since she had felt pleasure like this, and it just kept building, and building, and building until Beth was sure she was going to explode.

When her orgasm finally did hit, she cried out her husband's name as her entire body went taut and then began to shake with the force of the pleasure flying through it. Her hips rocked, seeking more of what Axel continued to offer as she rode the wave for as long as he could keep her on it.

"Are you ready for me, wisp?" Axel asked. He never entered her body without making sure she was there with him, aware of who he was and where she was, safe in the knowledge that she was with someone who loved her.

"Can't wait," she managed to murmur, aftershocks of pleasure continuing to send tingles through her body.

"Watch me, wisp. Watch your husband make love to you."

Although the orgasm had left her sated and sleepy, Beth locked her gaze on her husband as he entered her in one thrust. There was no condom, never anything between them. Since condoms had set off a panic attack the first time he used one, Axel had gotten a vasectomy so she didn't have to worry about taking birth control, and they didn't have to use protection.

Now, as he began to thrust in and out, she wanted for the first time ever to be pregnant with his baby. Children had never been on her mind before, she'd just been happy to have a man who loved her, and cherished every second they spent together, but now she'd love to be carrying the baby of the man she loved inside her.

Axel's lips rained kisses down on her face before finally finding her lips. Tangling her fingers in his hair, she kissed him back as her legs lifted, hooking around his hips to pull him deeper inside her.

Like they were two halves of the same soul, they both found release at the same time. Pleasure tied them to one another as they rode the wave together this time.

As that pleasure began to fade, Axel didn't pull out of her, just held her close and rolled them so she was lying on top of him, his length still buried inside her. His love for her felt like a tangible thing. Alive. Perfect. Filling the holes inside of her and making her whole.

Snuggling deeper into his hold, Beth prayed that wherever he was, Leonid Baranov never got a chance to take this feeling away from her.

She'd been through so much, but in Axel's arms none of it mattered.

Leonid Baranov didn't get to ruin that for her.

CHAPTER Nine

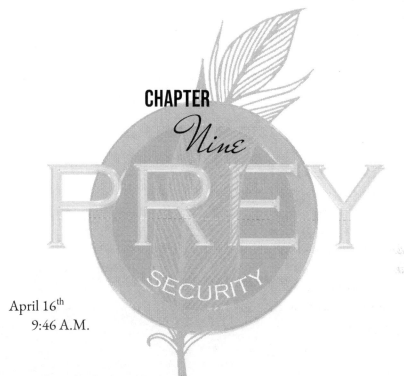

April 16th
9:46 A.M.

Something hit him on the head.

A small pink ball bounced onto the floor at his feet then rolled off across the gym floor.

Turning, Axe glared at his friends as he continued with the set of bicep curls he was doing.

"Did you just throw that at me?" he growled.

Panther shrugged, completely unapologetic. "I called your name half a dozen times and you didn't respond."

"So you threw a ball at me?" he grumbled.

Another shrug, this one accompanied with a grin. "Worked."

"Still a ball," he muttered.

"A *pink* ball," Scorpion amended, clearly amused.

"Ruthie's," Panther said as a way of explanation, his smile growing as he mentioned the little girl who had captured his heart along with her mother.

"Pink your new favorite color?" Scorpion teased.

"Sure is," Panther replied good-naturedly. "And if the baby turns out to be a girl, we're going to be swimming in everything pink." Neither Panther nor Elle wanted to know the baby's sex, deciding to wait to be surprised when their little one was born. From what Axe could gather since Panther already had a son, eight-year-old Andy, he was hoping for a girl, and since Elle already had a daughter, seven-year-old Ruthie, she was hoping for a boy. Although he knew that boy or girl, both of them would be thrilled to bring a new baby into the world, one that would officially join their little family together.

"Hey, aren't you having a girl," Tank taunted Scorpion. "You think you're not going to be living in a world of pink?"

Scorpion froze, arm with a dumbbell in his hand paused halfway between his side and shoulder, then groaned. "I would have thought Jess wasn't the kind of woman to go all pink crazy, but now that you mention it, I'm totally wrong. She's been buying baby stuff, and over half of it is pink."

The horrified look on Scorpion's face made them all laugh, which only made Scorpion scowl at them.

"You think your women won't be any different?" Scorpion asked them. "You're getting married next weekend," he said to Tank. "Tillie has been saying for months now that she wants to do one thing at a time. How long after the wedding do you think it'll be before she starts talking about adding to your little family?"

For a moment, the grin on Tank's face faltered, but then it only grew wider. "When we get pregnant, if it's a girl and my pixie wants to deck things out in pink, I'll paint the whole house inside and out if that will make her happy."

It was plain for anyone to see how much Tank loved Tillie. He'd met the woman when she'd become a Prey case the same day that Beth had reappeared on the compound. While it had been a bumpy start for the couple given the job Tank had to do, they were now so in love and ready to spend their lives together. Axe felt awful that because of him being in a coma the couple had decided to postpone their wedding a couple of weeks.

"Suck up," Scorpion muttered before turning his sly grin on Rock. "What about you? You pined over Ariel for two decades before you finally got her back. You're getting married in the summer. Do you think you two can even make it to the wedding before we hear you're expecting the pitter-patter of little feet?"

The smile on Rock's face was positively giddy. "Can't wait to get my girl pregnant. As soon as she's ready, I'm ready. And I'm with Tank. If we're having a girl and Ariel wants the whole house pink, I'm down for painting the whole woods pink. Whatever my girl wants, she gets. I owe her. Big time."

Ever since they'd known Rock, he had been in love with a woman from his past who they knew he had hurt even though they didn't have any details. Ever since Ariel came back into his life, Rock had been a different man. Happier, calmer, and more relaxed.

It was what love did to you.

It changed everything for the better, and there was no better feeling in the world than holding the woman you loved close.

"Another suck up. And you?" Scorpion turned to Trick. "Just because you and the lovely Stephanie have only been together a few months doesn't mean marriage and babies aren't in the near future for you two lovebirds."

"Can't wait." Trick grinned. "Steph is it for me and I already bought a ring."

That cut off the talk on pink for the moment as they all offered congratulations. They had all known it was a matter of time, it was plain to see that the darkness Trick and Stephanie had met in had since blossomed into the most beautiful of lights. None of them were surprised to hear that Trick was already preparing to pop the question.

"Now you," Scorpion said, turning to him. "You want to tell us what that goofy look on your face is and why you've been here but not here all morning? Can we assume it has something to do with our girl?"

Knowing how much these guys loved his wife, that they all thought of her as a little sister and would do anything to protect her, meant more to him than he could ever express to them. They'd been rock solid this past year, simultaneously supporting him and Beth as well as helping him hunt for Leonid Baranov, and falling in love along the way.

While it had sucked watching Beth bit by bit lower her guard with his friends, all he had ever wanted was for her to be happy. So as hard as it had been for him, he'd relaxed a little as he'd seen the small progress Beth had made. The worst feeling in the world for him was knowing that Beth was alone. She'd suffered through so much without any support, and it made him physically ache to see her shutting herself off from all of them.

But not anymore.

His Beth was back, and the weight of the world seemed to have lifted from his shoulders.

"Last night Beth got her memories back of our lives together," he told the guys. It wasn't that he had been purposefully withholding that from them. After sleeping with his wife in his arms, they'd made love this morning before he cooked her breakfast and walked her over to Tank and Tillie's place to spend time with the others while he and his team had a PT session. When he'd gotten there, he'd been too lost in thought about how amazing last night had been to do anything else but daydream about it.

"All of them?" Trick asked.

"Everything up until she was taken," he confirmed.

"That's awesome, man." Panther, who was closest to him, slapped him on the shoulder.

"It's more than awesome, it's perfect. I finally have my wife back." While Axe couldn't say that he had ever given up hope that Beth's memories would return, he had begun to feel like there was a chance it would never happen. She'd been slipping away, and he hadn't known how to reach out to help her when she wouldn't let him get close enough. But now she was back, and she was his again in every sense of the word and he was never going to let her go.

"I hate to sound like a wet blanket," Tank started, "but we're no closer to finding Leonid Baranov than when we first raided his house six years ago. As long as he's out there none of us are safe."

More like a bucket of ice water than a wet blanket, Axe refused to let anything dampen his mood this morning. Reality would still be there tomorrow, but today, he was going to focus only on the positives, not the negatives.

There would always be a reason to worry about safety in their line of work. And while he didn't disagree that Baranov was a major threat and the reason he and his team had been forced out of Delta Force, today was about gratefulness.

Thankful Beth was alive.

Thankful he was alive.

Thankful they were together.

Thankful her memories had returned.

Thankful that his teammates were all happy and in love and planning wonderful futures.

"Leonid Baranov is as close to the devil as we've ever gotten. He's pure evil and is a threat as long as he's alive. But if there is one thing this whole thing with Beth and her abduction and amnesia has taught me it's that even on the darkest of days, where the clouds are so thick that barely any light gets through, the sun is still there. It's still shining. The sun never moves, we do. Life does. Some days we bathe in the sun's rays, others it's so dark we can't see it. Love. The sun is love. It's always there, Beth's love, my love for her, your love for your women, and theirs for you. No matter what happens nothing can touch it. It's like the sun, there will be days when it's so bright it's blinding and days it's so dark you'll feel lost. But it's there. It's always there. That's why I know we'll bring Baranov down. There is no sun in his world, no love. He doesn't understand it. But we do. We love our families, and that's why there is nothing that will stop us from destroying the devil."

～

April 16th
12:13 P.M.

It felt so good to laugh again.

To relax.

To be free and have fun.

To be normal.

It felt like normal was the one thing she had never been. Beth knew that very few people in the world had lived a life like hers, and in some ways, it made it hard to connect to people. What could they possibly understand about growing up as she had? Of being sold and tortured?

But here, with Axel and the guys and the women they had fallen in love with she didn't feel isolated. Maybe it was because of the darkness Bravo Team had seen for themselves, first in their careers in Delta Force and then with Prey. They had seen firsthand what had happened to her, so she knew they got it even if they hadn't lived it.

These women sitting around her now got it, too.

Each one of them had lived through something horrific. Tillie's childhood trauma with her father and having a hit put on her by a crime boss. Ariel's abduction by a human trafficker, Jessica's childhood abuse, Stephanie's torture at the hands of a terrorist militia, and Elle's brush with a stalker meant they knew how evil the world could be.

This right here was her family. They got her, accepted her, and made her feel like she was completely normal.

"So, girl, you have to dish on what our guys were like before we met them," Jessica told her as they sat around Tillie's living room, finishing off things for the wedding that was supposed to happen a couple of weeks ago.

"Pretty much like they are now," she replied. Even though she had only known these women after she had amnesia, now that she had her memories back she felt closer to them. It was weird, and she didn't know why, they had all accepted her as she was, maybe it was because now she remembered the guys from before it made her feel closer to everyone.

"Big teddy bears, aren't they?" Ariel said, a dreamy look on her face. "Warriors on the outside, but inside they're so caring and soft, there's nothing they wouldn't do for someone they love."

"They're amazing," Beth said. Honestly, she didn't know how she would have survived those first few months without every single one of those men. "They were there for me unconditionally after they found me and pretty much adopted me. Leonid Baranov put targets on their backs, they were forced to leave their jobs, their homes, they were building this place, joining Prey, they had so much on their plates already, and yet they didn't hesitate to take me under their wings."

"They all love you so much," Stephanie said softly. Of all of the women, Stephanie had become the closest to Axel over the last couple of months. It had been a shock to Beth when she first saw the other woman hug Axel and had gotten a burst of jealousy. She hadn't been able to let Axel get close then and she'd known that Stephanie was in love with Trick, but still seeing another woman touching her husband had felt weird. And not good weird.

A soft smile touched her lips as she thought of her newly restored memories. "Axel used to read to me, and when he learned I didn't know how because I'd never been to school, he made it his mission to teach me everything I should have learned as a child. Trick taught me to bake, he'd spend hours with me in the kitchen," she said to Stephanie.

"Huh, I didn't know that. He's been holding out on me, I didn't know he was a baker," Stephanie said. "I think he's going to have to make that up to me."

They all laughed.

"Tell him to make you brownies, his recipe is to die for," Beth said. "Panther taught me all about phones, computers, and the internet. I didn't even know they existed. We literally lived on a farm with no running water and a generator that ran the lights. Panther gave me my first phone and made me feel normal for probably the first time ever. He was so patient, and he's such a good dad. I remember Andy bouncing about our feet while he taught me how to use the phone, he never once got frustrated with either of us even though it took me a while to figure things out."

"His patience with Andy and Ruthie is one of the things I love most about him," Elle said, her smile warm, eyes soft.

"I know it's totally weird and not really a useful, practical life skill, but Scorpion taught me how to make balloon animals," she said with a laugh.

Jessica's eyes widened. "Balloon animals?"

"Told you it was weird, but it was just ... fun. Maybe the first time in my life I was ever just playful and silly. Those were some of the happiest memories I have." Beth smiled fondly as she recalled those hours she'd spent with Scorpion.

"I had no idea he could do that," Jessica said.

"I think he was a little embarrassed about it. I don't think any of the guys know," Beth explained.

"Well, he better plan on doing that for the baby." Jessica huffed, but there was no real anger in her tone.

"You know he will," Beth said. Turning to Ariel, she smiled again. "Your guy taught me to shoot. Not so much fun, but I definitely felt a whole lot safer once I knew how to defend myself. Although Axel did about have a heart attack when he learned Rock was not just letting me touch a gun but actively teaching me how to use it."

"He worries about you," Ariel said. "All our guys are worriers."

"Can you blame them?" Jessica asked wryly.

"I guess we *do* have a bit of a habit of finding ourselves in sticky situations," Tillie conceded with a giggle.

"Sticky?" Elle snorted. "Try Gorilla Glue level stuck."

"Can't argue with that." Stephanie laughed, the darkness that lingered in her eyes was fading with each passing day, but it would never completely disappear.

"What did Tank teach you?" Tillie asked.

"So much," Beth replied. "He ran me through self-defense techniques for hours every single day. Not only did it help me learn how to get out of situations I might find myself in, but it also helped build up my strength and stamina, both of which were severely lacking after spending months locked in a cage in Leonid Baranov's basement. Axel didn't like Tank teaching me all that stuff, not because he didn't want me to be able to protect myself if I had to, but because he didn't want to think of me ever having to be in a situation where I would have to use it. But I'm so grateful for everything Tank taught me because if he hadn't, I would be dead right now."

It took a second for what she'd just said to sink in, but once it did, Beth was immediately gripped by more memory flashes.

"You want to live then you have to fight for it," a man told her.

A man she remembered.

He was Tomas Butcher, Leonid Baranov's right-hand man.

But what did he mean she had to fight to live?

Fight who?

Where?

Why?

Beth supposed the why didn't really matter.

She knew better than to go off alone, even if it was chasing after what looked like a dirty, tiny, abandoned kitten. All she'd wanted to do was find the poor little thing and take it to a shelter. Or take it home. She'd been thinking of getting a pet.

Only when she'd followed the small animal into an abandoned lot, she'd suddenly been grabbed, subdued, shoved into the back of a waiting van, and drugged.

Baranov had come for her.

Ever since Axel had saved her, she had worried this day would come.

Now that it had, it wasn't what she had expected.

Yes, she was once again back in a cage, only unlike last time, there was no rusty metal collar around her neck, attached with a chain to the door of her small cage. This cage was bigger, there was a metal toilet and a sink, and there was a metal bed frame in the corner with a mattress even worse looking than the one she had slept on as a child on top of it.

Three walls of her cage were concrete, and the fourth was metal bars running from the concrete floor to the concrete ceiling. Everything was painted white, and there were no windows, so she had no way of knowing how long it had been since she'd been kidnapped.

Beth understood why Baranov had taken her, he hadn't broken her yet, and he liked to play with his toys until they were ruined. But she had no idea what fighting for her life meant.

"Let's go," Tomas ordered.

Since he had one of his men unlock her cage and reach in and grab her arm to pull her out, she had no choice but to go where she was taken.

Still a little woozy from whatever drugs she'd been given, she did what Axel and her guys had taught her and paid attention to every detail. Figuring out the place's strengths and weaknesses might wind up saving her life. Of course, her husband would be looking for her, but she wasn't going to be a damsel in distress, she was going to fight for her freedom and her life.

Taken into a large room with a raised platform in the middle and seats all around, she looked about, totally confused.

What did they expect her to do?

Men were sitting in the seats, and on the platform in the middle was a man she was sure she recognized as one of Baranov's guards.

She was led up onto the platform, and then the man who had dragged her there stepped away.

Tomas silenced the men, and dread pooled in her stomach when he looked at her. Whatever was going on here was bad.

Really bad.

Maybe even worse than what Baranov had done to her before.

"Our first fight is ready to begin. No rules, the winner is whoever kills the other first," Tomas announced.

Kill?

They expected her to try to kill someone?

That was what they meant by fight for her life?

Either she killed the man who was a foot taller and had to outweigh her by more than a hundred pounds, or he killed her.

CHAPTER Ten

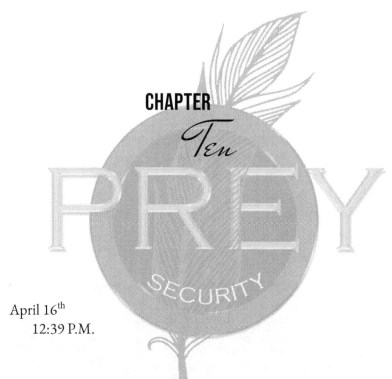

April 16th
12:39 P.M.

"Tuxedos are the worst," Scorpion grumbled as he tried his on.

Although Tank and Tillie were following in his and Beth's footsteps and getting married on the compound, while his wedding had been simple, the guys—including him—had worn jeans and shirts, Beth had worn a stunning white dress but not a wedding dress, Tillie wanted to go all out with the fairytale look. Which meant tuxedos for all the guys, including Andy who was going to be the ringbearer, formal dresses for the girls—in what he had to admit was a beautiful shade of green—and a full-on wedding dress with lace and beads for both the bride and Ruthie the flower girl.

"You'll be eating your words when Jess makes you wear one," Tank grumbled, looking no more pleased about having to wear a tux than any of the others.

Axe didn't mind them. He wasn't a fan, but growing up in a wealthy family meant attending a lot of formal events and wearing a lot of tuxes. From charity fundraisers to weddings, he had to have attended dozens over the years before he finally broke away from his family when they wouldn't accept his choices for his own life.

Scorpion likely made some snappy comeback, but when Axe's phone rang, he diverted his attention to it. Since this was the first time he'd been away from Beth—even if she was only in another building on the compound—since he woke up from his coma and they finally reconnected, they were both a little on edge. They'd already spoken and texted a few times, but he couldn't deny he was anxious to hear her voice again.

"Hey, wisp," he said as he answered the call.

Instead of Beth's voice greeting him, it was Jessica's, and she sounded panicked. Not a good thing considering not much made the former undercover cop panic.

"Axe, you need to get over here, now," Jessica told him without preamble.

He was already moving as he asked, "What's wrong? What happened?"

"Beth just zoned out. Went completely blank, eyes open but vacant, mouth moving but no words coming out. We know she had flashbacks and checked out a couple of days ago so we just kept talking to her, reminding her where she was and that she was okay. It seemed to be working, and we were going to call you and let you know that she was okay, but that you needed to come. Only then ..."

"Then what?" he demanded, waving at the guys to follow him and running toward Tank and Tillie's cabin.

"Then she started freaking out." It was clear from Jessica's tone that she was equally as freaked out.

"What do you mean freaking out?" Dread pooled in Axel's stomach. So far, she had coped well with having such horrific memories return, but there were one lot of memories none of them knew about yet. One lot that had triggered her amnesia in the first place.

Those of the eight months she was missing.

A lot could happen in eight months.

While they had, of course, had her completely checked out physically, there had been no explanation for what had caused the healed and mostly healed broken bones or the bruises in various stages of healing littering most of her body. The only one who could provide those answers was Beth herself, and with her amnesia, there was no way she could do that.

Those bruises, those broken bones had haunted him for a year now. As much as he wanted to know what had happened to his wife during those months, he was equally as terrified. Especially of her getting those memories back when he wasn't there beside her.

"She's screaming and sobbing, won't let anyone touch her. When we tried to console her, she just freaked more and started throwing punches. Ariel's okay, but Beth managed to knock her down when she tried to help. We don't know what to do for her, Axe." Jessica's voice held no anger or judgment, and the only fear was for Beth, not herself and the others. The only thing Beth had said about those missing months was a cryptic comment she'd mumbled when they'd first found her running onto the compound.

After begging them not to hurt her, she'd told them that to survive you had to fight.

None of them knew what she meant, and when they'd asked her about it after she had been calmed down and given a medical examination, she hadn't even remembered speaking the words.

"Just keep talking to her, make sure she knows she's safe, but don't get too close to her." The last thing they needed was for Beth to accidentally hurt one of her friends. She was going to be in rough enough shape when she finally snapped out of her meltdown without having to learn she had hurt someone she loved and cared about.

It seemed to take forever to run from Trick's place, where they'd been trying on the tuxes, to Tank's where Beth and the others were. Logically, Axe knew it wasn't more than minutes, but it felt more like hours before he was bursting through the door.

His heart broke at the sight before him.

Huddled in a corner was Beth. Her eyes were open and wild, it was obvious that whatever she saw wasn't the sweet cabin. Tears streamed down her cheeks, her skin was much too pale, and her entire body was trembling violently, enough that he could see it from across the room.

Without hesitation, he ran to his wife.

"No, no, I don't want to hurt him," she wailed as he approached.

When he didn't stop moving, she began to kick out with her feet and fling out her fists. Her moves weren't random, they showed near-perfect technique, strength, and purpose.

Fight to survive.

The sick feeling in his stomach told him he knew exactly what had happened to his wife.

"It's okay, Beth. It's Axel," he said, fighting to keep his voice calm and soothing as he evaded a punch and managed to use his superior skill to grab hold of her.

She was fighting like her life really did depend on it, and it was a struggle for him to keep hold of her without hurting her. Since he didn't want her to hurt herself, he tightened his grip a little, so very aware of how fragile his wife felt in his arms. If she were a threat, he could easily have neutralized her by now even though she was doing exactly what she should to get out of his hold.

"Calm down, wisp. You're safe here. You're home. It's just me holding you, just your husband, you don't need to fight anymore. You did so good though, honey. So good. You did fight, and you did survive, but now you don't have to fight anymore. You don't have to fight here, wisp. Because this is home, this is your safe place, and you're surrounded by all the people who love you. Come back to me, Beth."

Sitting on the floor as he was, with Beth's back pressed to his front, one of his legs thrown over hers, and his arms locked around her torso, pinning her arms to her side, he'd subdued her enough that he was able to touch a kiss to her temple.

"Come on, Beth, it's time to come back to me."

As the fight slowly drained out of her, he wasn't sure if it was because she was giving in to whatever was happening in her mind or if she was starting to wake up. Whatever the reason, he began to rock her as he cradled her on his lap, touching more kisses to her face, gentling his hold so it wasn't as restricting to help her know she was safe.

"Please, wisp, wake up now. Come back to me."

For what had to be a solid ten minutes, Axe sat there, holding his wife, murmuring reassuringly to her, rocking her, kissing her. Slowly, she began to relax in his hold, her attempts to get away faded until she was completely limp, her tears began to slow until they were nothing more than a trickle, and her wails quietened until it was only the sound of his voice and her ragged breathing that filled the cabin.

When he felt her stiffen all of a sudden, he straightened and shifted his hold on her so that she was facing him. "Wisp?"

One slow blink and the vacant look in her eyes cleared, and fresh tears welled. "Axel."

"Right here, honey. Right here," he promised.

"I ... I ... my memories ... I remember everything," she stammered through her tears. "They took me. Tomas Butcher told me I had to fight the men if I wanted to live. I had to kill them. I had to kill them," she repeated, pure shocked horror in her broken voice. "They were Baranov's men, I'm sure, I remember them from his house. Baranov was there, I remember him ... watching. I did everything Tank taught me, and I fought them, and I survived. I killed them. At least half a dozen men. I killed them, Axel. I took lives."

On those words, Beth's overwrought mind gave out, her eyes rolled back in her head and she slumped against his chest as she passed out.

~

April 17th
  8:01 A.M.

Waking alone in bed was not how she wanted to start her day.

Disappointment over Axel leaving her alone made Beth want to curl back up into a ball, pull the covers over her head, and hide.

But she'd done enough of that yesterday.

After the horrific memories of being forced to kill those men—good men or bad, they were still human beings, and taking a life hurt—she'd reached the edge of her endurance, and her mind and body had crashed. By the time she woke up after passing out in Axel's arms, he had already brought her back to their cabin and tucked her into bed, curling his own body protectively around hers.

That was how they had spent most of the day. When she wasn't sleeping in bed tucked into her husband's arms, she was sitting on the couch in their living room tucked into her husband's arms. Axel had been there beside her every second, he'd even run her a bath and sat in it with her, his gentle hands washing her body and her hair.

Axel wasn't the only one that had rallied around her.

All of Bravo Team had hung out in their living room for most of the day. They hadn't asked anything of her or pushed any expectations onto her. It didn't matter if she didn't contribute to the conversation or do more than pick at her sandwich. They showed her with their words and their actions that she was family, that they loved her, cared about her, and supported her.

Honestly, it was the only thing that got her through those first few hours.

But now it was a new morning, a new day, and she wasn't going to hide.

Fight.

That had been ingrained in her from birth.

Life was just one big, long battle, and if you wanted to survive to see another day you had to stand tall and face whatever came before you.

So that was what she was going to do, Beth just wished her partner was right here by her side.

Just as she swung her legs over the side of the bed, Axel stepped out of their ensuite.

"Trust you to wake up the second I go to the bathroom," he teased as he crossed the room and grabbed her biceps, pulling her up and into his arms. "How are you doing this morning?"

"I thought you had left," she said honestly. After losing her entire self and life to her trauma, then lacking the confidence to speak up and say what she needed for almost a year, there was no way she wasn't going to be one hundred percent honest from here on out.

A soft kiss touched her forehead. "Never, wisp. Wherever you are, I will be, too."

That made her smile, and she framed her husband's face and tugged it down so she could kiss him properly.

Hand in hand, they walked downstairs and into the kitchen. It didn't even need to be a question, they both knew they would be making waffles for breakfast again. As Axel began mixing the batter, Beth grabbed glasses and juice from the fridge.

Expecting some sort of argument when she said what she'd woken up knowing with absolute certainty, Beth made sure she kept her voice calm and confident. Getting too emotional right now, while totally understandable given she'd just relived a lifetime of trauma in a couple of weeks, was only going to convince Axel she couldn't do this.

But she could.

More than that, she had to.

So calm and confident it was.

"Axel, I want to help," Beth announced.

"With breakfast? I got it, wisp. If I'm here in the morning I cook you breakfast, simple as that."

A small smile curled her lips even as the ball of nausea that sat heavily in her gut churned faster. She knew that, although those first few weeks they'd lived together, it had taken a while for her to get it. Taking care of the family's needs had been one of her jobs as a child, nobody had ever bothered to take care of her, and it had taken some getting used to when Axel announced it was now his job.

Today, though, that wasn't what she was talking about.

"Not with breakfast. With finding him," she said quickly before she lost her nerve.

The glass bowl Axel had been mixing the batter in dropped from his hands as he spun to face her, shattering at his feet with a loud crash and sending glass shards and waffle batter flying across the floor.

"What did you just say?"

Even though Beth knew Axel would never lay a hand on her in anger, never touch her and cause her pain, she couldn't help but wince at the pure, unbridled fury in his voice.

This was the warrior he rarely let her see.

Her husband was always so calm and in control, he oozed confidence and reliability, he knew what she needed, peace and security, and he gave it to her without hesitation.

Standing before her now wasn't her sweet, gentle husband, it was the man who had joined Delta Force, the man who was a lethal weapon, who could kill with his bare hands in a dozen different ways, who fought to make the world a safer place, and who rescued victims.

Two sides of the same man, only this side was new to her and scared her a little.

Still, this was one fight she wasn't backing down from.

"I have my memories back now, I can find my way back to wherever I was being held. I'm sure I can," she said. Beth stuck with her plan to sound calm and confident even if her heart was beating so hard it took everything she had not to rub her chest to soothe the ache.

"We don't need your help," he snarled. It hurt a little, but she knew his anger was coming from a place of fear and nothing else.

Besides, they both knew that wasn't true. She'd been home for a year, and missing for eight months before that. If they had been going to find where she had been taken and held against her will without her help they would have done it by now.

Truth was *she* was their best bet now that she had her memories.

"I need to help," she said, meeting his gaze squarely and not allowing the terror that threatened to crush her show.

A vicious curse fell from his lips.

"No," Axel said like it was as simple as that.

The problem was, nothing about this was simple.

"Besides, we thought the warehouse that blew up was where you were being kept," Axel said as though that put an end to the entire conversation.

For her it did not.

A warehouse didn't jive with what she recalled.

The place she had been kept hadn't felt like a warehouse, and what she'd seen of it didn't look like one either. It was too big, and there weren't any windows in most of it. The place she had been held felt more like it was underground.

"I don't think I was kept at that warehouse," she said slowly.

Axel sputtered, but there was nothing he could say to that. None of them knew for sure where she had been, but of all of them, she had the best chance at figuring it out.

Carefully crossing the room to stand before her husband, she took both his hands in hers, squeezing a little. "I'm not asking you to put me on the front line, Axel. I just want to help. I need to help. Leonid Baranov stole everything from me, he almost made me lose you. I want to be part of helping take him down. I just want to help you retrace my steps and find the place where I was held. I doubt anyone is still there, it would be too big of a risk, but there could be clues. Once I help you find the place I'll come back here and stay safe while you and your team do your thing."

His fingers curled around hers until they were almost painfully tight. Then he growled and dragged her closer until she was flush against him. "I can't lose you, Beth. Don't you get that? You can't ask me to put you in a potentially dangerous situation after I only just got you back."

"I'm not. I'm asking you to trust me the same way I trust you to keep me safe. I killed men twice my size, I did it because I had to come home to you. You're my everything, but as long as that man is still out there, we will always be looking over our shoulders waiting for another attack. All I'm asking is that you let me help bring him down so we can have the future we deserve."

Even before he let his forehead drop to rest against hers, Beth knew that he was going to allow her to work with him and his team. It didn't really feel like a victory, though, because this was terrifying and dangerous.

But it had to be done.

As Axel's mouth crashed to hers, she just prayed she was making the right decision for all of their sakes.

CHAPTER
Eleven

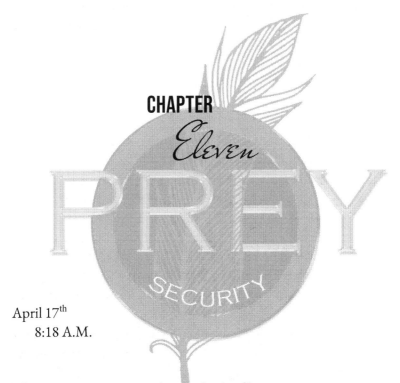

April 17th
  8:18 A.M.

This woman was going to be the death of him.

She consumed him, drove him crazy, made him irrational with a need to keep her safe, drove every single one of his protective instincts into overdrive, and made his heart swell with so much love that he wondered how it still fit in his chest.

Beth was his everything, and the thought of her being hurt was making him lose control.

Knowing what he did about Beth's past and how she had been abused and tortured, Axe always made sure that when he touched her, it was with the gentleness and reverence that she deserved. Sex between them was soft and sweet, but what was arcing through the air in this moment was the opposite.

When her hands fumbled at the waistband of his pajama pants, trying to shove them down his hips, her greedy hands reaching for his already rock-hard length, some of his common sense returned.

He couldn't maul her like she had been used and abused by every other person in her life. Beth deserved the world, she deserved to be worshipped, not thrown down on the kitchen table and ravished like he was some horny, hungry teenager.

"Wait," he said, managing to get a grip on Beth's wrists, stilling her almost frenetic movements.

"Wait? Why?" Beth asked with a pout. An actual pout.

Smiling despite the desire coursing through his veins, he held onto her wrists with one hand and, with his other, smoothed a lock of hair off her cheek, tucking it behind her ear. "Because I need to slow down a little or I'm going to pick you up, carry you upstairs, strip you naked, and throw you down on the bed."

A shiver rocketed through her, and heat burned brightly in her eyes making them appear to glow on her otherwise pale face. "Do that," she said in a breathy whisper.

"Can't, wisp," he said, although his body was totally on board.

"Why?"

Her voice had a thread of vulnerability, and he ached to wash it away. "Because you deserve sweet, soft, and gentle. You deserve everything."

"Then give me everything." Although he still held her wrists, she shifted the rest of her body closer. "You've given me sweet, soft, and gentle, and you were right, there was a time when that was what I needed. When it was all I could handle. But I'm stronger now, Axel. *You* helped me become strong. You shared your friends with me, and every single one of you taught me what I needed to survive hell. I can never change my past, Axel. I can never go back and do it over, but I want a future, a future with you. You give me everything I need, so don't hold back now. Give me everything, make love to me like I'm not a woman who's been abused her whole life."

Never able to deny his wife anything, Axel grabbed her hips and lifted her, grinding his erection against her center. "Are you sure?"

"Positive," she said, squirming in his arms. His length jerked at the friction, and he tightened his grip on her hips to hold her still.

"And you'll tell me if you feel uncomfortable and need me to stop?

Nonnegotiable," he added as he began to carry her toward the stairs. "I won't ever do anything to hurt or traumatize you."

"I know. That's why I trust you to make love to me any way you want. I just want to be normal, Axel. For one moment, I want to be completely normal."

"Normal is overrated," he said as he reached their room and tossed her onto the bed.

Beth landed with a bounce and squealed in delight, the gleam in her eyes told him she was all in. If she was just doing this as a way to prove some sort of point, either to him or to herself, then he wouldn't go through with it. Axe meant it when he said he wasn't going to do anything to hurt or traumatize her. She'd been through enough, but if this was what she wanted, to be treated like any other woman then he could give her that.

Even if she wasn't any other woman.

She was his woman.

His to love, his to protect, his to pleasure.

Which was exactly what he intended to do.

Shoving off his pajama pants, he left them where they dropped and climbed onto the bed. All Beth was wearing was one of his T-shirts so it didn't take more than a couple of seconds to grab the hem and yank it up and over her head, throwing it onto the floor.

Delectably naked and ready for him.

"Touch yourself, honey," he ordered as he shifted so he was on the bed, his knees on either side of her legs, looking down at her.

Beth's eyes widened. He was pretty sure she had never touched herself. Her life had never been the kind that was conducive to her learning about her body or even having the time to think about what brought her pleasure.

Her hand trembled as she moved it between her legs, but there was no hesitation on her part, and he watched in fascination as her slender fingers slid along her wet center and came to rest on her swollen bud. She swirled the pad of her finger on it before bringing it to her opening and slipping it inside, Axe began to stroke his hand up and down his length. Sex with Beth was always perfection, it didn't matter to him if it was slow and sweet, or hot and passionate, but seeing his wife like this, no inhibitions, no timidity, he knew hot and passionate was going to be in the cards a lot more frequently.

Alternating between pumping her fingers in and out and working her bundle of nerves, Beth whimpered, her breathing growing ragged as she began to writhe on the bed as pleasure built inside her.

His length jerked as he watched her, and as much as he loved watching her pleasure herself, if she didn't come soon, he was going to and he wasn't coming until he was buried inside his wife.

"Faster, babe," he said as his free hand circled her wrist and his finger touched the top of hers, adding pressure to her bud as they worked it together.

"I'm close, Axel," she said with a moan as he moved both their hands to her opening.

Taking her hand, he curled her fingers into her palm one by one until only her forefinger was left up. Then Axe covered her hand with his, keeping his own forefinger straight, and plunged both their fingers inside her.

She was hot, tight, and utterly perfect, and he couldn't get enough of her as they slid their fingers in and out. Both their movements grew jerky when he withdrew their fingers and moved them to her bud, working it hard and fast.

"Come, babe, now," he ordered her, and just as he dipped their fingers back inside her, grazing the spot that would make her see stars, she exploded. Crying out her pleasure, her internal muscles clamped around their fingers as he continued to thrust them in and out as his thumb brushed across her bud, prolonging her pleasure.

While she was still quivering, Axe released her hand and grabbed her hips, burying himself inside her in one smooth move. Beth cried out her pleasure again as her quivering muscles continued to pulse around his length, and he grabbed her bundle of nerves between his thumb and forefinger, rolling it a few times then pinching it hard, and a second orgasm rolled through her.

Thrusting roughly into her, it only took a few seconds before he found his release and he came with a grunt. Waves of pleasure seemed to go on and on, and he realized that he'd been treating his wife like she was a lot more fragile than, in reality, she was. Beth had been bent in all number of directions, but she hadn't broken. She was strong, so much stronger than him, and while he would always feel the need to protect her, he also had to encourage her to find her wings and learn to fly.

Because she would never fly away. His Beth was smart and capable and could do anything she put her mind to.

Including helping him and his team find the building where she had been held prisoner.

Sinking down onto his wife, careful to keep his much larger body from crushing hers, he held her tight, rolling them to their sides so they were facing each other, him still buried inside her.

"Thank you," she whispered, feathering a kiss to his lips.

"Thank *you*," he countered. "For being strong enough to survive and come back to me. For being the most amazing woman ever to have existed. For loving me despite my faults."

"You don't have any faults."

Axe chuckled. "Spoken like a woman in love. I don't think you have any either."

"You're going to let me help, aren't you?"

"On one condition."

"I won't do anything stupid. I won't do anything dangerous. I'll do everything you tell me without arguing or trying to discuss it with you first."

"Not what I was going to say, but good to know. The condition is today you just get to be my wife. Nothing else. No madman trafficker hunting us, no danger, no pain, no fear, nothing but you and me and this bed. Oh, and maybe the bath, and the shower, and definitely the kitchen. I've always wanted to taste you in the kitchen. Tomorrow, we'll let our problems back in, but today, we're just going to be a regular husband and wife."

~

April 18th
    11:14 A.M.

. . .

She was getting frustrated with herself.

Okay, so she was well past frustrated, Beth was absolutely annoyed with herself. The worst part was she couldn't even lie to herself and say that she had a terrible sense of direction, which was why she struggled to figure out the path she had taken a year ago. As a child, they had lived on a remote mountain farm, and she had known every inch of those woods. Known the perfect places to hide so nobody would find her. Although, she only hid out there when she needed a break because there was always a punishment waiting for her when she got home.

It wasn't even the fact that a year had passed since she ran through these woods, her desperate mind knowing only one thing. That she needed to get home to her husband. Just because a year had passed in real time, since she only got her memories back a couple of days ago, they felt much fresher, more like they had just happened.

So far, they'd been at this all morning, and she was yet to lead them more than about fifteen minutes away from the compound where she'd set off the alarm when she'd entered it that night. How were they ever going to find their way to wherever she'd been kept at this rate? It would take them days, weeks even.

"Hey, you're doing fine," Axel soothed from where he stood right beside her.

Frustration simmering over, she whirled around to face him. "That's a lie and we all know it," she snapped.

Eyes widening in surprise, they then softened in understanding. "It's not a lie, wisp."

"Of course it is," she said with an eye roll. While totally aware she was being unfair, her husband had been nothing but supportive even though she knew he didn't want her to do this, she couldn't seem to help herself.

"No, Beth, it's not," Axel said, firmer this time. "Nobody thought this was going to be easy for you. Nobody thought you were just going to waltz out of the estate and lead us on a trail back to where you were held in under five minutes."

"I did." She huffed.

"Think you need to readjust your expectations then, Bethie," Tank spoke up.

"You *are* doing a great job," Axel assured her.

"You *have* to say that because you're my husband."

"You *are* doing a great job," Scorpion repeated Axel's words as he slung an arm around her shoulder and pulled her in for a brotherly hug. "And Jessica would kill me—slowly—if I married anyone but her."

His teasing helped her to relax a little, and that eased some of the pressure inside her. Maybe she really *was* putting too much pressure on herself, having unrealistic expectations.

"Okay, I'll try not push myself so hard," she agreed.

"The harder you push yourself, the less likely you are to remember anything," Rock said.

"Really?" she asked, turning to look at him. She'd thought the harder she pushed herself, the better she would remember things, and she was pushing as hard as she could which was why she was getting so frustrated with herself.

"Definitely," Rock said. "You're trying to force your brain to do something it only just decided you were in a place where you could safely remember without causing more damage."

"And remember when you ran back to the estate you weren't in a good frame of mind," Trick added. "You were hurt and traumatized, you were running for your life, you weren't taking notes so you could find your way back."

"That's true," she agreed slowly. They also had no idea when her amnesia had kicked in. Had she forgotten who she was sometime while she was being held prisoner and being forced to kill to survive? Had she lost her memory while running through the woods? Had she lost her memory when she finally knew she was in a place where she was safe? When her memories had come back, they'd all come back so she had no idea when she'd lost them, although if she had to guess, it was the second she stepped onto the estate and knew without a shadow of a doubt that she was now safe.

"Elle does this cute thing with the kids when they can't remember something. It's kind of silly, but do you want to try it?" Panther asked.

"I'll try anything," Beth answered quickly. There was a lot of pressure on her to do this. From herself, at least, since the guys had only reluctantly agreed to let her try this and kept reassuring her that she was doing fine.

"Okay, close your eyes," Panther instructed. Once she had, he continued, "Now think of the last time you laughed. When was it?"

A smile was already on her face as she answered. "Last night, Axel thought he was so clever making me a chocolate dessert smorgasbord. I told him not to try to carry everything at once and offered to help, but he was being all alpha macho man and wouldn't let me. Of course, he dropped it and chocolate went everywhere. And I do mean everywhere. Took us an hour to clean up, and I'm still not convinced we won't come home to find the kitchen swarming with ants who found everything we missed."

There were snorts and snickers all around, but Beth kept her eyes closed, enjoying reliving the perfectly ordinary, normal person's life moment in her head.

"Good one." Panther chuckled. "Okay, now you're just going to let yourself relax and picture your mind right where you want it to be. This is the last place you remember being so just let your mind drift back there. No putting pressure on yourself, and any time you feel yourself getting all tense and stressed, you just picture that moment where soldier clumsy here thought he could do everything himself."

Letting go of the pressure, Beth allowed herself to relax and picture herself a year ago running through these woods desperate to get home to the people who loved her.

There had been no other thought in her mind.

A singular purpose.

Get home.

Get to Axel.

Then she'd be safe.

So obviously, she still had her memories while she was running home. She hadn't found the compound because its location was buried in her subconscious, she knew where it was and was heading there on purpose. Once she got there, unable to process any more trauma, her mind had just shut itself down.

But she knew where she was going.

Which meant she had known she was close to the compound.

That meant she must have recognized something in the place where she was being held or the surroundings when she first escaped, and knew she was close to home.

Relaxed now, no longer trying to force herself to figure out the path she had taken that night, Beth found that images began to play in her mind.

Opening her eyes, she turned a little to her left. "I came from this way," she told Axel and the guys, pointing in the direction she remembered herself running.

"Knew you could do it," Axel said, grabbing her hand and tugging her closer so he could give her a quick kiss.

"Sorry for taking my frustration out on you, it wasn't your fault I couldn't figure it out," she whispered, touching another kiss to his lips.

"Not mad at you, wisp, but you're forgiven."

"I love you, more than anything," she said, compelled to make sure he truly understood the depths of her love. He was the first person to ever love her, to ever even care about her, and she treasured that gift like the precious thing it was.

"Love you right back."

Keeping a hold on her husband's hand, for the next couple of hours Beth led the men through the woods. It wasn't always easy. There were times she could feel her frustration level rising again, but every time it did, she stopped, closed her eyes, and pictured something that made her laugh. It was like a mind cleanser, and after, she could always push away the irritation, focus again, and figure out where she had come from.

Every so often the guys made her stop, take a moment to rest, drink some water, and eat a piece of fruit. It wasn't particularly hard hiking out there, but they were deep in the forest, and with the combined physical and mental work she was doing, Beth was beginning to weary.

"We should stop soon, head back, start again tomorrow," Axel announced. "We'll mark the spot so we know where we got to, and Panther can start running checks on this area, see if we can figure out where you were."

Ignoring him, something tickled the back of Beth's mind.

There was something about this place that ... freaked her out.

The trees looked the same, but the hairs on the back of her neck stood up, and her heart rate accelerated even as she stood still.

"Axel?"

"What's wrong?" he asked, sensing her growing distress.

"I think we're—"

Before she could finish her sentence, gunshots broke out around them, and she was thrown to the ground, her husband's body covering her and pinning her down.

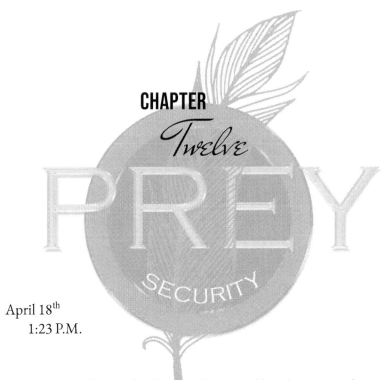

CHAPTER *Twelve*

April 18th
   1:23 P.M.

"Are you shot?" Axe asked Beth as he pressed her down into the ground, covering her entire body with his own.

Panic drummed a steady beat inside him.

The gunshots had come out of nowhere. He and his team were highly trained, and they hadn't detected any other presence in the woods.

Whoever these guys were, they were good.

Almost too good, considering he and Beth were sitting ducks out there.

While his team had all taken cover behind trees, Axe's only thought had been Beth and keeping her from getting hit. If she hadn't been already. Now with gunshots continuing to be fired at them, there was nowhere for him to go. For now, they were stuck where they were, and if Beth had been hit and was bleeding out, there would be nothing he could do for her.

He'd be forced to lie there and watch her bleed out beneath him.

"N-no," Beth stammered. "Are y-you?"

Honestly, with fear consuming every inch of him like the greedy monster it was, he couldn't tell. There was no searing pain coming from any part of his body, not even a sting, so he took that to mean he hadn't been shot, but with so much adrenalin flooding his body any pain could be quite easily masked.

"I'm not hit," he assured her.

Another shot hit close enough that he could feel the dirt fly up onto his face. From the way she flinched beneath him, he knew Beth had felt it, too.

They were too exposed out there, but the only way to get to cover was to move, and that meant exposing Beth to the flying bullets.

Which he was not prepared to do.

Cursing the fact that they weren't wearing comms because they hadn't thought it would be necessary, Axe wished he could communicate with his team without having to yell out and give the enemy more information about them, their exact positions, how many of them there were, and that they had an unarmed, untrained woman with them.

"Axel, I remember this place, we're close," Beth whispered.

It never even occurred to him to ask her if she was sure. Beth had been an absolute rockstar. Even though she had struggled, getting frustrated with herself when she couldn't just walk them in a straight line to the place she'd been held captive, she had fought through her annoyance, focused herself, and led them all the way to there.

Even if his faith in his wife wasn't as strong as it was, the fact that they were being shot at confirmed that wherever the facility was that Beth had been held at, it had to be nearby.

There was no other reason someone would be shooting at them.

Deciding to risk calling out to his team was better than grabbing Beth and running with her to hide behind the trees, Axe asked, "We got eyes on them?"

"Negative," Scorpion's voice called back.

"Has to be at least four of them from the direction of the shots," Trick added.

"Angle suggests they're above us," Panther said.

That made no sense. If the men were in the trees shooting at them, they should be able to pin down the location of the shots much easier.

But now that he was ruthlessly shoving back the terror at Beth being stuck in the center of a gunfight, he realized that the shots were somewhat chaotic. While several had come close to hitting him and Beth, others seemed to fly about randomly.

"Anyone hit?" he asked.

Five negatives somewhat soothed his frazzled nerves but didn't explain the haphazard shots. How could these men be good enough to remain undetected, but not good enough to pick them off one by one?

In reality, all seven of them should already be dead.

They should have been shot before they even realized they were being watched.

"Shots don't seem to be directed at any of us specifically," Tank said, echoing Axe's own concerns.

"And they're not coming closer and haven't responded to us talking," Rock added.

Something felt wrong, but he had no idea what it was. Were they hoping to confuse them, wait for one of them to make a move, and then take them out? Maybe they wanted to be able to say they had been shot at first so they didn't have to explain seven dead bodies? Or maybe they were trying to lure them into some sort of trap?

A cry fell from Beth's lips as another bullet hit the ground right where the one before had, a mere three inches from their heads.

What were the chances someone would hit that same exact spot?

"Axel, the guns, I remember, it's not people. They're programmed to shoot when something sets off the motion sensors. I remember almost getting hit when I ran," Beth said in a rush.

Again, he didn't doubt his wife for a second. She hadn't only been strong enough to survive what Baranov had done to her, but she'd been smart enough to escape as well.

"Guys, no one is shooting at us, it's a security system set up to shoot at movement," he called out.

"Genius," Panther muttered, and Axe rolled his eyes at the tech genius who could find something about this to be excited about.

"We need to get close to the system so we can shut it down. We can't stay here forever," Axe said. Because while there might not be an actual person shooting at them, the system would be set to alert whatever human guards were nearby, and soon they would all be converging on this area.

"If I can get close enough I can shut it down," Panther said confidently.

"Or we just shoot them down," Scorpion muttered.

"Panther's plan first, otherwise, have at it," Axe ordered.

The seconds felt interminably long as he lay there, forced to wait while his team took care of the threat. But nothing would make him move and put his wife at risk. If they stayed exactly where they were, they wouldn't be hit. The guns could fire only in the same directions time and time again, and they were in a safe spot so he didn't dare move and put Beth in danger.

Sooner or later, the weapons would run out of ammo, but he had no intention of hanging around until then. The need to get Beth out of there, somewhere safe, somewhere far away from the place that had tortured her so badly her mind had needed to shut down just to survive, was almost too strong to ignore.

Knowing how close this place was to the compound made him want to pack up Beth, and the others, and ship them off to hole up at Prey's main office building. The place was in the middle of Manhattan and had several secure apartments. Leonid Baranov managing to get to Beth there would be impossible.

Ever since Beth returned a year ago, they had known the place she'd been kept had to be close to the compound, but they had checked out the entire area and found nothing indicating a facility where she could have been held captive. Knowing it was close to the compound, and now *knowing* it were two different things, and the safe home they had built no longer felt all that safe.

Baranov could have come for them at any time.

Why hadn't he?

What had stopped him from annihilating Bravo Team when he had already put out hits on them six years ago?

None of it made sense.

The Russian oligarch had been there when Beth was held captive, she said she remembered him watching her as she fought for her life, but her only interactions appeared to have been with Tomas Butcher.

That had to mean something, but as another bullet slammed into the earth inches from his wife's head, it was hard to concentrate long enough to figure out what.

"Hold on, wisp, I got you," he murmured, hoping to soothe her a little. Just because she wasn't complaining, screaming, or crying didn't mean she wasn't terrified. He could feel how badly she was shaking.

"You always have me," she whispered back.

"Always," he agreed. There would never be a time when he wasn't prepared to put his body between her and a bullet.

As soon as this was over, he was tucking his wife safely away at Prey. Then he was going to do whatever it took to finally bring down Leonid Baranov once and for all.

If only they could hurry up and move from this spot.

Come on, Panther.

The number of bullets flying had decreased, implying that one of the guns shooting at them had been disabled. Still, the occasional bullet hit the ground or a tree nearby which meant there was at least one more in operation, probably more.

Seconds ticked by feeling more like hours.

Until finally, everything went quiet.

Deadly quiet.

The kind of quiet that was like being in the eye of a hurricane.

~

April 18th
    1:58 P.M.

"D-did Panther get the g-guns to turn o-off?" Beth asked. As much as she hated that her voice was shaking along with the rest of her, there was nothing she could do about it.

Knowing what she had survived, knowing she had killed to stay alive, none of it meant anything in this moment. Because deep down inside, she was no trained warrior, she was just a woman who had been forced to learn how to live through terror because it was either that or die.

Literally, those were her only two options.

The men there with her knew what they were doing, they were confident in their abilities, and while she had no doubt Axel was terrified for her safety, and all the other men on Bravo Team were afraid of not making it home to their loved ones, they weren't rocked by tremors like she was.

"I think he did, wisp," Axel replied. His voice was soft and soothing. If it wasn't for the way he pressed her down into the ground hard enough that it hurt and felt like she was being crushed, she would think he wasn't affected by the gunshots.

"Then why aren't we getting up?" she asked, pleased when she managed to keep the shakes out of her voice that time.

"Because we don't move until Panther himself tells us we're all clear," he replied evenly.

"But no more shots have come," she reminded him. She wanted to get up, find that place, and tear it to the ground so no one else could ever be hurt there again.

"I won't risk you," Axel said in a voice that very clearly communicated that arguing would be pointless.

Not that she wanted to argue anyway. Beth trusted her husband and these men who were the big brothers she'd dreamed of having as a child implicitly. But ...

How could she ask them to keep risking their lives for her?

Just because she'd had amnesia and had been doing her best to keep her distance from all of Bravo Team not just her husband didn't mean she wasn't aware of how many times they'd gone out hunting down a lead. Of course, she knew that they weren't in danger just because of her and what had happened to her. This was the job they had picked, the life they had chosen, and if it wasn't she might never have survived Leonid Baranov's House of Horrors.

But knowing they put themselves in danger to make the world a safer place, to save people like her, to kill people like Leonid Baranov, and knowing they were putting themselves in danger specifically for her because they loved her was so very different.

"We've gotta get out of here," Panther called out, sounding breathless as footsteps suddenly pounded the ground around them.

In one smooth move, Axel hooked his arm around her waist and pulled her up with him. "What did you find?" he demanded.

"There were four stations with guns aimed in all directions. I disabled all four of them," Panther replied.

To Beth, that sounded great, but obviously there was more bad news coming.

Seemed there was always bad news coming.

Why for once in her twenty-four years couldn't something go right for her?

Seriously, did the universe hate her or something? It gave her a family right out of a nightmare, then threw her from the frying pan into the fire, then when it finally gave her a break and a wonderful man to love her, it then took it all away.

No more.

Please no more. I don't think I can take another bad thing.

Was that why she had really been so hesitant to let Axel get close when she had amnesia? Was it because, at the back of her mind, she feared that something else would happen and it would be the final straw that broke the camel's back and destroyed her?

As much as she wanted to pretend she was strong enough to survive anything, the truth was she wasn't. Nobody was. Sooner or later, she'd break under the pressure life kept piling on her shoulders.

"What are you doing?" she asked, startled when Axel suddenly picked her up and pushed her up toward the branches of a nearby tree.

"Weren't you listening?" he asked.

"Umm ... I might have been distracted," she admitted.

"Whoever set those guns up was alerted as soon as they started firing. Panther, Rock, and Tank saw them when they went to disable the guns," Axel summarized for her. She didn't have to ask to know that Scorpion and Trick had stayed there watching over her and Axel while the others had gone to disable the weapons.

But she did have to ask why he was putting her in a tree instead of all of them running. "So, we have to get out of here then," she said, wriggling in her husband's hold.

"No time."

The grimness in Axel's tone made her blood turn to ice. It sounded so ... final. "Maybe there is," she said desperately, fighting the fresh wave of terror mounting inside her.

"No, wisp, there isn't," Axel said with a calm she knew he didn't feel. "You're going to hide. Panther saw at least a dozen men, but there could be more. Depending on how well trained they are, we might stand a chance."

She could barely breathe let alone speak. "And if you don't?"

Although she asked the question, they all knew the answer.

If Bravo Team couldn't fight off the men, they would all die in these woods. Tillie would never get to marry the man she loved after putting off the wedding twice already. Likewise, Ariel would never get to marry her lifelong crush and soulmate. Jessica wouldn't marry Scorpion and would raise their daughter alone. Stephanie would never get to say yes when Trick asked her to marry him. And Elle would be left raising her daughter, Panther's son, and their unborn child alone.

All because of her.

"You can't die," she said, clawing at Axel, desperate to latch onto him so he couldn't leave her.

"Don't plan on dying, wisp, I can promise you that," Axel said, his voice soothing even as his eyes were tumultuous, filled with fear, regret, and pain. He might not be planning on dying, but it didn't mean it wouldn't happen.

"No one on our side is dying here today," Rock said confidently.

"Amen, brother," Trick added.

"You forgotten who you're talking to, Bethie?" Tank asked, determination in his dark eyes.

"We're taking them down," Scorpion said.

"Because no one is hurting the people we love ever again," Panther declared.

"We're going to do everything we can, wisp. None of us will go down without a fight. But we need to know you're safe and out of the way. You're going to stay there and not come down. Not for anything," Axel clarified.

Aware she was wasting time with her panicking, Beth gave a shaky nod. "Kiss me?" she asked, all too aware it might be the last time she ever got to kiss her husband.

Crushing his mouth to hers in a quick but heartfelt kiss, Axel then lifted her up into the tree.

Beth's hands were shaking badly as she grabbed a branch and began to pull herself higher. Axel and the guys had disappeared as if into thin air, although she felt them nearby when she chanced a quick glance down.

When she thought she had gone high enough that nobody would see her she stopped. Wrapping her legs around the branch she was sitting on, Beth leaned against the tree trunk and squeezed her eyes closed as though that could make everything go away.

No sooner had she caught her breath than gunfire erupted below her.

No stranger to fear, there was something different about knowing it wasn't you who was in immediate danger but the man you loved. The people you loved. People who hadn't hesitated to take her under their wing, shower her with love and care, and be there for her in all the ways she hadn't even known she needed.

Now they were down there putting their very lives on the line for her.

While Axel was her heart, her soul, her everything, she loved every single one of those men and would do anything for them.

Tears streamed down her cheeks, and she pressed her hands to her ears in a desperate but pointless attempt to block out the sound of firing guns. Had Axel been hit? One of the guys? Or were they slowly eliminating the enemy?

There was no way for her to know from up there.

"Beth," the sound of her name being called by a voice she recognized from her nightmares had her eyes popping open, her hands dropping from her ears.

She didn't hear Axel.

Didn't hear any of the others.

Did that mean they were all already dead?

Was it over?

Had they lost?

"I know you're close by, Beth," Tomas Butcher's voice continued. "And if you don't come out from wherever you're hiding in the next sixty seconds, I'm going to put a bullet in the brain of one of your friends here. Then, another sixty seconds after that I'll kill another, and another, until your husband is all that's left. Then I'll torture him and kill him slowly until the sounds of his screams pull you in."

CHAPTER
Thirteen

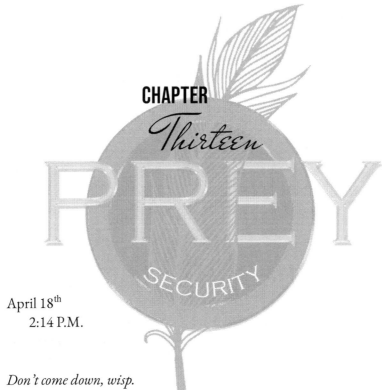

April 18th
   2:14 P.M.

Don't come down, wisp.
   Please don't come down.

Even as Axe sent the silent prayer into the universe, he knew it was already a lost cause.

Of course, his girl was going to come down.

There was no way on Earth Beth was going to stay hiding in a tree while Tomas Butcher and his men killed her friends. Tomas wouldn't even have to get to the part of his threat about torturing Axe before Beth would be shimmying down that tree.

Damn his wife and her big heart.

How had life not taught her that people were rotten, evil, undeserving of her love?

It didn't matter that his team weren't any of those things, he didn't want her putting her life in danger. Not that he wanted any of his friends to die, he loved these men like brothers, but they had all signed up for this life, knowing what they were doing, what they were risking.

Beth was a completely innocent victim and didn't deserve any of what had happened to her.

Lined up on their knees with their hands behind their head, weapons pointed at them, they were about ten yards away from the tree he knew Beth was in. They had managed to take out about a dozen men before they were outnumbered, but Tomas still had about two dozen with him.

From the number of guards and the fact that Tomas himself, Baranov's right-hand man, were all there it was obvious that the facility Beth had been held at was still operational. So why hadn't they managed to locate it? And why hadn't Baranov made a move before now? He had to know where Bravo Team's compound was, and he clearly had the manpower to run a successful raid. So why hadn't he?

What vital piece of the puzzle were they missing?

A mere ten seconds after being given an ultimatum, Beth's terrified voice called out. "Don't shoot anyone. I'm coming, but it's going to take me longer than a minute to climb down from this tree."

Victory bloomed on Tomas' face as he immediately pinpointed the tree Beth's voice had come from and stalked over to it, four of his men following behind him. "You try anything stupid, and I'll kill one of them," Tomas warned.

"What stupid thing am I going to try?" Beth huffed. It was clear she was afraid from her tone, but there was strength there, too. She was a survivor, and she had learned at a young age how to not let her fear control her.

Hold onto that strength for me, wisp.

I promise you it's not over.

We'll get you home.

We all have too much to live for to let it end like this.

Part of him wished they'd given Beth a gun so she could take down some of these monsters, but the more sensible part knew she couldn't take them all out, and in the resulting shootout, she would more than likely wind up getting shot.

Before her feet even touched the ground, Tomas gestured to a couple of his men who reached up and grabbed her roughly. A growl rumbled through Axe's chest without him even realizing it at the sight of the men manhandling his wife.

As soon as he figured out a plan to get them all out of this alive, he was going to take great pleasure in killing those men slowly and painfully.

Beth was dragged over to where the rest of them were standing, and Axe could feel the anger raging from the rest of his team. They all loved Beth, and seeing anyone hurt her was unacceptable.

"You should have left it alone," Tomas said as he stood in front of them. Something in his voice hinted there was more going on here than they were all aware of, and Axe believed it.

There were too many questions without answers, too many things that didn't make sense, and there was something they were missing, and he wanted to know what it was. The lives of his wife, his team, and his teams' families were all in danger so long as Baranov was out there.

It was time to end this.

"We're all going to walk together down to the building I'm guessing you were out here to find. Since you've gotten closer than you should have, we'll have to transport you to another facility," Tomas said, although it seemed he was speaking more to himself than to them. "Since I suspect threatening your own safety isn't as likely to garner the cooperation I want, I'll just remind you that if you try anything, our sweet Beth here will be the one to suffer."

To highlight his point, he tangled his fingers in Beth's hair and yanked hard enough to make her wince, although she clamped her lips together and didn't utter a sound.

Men moved behind him and the others, grabbing their hands and yanking them down, tying their wrists together. Then he was hauled to his feet and nudged with the barrel of a weapon.

For the next twenty minutes or so they were marched through the woods. Tomas was up the front, his hand still in Beth's hair, dragging her along with him, moving faster than her much shorter legs could move.

As he watched, his anger burned brighter. Tomas was a dead man. He was hurting Beth just to make a point, to remind them all that he was the one with the power. Only Axe didn't believe that. For now, yes,

Tomas had the numbers advantage, but that was it. The ropes around his wrists had been tied tight enough, but he could get out of them in minutes at the most, which meant these men weren't as trained as he and his team.

All they needed was for some of the men to leave and then they could make their move.

It took Axe a moment to realize what he was seeing when they were all stopped. They were in a small clearing, but there didn't appear to be anything there other than a few vans parked near the end of what was barely a road, more a vague track through the trees. Over by one end of the clearing was what looked like a rock formation, but as Axe looked closer, he realized it was actually disguising a door.

No wonder when they had run searches of the area, sending out drones and analyzing satellite images, they hadn't been able to find the location of where Beth had been kept. They hadn't been looking for an underground facility, one that was likely purpose-built to be undetectable.

"Put them in a van and take them to facility three," Tomas ordered his men. "I'll be there later tonight, and we'll decide what to do with them."

Perfect.

There was no way more than a handful of men could accompany them in a van. That was all the edge his team would need. Now they knew about this place, as soon as they were free, they would bring down the entire might of Prey on Baranov and Butcher. Then finally ... *finally* ... this whole nightmare would be over.

All seven of them were shoved inside the back of a van, and two well-armed guards climbed in with them.

Amateurs.

If Butcher thought two guards were enough to keep six highly trained, highly honed killing machines under control then he was an idiot.

As soon as the van doors were closed, he exchanged glances with his team. Since they had been together for so many years, they didn't need to communicate with words. All it took was a look to know they were all on the same page. There were no seats in there, and nothing to hold onto. The two guards were standing by the door, so Axe nudged Beth into the back corner and braced their bodies as the van started driving.

"You okay, wisp?" he whispered, his lips on her ear so he could speak without being overheard.

Beth gave a jerky nod and leaned her body closer to his.

"Hold on just a bit longer for me," he urged, knowing Beth could do it. "Need you to untie my hands." Although he could do it himself, it would be less obtrusive to have Beth do it, and they hadn't bothered to tie her up. Stupid of them, they must have forgotten already that she had killed to survive the last time they kidnapped her.

Angling his body so they wouldn't be seen, he threw a glare at the guards, hoping they would think he was just angry that they had put their hands on his wife. Beth's nimble fingers worked quickly, and moments later he was free.

As soon as he was, Axel moved carefully, bringing his arms around in front of him and working on untying Trick. The dim light meant it wouldn't be easy for the guards to see what they were doing, and it didn't look like they were paying much attention anyway. They thought they had the upper hand and that everything was going to go smoothly.

They didn't know that now three of their seven prisoners were free, and in a moment all seven of them would be.

Then they'd be making their move.

~

April 18th
3:22 P.M.

The anticipation was killing her.

Beth didn't know exactly what Axel and the guys had planned, but she knew it was something. Because she didn't speak their private silent code, she had no idea what the exchanged looks meant, but she knew these men well enough to know that they were going to make a move as soon as they believed the time was right.

It wasn't that she didn't trust them because she absolutely did, it was just the waiting was keeping her on edge, and she was already completely strung out.

Hearing someone threaten to kill her friends, to torture her husband ... there were no words to describe that.

All she wanted to do was simultaneously grab Axel and hold on to him, never letting him go, and get away as far and as fast as she could from all six of these men because they were in danger now because of her.

Because they loved her.

As wonderful as it was to have people who loved her, it was weird, too. Growing up, her parents, aunts, uncles, cousins, and siblings hadn't cared about her at all, but there had been a couple of other girl cousins who had been treated the same way she had. Beth had tried her best to shield them in whatever way she could, and she knew that fear and trauma had bonded them together.

But it wasn't real love.

Not like this.

Not like what Axel had showered upon her from the moment he saved her life.

Not like what these men had shown her over the last six years.

They had taught her what love was, they had made her feel special like she belonged. They hadn't done it because they had to, they'd just done it because they wanted to, because they chose to.

Because they loved her.

And in return, she loved them with everything she had to give.

Only right now, her love was hurting them not helping them, and she hated it.

If it wasn't for the fact that Axel suddenly shoved her backward, pressing her body between his and the side of the van, she wouldn't have even known it was coming.

One moment, the men were standing in the back of the van, their arms behind their backs even though she knew they had all untied one another and no one's wrists were currently bound with rope, the next, they were moving so fast they were nothing more than a blur.

They pounced with every ounce of their skill and training on display.

They disarmed both guards before the men even knew what was happening. They snapped the neck of one of the guards, letting his body drop onto the floor, the other was yanked up against Trick's chest, his arm across the man's throat.

Whoa.

Beth had never seen them in action like that before.

When they'd rescued her, Axel had protected her from most of the violence, and by the time they found her, they'd killed almost all the men who had been at the house. Tank and Rock might have trained her in shooting and self-defense, and she had seen them run training drills plenty of times before.

But this was different.

This was *real.*

Their lives were truly on the line, and they were prepared to do whatever it took to keep themselves alive.

"Tell your pals in the front there to pull over," Trick ordered.

Instead of answering, the man attempted to fight his way out of Trick's hold.

From the way the man's eyes suddenly bulged and he clawed at Trick's arm, Beth could guess that her friend was currently cutting off his air supply.

"I've got a ring sitting in the drawer of my nightstand, you think I'm going to let you kill me before I get a chance to ask my girl to marry me?" Trick snarled in a voice so cold, deadly, and ruthless that Beth shuddered.

She wasn't stupid, and she wasn't new to danger, she knew the stakes here, knew one wrong move, one careless move, would get them all killed. But she'd never heard sweet, easy-going, lighthearted Trick speak in that tone before. He was always the goofy one, doing his magic tricks, breaking the tension, and keeping things light.

Not now.

Now he looked every bit the lethal warrior he was.

Axel's fingers found hers and squeezed reassuringly and she leaned into him, so very grateful for his presence even as she wished he were a million miles away from any danger.

"What's the code word?" Panther asked as he reached out and grabbed the radio from the living guard's belt.

Trick must have eased up a little on the pressure on the man's neck because his eyes no longer bulged, but his expression was sullen, and he didn't answer Panther's question.

"Don't have one, huh?" Panther mocked with what she would describe as a more menacing snarl than an actual smile. "Need help back here, pull over," he spoke in a low voice into the radio. With the way he'd spoken, it would be hard for the driver to identify whether it was actually one of his colleagues or a prisoner.

Looking at Axel, when her husband nodded his head, Trick snapped the guard's neck and let the body drop to the floor at his feet. With everyone free, both guards dead, and Tank and Rock now sporting the guards' weapons, Beth felt like maybe they would make it out of this alive.

At least they now stood a chance.

Obviously, believing it was one of his colleagues needing assistance, the driver pulled the vehicle over to the side of the road, and a moment later, they could all hear the thump as he got out and closed his door behind him.

"Cover your ears," Axel ordered, taking the hand he still held and lifting it to place it over her left ear.

Her other hand was shaking as she lifted it and covered her right ear. While this certainly wouldn't be the first death she witnessed, Beth knew she didn't want to see what was coming. So much death, so much darkness, so much pain, it seemed to coat her skin, sealing some of that darkness inside her.

She just wanted this to all be over. She wanted to live like a normal woman, not haunted by a past that wouldn't stay dead. Not constantly battling to keep her trauma contained so she could make the most of the second chance at life she had been handed.

All she wanted was to be free.

"Don't look, honey," Axel whispered, turning her so she was tucked against him, her face pressed into his chest.

Even though she was expecting it, the bang of the gun going off was much too loud in the contained space of the back of the van. Not that it seemed to faze anyone but herself.

As soon as the weapon went off, she assumed killing the driver and a passenger if there had been one, the guys began moving. Axel scooped her up, carrying her out of the van and into the afternoon sunshine.

The sun was too bright even against her closed lids, and Beth was suddenly so drained she barely had the energy to breathe, let alone anything else. Unable to lift her head from where it had lolled against Axel's shoulder when he picked her up, her hands still pressed to her ears even though there were no loud sounds to shield them from, she just hung limply in his grip.

It didn't seem to bother him, she could hear the buzz of his words through her hands on her ears, and he walked about with her as though she weighed nothing as she presumed, he and the guys came up with a plan.

She was so tired of plans.

Why couldn't her life just be simple for once?

Why did the very fact that she was here and alive mean so many people had to be in danger?

Her mind flashed with images of the guys on their knees with guns pointed at their heads. Tomas' voice echoed in her mind, telling her he would kill them one by one if she didn't surrender herself.

That he would torture her husband just to get to her.

Then she thought of the women behind at home. Women who hadn't hesitated to accept her and her place in the lives of the men they were falling in love with. Nobody had resented the guys constantly rushing off to search for clues as to what had happened to her.

They had just ... loved her ... because she was important to their men.

Because of her, they could have lost the men they loved.

It wouldn't have been anyone's fault but hers.

"Beth?" Axel called her name as he set her on her feet. Keeping one arm around her waist to keep her on her feet, his other hand circled first one wrist and then the other, tugging her hands away from her ears. "It's okay now, wisp."

Only it wasn't.

Not really.

"Open your eyes, Beth." Axel's large hands framed her face, and his thumbs brushed softly beneath her eyes.

When she complied and saw the love for her shining in Axel's warm brown eyes, she knew what she had to do. Tomas had made it clear that it was her he wanted, otherwise he wouldn't have threatened the others just to get her to show herself. The guys knew where the building she had been kept was, but surely Baranov was smart enough to already be clearing it out and wiping it free of any potential evidence against him.

So long as she was in the picture, the guys would keep putting themselves in danger, and she just couldn't stomach the thought of anything happening to them because of her.

"You doing okay, wisp?" Axel asked.

Managing a shaky nod, she grabbed his shoulders and pulled him down so she could kiss him. "I'm okay," she whispered against his lips.

"That's my girl. Always so brave."

Brave enough to do what had to be done she hoped.

"Why don't you sit down and rest for a bit? You'll be back home soon."

Nodding because she no longer trusted herself to talk, she kissed Axel back when he dropped a quick kiss to her lips before going off to join his team who were standing by the van. Then with a last look at her husband and the men she considered her big brothers, Beth turned and ran off into the trees, praying that her distance was enough to keep her family safe and alive.

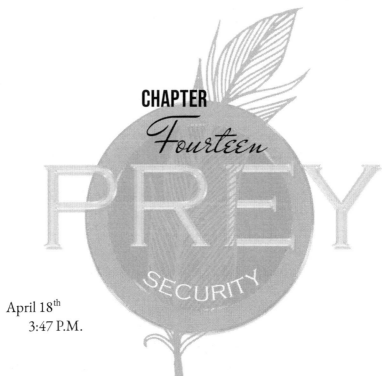

CHAPTER

Fourteen

April 18th
    3:47 P.M.

"Uh, Axe, I think we have a problem."

At Tank's words, Axe looked up from the phone they'd stolen from the driver which he was using to fire off texts to Eagle about the situation. "What's wrong?" he asked.

Tank merely nodded his head toward where Beth was resting. Even in the split second it took to turn his head, a million thoughts flew through his mind. Had Beth been injured and he hadn't realized it? Had they been found and someone was holding a gun on his wife?

What he wasn't expecting to find was the spot he'd last seen Beth empty.

She was gone.

"Someone grab her?" Rock asked.

They were sure the van they were being transported in would be tracked, and they were prepared for an attack, although Axe was hoping it didn't happen until after Prey sent in reinforcements. The last thing he wanted was his wife in danger again.

Ever again.

But he didn't think that Baranov's men had tracked them already. He had a pretty good idea why Beth wasn't where he'd left her, and it wasn't because she had been taken against her will.

Sighing, he rubbed at his temples, his heart aching for his wife's pain but also furious with her for bailing on him no matter the reason. Cutting her slack only because he knew she was traumatized and not thinking clearly, but when he found her, he was going to make damn sure Beth knew she was never to attempt to handle anything like this on her own again.

"Should I call Eagle back? Tell him we need a search and rescue team?" Scorpion asked.

"No," he said simply. "I don't think Beth was taken against her will."

"Then where is she?" Panther asked, clearly confused.

"My sweet, silly wife has apparently decided she's more trouble than she's worth," Axe replied.

"That's crazy. Beth can't possibly believe we wouldn't do whatever it took to keep her safe," Rock said.

"Exactly. I think that's the problem. She knows we'll do anything to keep her safe, and she also knows you all have families waiting for you at home," he explained.

"So, you going to go find and talk some sense into our girl?" Tank asked.

"That's the plan. I'll find Beth, you guys stay here in case Butcher and his goons show up. Try to keep one alive. We know where one of the facilities is, but we need to find at least two others if we want to end this once and for all," Axe said. And that was exactly what he had planned.

Leaving the guys to handle things, he took off into the woods. It wasn't hard to follow Beth's trail. If she was trying to hide where she was going, she was doing a terrible job of it. She may as well have posted big signs with blinking lights and arrows.

Was she leaving behind a trail because she was too mentally and physically exhausted to do anything about it? Or was it because she really wanted him to follow after her?

Axe knew the last thing Beth truly wanted was to be alone. Fear was motivating and controlling her. He knew his wife, and he would bet anything that, at the moment, the only thing she was thinking about was sitting in that tree and hearing a man from her nightmares threaten to kill the people she loved unless she handed herself over to him.

But running wasn't the answer.

It was, in fact, only putting all of them in more danger.

As if they were really going to just let Beth go off alone when they knew that Baranov was after all of them. If she was thinking clearly, she would know that he was going to go after her, but that weakened his team because now they weren't six strong, they were five and one.

The problem was, Beth *wasn't* thinking clearly right now.

A problem he was going to fix as soon as he caught up to her.

Exhausted as she was, she hadn't made fast progress, and she couldn't have been gone all that long before Tank noticed she was no longer by the tree where they'd left her. Maybe thirty minutes after realizing she was gone, he heard the sounds of her labored breathing and stumbling steps.

Scanning the area first to make sure she wasn't being followed, Axe then circled around so he was in front of her, and propped a shoulder against a tree, waiting for her to notice him.

Because of her exhaustion, she was practically on him before realizing he was there.

A squeal fell from her lips before she obviously realized it was him.

Anger that she would run from him, that she thought he would let her run from him, made his voice harsher than it should have been. "Fancy meeting you out here."

"I ... umm ... what are you ...? How did you ...?"

"What are *you* doing out here?" he demanded.

"I ... I had to ..."

"Had to what?" It came out like a snarl, but Beth wasn't the only one teetering on the edge here. He'd been forced to sit there and watch his wife be manhandled, watched her afraid for her life and the lives of those she loved, and had her far too close to danger. "What exactly was your plan, Beth?"

Tears shimmered in her eyes, and she took a step back at the ruthlessness in his tone. Axe knew he should calm down and attempt to soothe her fears rather than yell at her for reacting badly, but there was no way in hell he was letting his wife think that her running was the right answer.

A year.

That was how much time they had lost together because he had sat back, not spoken up, and not told his wife how much she meant to him. Beth was the one who had been traumatized, she had been the one with amnesia, the distance that had grown between them was on him, not her.

"Where were you going? How were you going to defend yourself if you were caught? Where were you going to stay? How were you going to support yourself? How were you going to buy food, or get a job, or find a house? What were you going to do when Baranov found you and dragged you back to his hellhole?"

Tears streamed down Beth's cheeks as his voice grew louder with each word, and just like that, his anger was gone. Reaching for her, Axe grabbed her and yanked her up against him.

"Don't you *ever* do that to me again. Together. We deal with things together. Not apart."

"Together," Beth echoed. "I'm sorry, Axel. I just couldn't let anyone else get hurt because of me. I couldn't stand the thought of you or one of those guys getting killed. It would have been all my fault."

"Wrong. It would have been Baranov's fault and no one else's. Did you really think we would stop hunting him just because you weren't there?"

"I ... wasn't thinking. I just ... panicked," Beth admitted.

"Panicking is fine, understandable, but you don't leave me ever again. Hear me?" he demanded, gripping her face and forcing her to look at him.

"I hear you," she whispered. "I'm sorry."

Lifting her off the ground, Beth immediately wrapped her legs around his hips as he crushed his mouth to hers. "Damn, don't be sorry, wisp. I know you've been through hell, I just can't ... won't ... lose you again. Not to anything. Not even to you and your misguided sense of right and wrong. I love you, Beth. More than anything."

"I love you, too."

Before the other night, Axe would never even have considered sex with Beth anywhere but in a bed where he could take his time and make love to her body. But right now, the tension crackling between them was too much for him to handle. From the desire burning in Beth's eyes, he knew he wasn't alone in wanting to do something about it.

"Hold onto me, wisp. This is going to be hard and fast."

Once her hands were gripping his shoulders, he backed her up against a tree, his hands making quick work of shoving both his pants and hers out of the way. Kissing her like she was his everything, because she was, he stroked her bud and dipped a finger into her tight, wet heat, preparing her for him.

When she began to moan, her hips thrusting against his finger, he withdrew and lined up, thrusting inside her in one smooth move.

Like he'd promised, this wasn't sweet and slow, it was hard and fast. Beth held on as he pumped into her with every ounce of desperation he'd felt when she'd been in danger, with every drop of love he felt for this woman who consumed him and completed him. His fingers worked her bud as he thrust into her, and seconds later she came around him, sending him hurtling into a powerful orgasm.

As they both rode that high, they clung to one another. Life hadn't been kind to Beth, but she was his now, to love, to protect, and Baranov wasn't going to take her away from him.

∼

April 18th
    4:30 P.M.

"Did we really just do that?" Beth asked, unable to truly believe that she'd just had sex out in the open in the middle of a forest.

Not just sex.

Great sex.

Maybe not the best sex of her life—that unequivocally had to be the first time Axel had ever made love to her and she learned what being intimate with a man was supposed to be like—but it was definitely in the top five.

Because this sex had been all about freedom.

Freedom from Baranov and his men, freedom from fear, freedom from the past. Freedom.

It was a wonderful, heady feeling, and Beth felt like she could take on the whole world and win. Not because sex or freedom gave her any particular power, it was because she and Axel were there together. And together it felt like there was nothing they couldn't do.

"Yeah, wisp, we did," Axel replied, amusement in his voice.

He was still inside her and she wanted to keep him there forever. Wanted to hold onto this feeling forever because it was just so wonderful. There was nothing in the world like knowing without a shadow of a doubt that you weren't alone.

If you'd never really experienced true loneliness, you couldn't quite understand what it felt like. Of course, Beth believed everybody had probably felt alone at least at one point in their life, but there was a difference between feeling it and actually being completely alone. Being alone had been her life before Axel and his team saved her. It had become normal, it just ... was. She didn't even know that anything else existed.

Running had been stupid.

A kneejerk reaction to her fear over what could so easily have happened. If they had been taken into the facility they'd been tracking when they'd been shot at, then they likely wouldn't have been able to escape. Just because she'd slipped away a year ago didn't mean that she could do it again. Or that seven of them could have escaped undetected. If they had been split up, or if there had been more guards in the back of the van, or if the guys hadn't been able to get free of their bonds, or any number of other things had been different, the outcome could have been as well.

Living with the guilt of knowing she had gotten her family killed would have been too much for her. There would have been no way she could ever have returned to the compound without Axel and the guys and face the women left behind.

But she should have had more faith in her family.

Together, they would take down their enemy, and then they would finally be free for real. Free forever.

"I'm sorry for running," she said again.

One arm supported her weight, his other hand lifted to cup her cheek. "I get it, Beth, I do. You were in shock and you panicked. I just need you to promise me you won't ever run from me again. Not for any reason. Not even if you think you're doing me a favor because I can assure you that you are not."

"I promise," she readily agreed. She didn't want to run from Axel, she'd done enough running this last year even if it was figurative rather than literal running. By now, she should have learned that running didn't solve anything. Running only made things worse.

A soft kiss feathered across her lips, and then Axel pulled out of her and gently set her down on her feet, righting her pants before he did his own. His touch was so soft, so tender, and Beth found tears pricking the backs of her eyes. She was lucky to have walked through the fire and come out the other end to a beautiful shower of rain. One that slowly soothed each burned part of her soul until she was healed and whole again.

"Much as I want to take you somewhere I can hold you, make love to you, be with you, I better get you back to my team. We're going to send you and the others into the city to stay in Prey's offices, and then the guys and I are going hunting," Axel told her as he reached for her hand and entwined their fingers.

Every fiber of her being wanted to rebel against that statement. She didn't want to go and hide away and allow her husband to go off into battle. But she fought against her instinct to beg him not to leave her.

This was something Axel needed to do, she got that, understood it, too.

While he hadn't known her when she was a child or when she had been sold to Baranov, so there was nothing he could have done to save her then, she knew he blamed himself for her second abduction. Just because she often went into town on her own, just because he'd done everything humanly possible to find her, and if he could have, he would have done whatever it took to bring her home, he blamed himself. He'd felt impotent when she was missing, and just as impotent when she returned with amnesia.

He needed to do this.

He needed to be the one to bring down Baranov and end the threat hanging over all their heads.

He needed to do something this time and not just sit around.

So, she didn't argue, didn't beg or plead, just rested her head against his shoulder and whispered, "Be safe, okay? I need you. I love you."

"I'm not letting him steal our future, wisp."

There was so much confidence in Axel's voice that a little of her fear dimmed. "Is Prey sending in another team?" It would dim more of her fear if she knew it wasn't just going to be Bravo Team against the whole might of Baranov's army.

"Not just one team," Axel replied. "Alpha Team and Delta Team. Charlie Team is out on something personal to them, otherwise, they'd be there, too. I think Eagle has called in some favors and got some SEAL teams on standby as well in case Baranov tries to flee the country. He also has Artemis Team and Fox and the guys on their way over here, too. Trust me, Baranov has no idea he's about to face the wrath of all of Prey Security. I think Eagle, Max, Falcon, Sparrow and Ethan, Hawk, and Isaac are all gearing up and coming, too. You might not have had a family worth anything in the past, wisp, but now you have an entire army at your back."

Those tears stinging her eyes earlier now began to run freely down her cheeks. "They're all doing that for me?" While she knew it wasn't for her specifically, Beth wasn't vain enough to think she was more important than bringing down an internationally wanted trafficker, she was still overwhelmed to know Prey was going all out to bring down her personal bogeyman.

Stopping, Axel turned her to face him, bending his knees so they were eye to eye. "Of course, Beth. All of Prey is your family, not just Bravo Team. Every single person there cares about bringing Baranov down not just because of who he is and how many innocent people he's hurt, but because *you* are one of those people."

Warmth spread through her. "But still, I mean *Eagle* coming out of retirement to be involved, that's ... wow." She'd met Eagle a few times, the man was the epitome of confidence. He was used to getting his own way, he didn't waste time doubting himself, and he went after what he wanted with a single-minded focus. Eagle was intimidating, but it was also clear when you were with him that he cared about every single person associated with his company. The billionaire might have created Prey after an injury ended his SEAL career, but he wasn't some remote boss, he was involved in every aspect of his business and the lives of the people who worked for him.

"Eagle told me he wouldn't miss out on this for anything. I think he's been looking for an excuse to get out of the office for a while and this is it."

Beth chuckled, and it felt so good to know she wasn't facing this monster alone. She'd done her part and led Axel and Bravo Team to one of Baranov's facilities, and now it was time for her to take a step back and know that her family was picking up the baton and fighting the fight for her.

An odd feeling for someone who had learned to fight on her own before she was old enough to talk, but she wasn't alone anymore. She had a whole big, tough, compassionate family of warriors who would use every weapon in their arsenal to end Leonid Baranov's reign of terror and finally set her free.

"I'm a lucky woman," she said softly, feeling that down to her bones.

Before Axel could respond, the sound of a car engine drew their attention. A vehicle appeared through the trees, and any hope that it hadn't spotted them went out the window when the SUV slowed, and a window lowered, the barrel of a gun appearing through it.

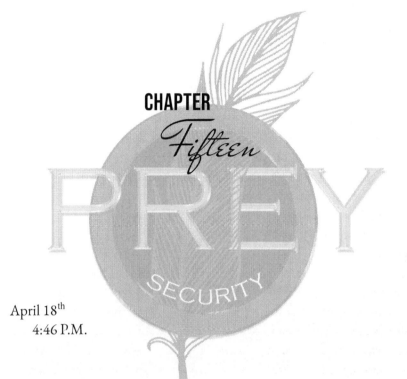

CHAPTER
Fifteen

April 18th
  4:46 P.M.

If Beth was killed for his mistake, Axe would never forgive himself.

Although, if they were caught, neither of them would be living all that long anyway.

He wasn't a rookie, and this wasn't his first op. Axe knew better than to have sex out in the open in an unsecured location when he knew there would be people out looking for them.

Letting his anger and fear get the best of him could be a mistake that cost them their lives. Just like he wasn't a rookie, he wasn't a teenager either, and he knew how to control his hormones instead of letting them control him.

What he should have done was pick Beth up, throw her over his shoulder, and sprint back to where his team was waiting near the vehicle. The conversation he'd wanted to have with Beth could have waited until they were someplace safe, and sex definitely could have waited.

Only in that moment, it had felt like it couldn't.

In that moment, it had felt like there was nothing more important in the world than purging the terror he'd felt seeing his wife in danger, and his anger that she was shutting him out again.

But he was wrong.

Because keeping Beth alive was more important than anything else.

Grabbing his wife's hand, they were already moving before the first shot was fired. That bullet missing wasn't doing anything more than buying them a couple of extra seconds. They were outmanned and outgunned, and he had Beth with him. Smart as she was, and with all the knowledge his team had given her on how to defend herself, she was still nowhere near ready for something like this.

If he hadn't been so impulsive, so intoxicated by his wife's mere presence, they would already be safe right now.

That knowledge made his stomach bitter as they ran through the woods.

Behind them, he could hear the vehicle getting closer, and a few more shots were fired, all of them missing their target. Staying and fighting wasn't an option until he was out of other choices. He only had one weapon on him, and Baranov's men were like cockroaches. There were always more of them. Just when you thought you had them all, more seemed to materialize out of thin air. Right now, there was only one vehicle, but they would have already radioed that they had spotted him and Beth, and more would be on the way.

The terrain was rocky and there was other debris and roots in the way as they ran, and both he and Beth were already tired from hiking all day and then being kidnapped. Still, his wife didn't complain, and she kept pace beside him, her long, slender legs pumping hard as she followed where he led her.

Dodging around a particularly large tree, Axe wished he knew the terrain better. If he knew exactly where he was and what was around him, he could better formulate a plan. Because his current plan of run and hope for the best wasn't cutting it.

"Axel, look. Up there. It's a river," Beth said.

He'd noted it, too, and it presented their best shot at getting away. If it was too deep for the vehicle then the men in the car would either have to stay and shoot at them or try to find a way across. The river wasn't too wide, and it wasn't running too fast, the temperature would still be cold because it was April, but they weren't going to become hypothermic.

They would be sitting ducks as soon as they left any protection the trees gave though.

Still, it was a risk they were going to have to take if they wanted a chance.

"You get in and swim to the other side without looking back," he ordered his wife as they approached the water's edge.

For a moment, it looked like she was going to argue with him, but this was non-negotiable. Laying down covering fire gave Beth the best chance at reaching the other side, and his wife was the priority here.

"Remember you promised me you'd be safe," she said as they splashed into the water.

"A promise I'll do my best to keep," he assured her as he gave her a shove to get her moving faster.

As soon as she was swimming, he turned just as the vehicle approached the river. Shooting at the people inside would take a whole lot longer than taking out the SUV itself.

Firing at the gas tank, he hit it, and then fired again, and again, until he was rewarded with a fiery explosion.

There was no hesitation as he dived under the water and began to swim for the other side. Pieces of the now burning car, and the bodies of those inside were strewn about, several landing in the water, but Axe ignored everything but his need to get to his wife.

Holding his breath for as long as he could, by the time he surfaced, he was already close to the other side where Beth was standing, water streaming off her, eyes panicked as she searched for any sign of him.

As soon as she spotted him, she ran toward him, into the water, grabbing him as he stood.

"I thought you got blown up, too, you had disappeared by the time I heard the explosion and turned," Beth babbled as she clung to him.

"No intention of leaving you alone out here, wisp," he assured her as he grabbed her hand and urged her on. As much as she needed time to rest, to process everything that had happened, time wasn't a luxury they had right now.

They had to keep moving, find a way to circle back to his team, or at least a place to hide out because that explosion would have alerted everyone in the vicinity, including his team, that something had happened.

So they did the only thing they could, and ran.

And ran.

And ran.

They kept running until Beth began to stumble and he was holding her up more than she was holding herself up.

"Let's take a quick break," he said as he stopped and pulled her into his arms.

"I can keep going," she said, voice uneven as she gasped for breath.

"We can afford a moment." They couldn't really, but his wife didn't need to know that, and she really did need this moment to catch her breath and refocus herself. "You're doing amazing."

"But not amazing enough if we don't get away," she said, burying her face against his chest and leaning into him, letting him take her weight, which he was more than happy to do.

"Shh, just close your eyes and rest. For this one second, don't worry about anything," he soothed, stroking her back with one hand while his other kept her locked against him.

Slowly, a little of the tension eased and her breathing began to slow. Giving her every second he could—giving *himself* every second he could —time passed far too quickly.

"You ready to run again?"

"Yeah. What's the plan?"

"There's my girl." Axe grinned down at her. "Plan is to run parallel to the river but not close enough to be spotted if Baranov's men are searching it. Sooner or later, it'll lead us to someone, a house, a town, a road, something."

"Let's hope for sooner *rather* than later."

"Amen."

Hand in hand, they began to run again. While Axe kept their pace brisk, he allowed them to go a little slower this time around. They had to have put a good bit of distance between themselves and the explosion, and hopefully, Baranov's men would be tied up there for a bit before they started looking. They had no way of knowing which side of the river he and Beth were on so that should help, too.

Another half an hour passed, and he was just about to give Beth another short break when he heard the rev of an engine. A different engine sound this time than before, so he knew it wasn't a car, probably an ATV if he had to guess.

More than one.

At least half a dozen.

"Axel," Beth's terrified voice said as she clung to him. He didn't have to explain to her how bad things were about to get. She already knew. Had already lived it.

"Sorry, honey," he whispered the heartfelt words, knowing he had just failed his wife who he had vowed to love and protect no matter what.

Since he wasn't going down without a fight, he shoved Beth behind him, pressed her back against a tree, so she was protected on two sides, and began to fire at the approaching men.

It was worse than he'd thought, there were at least a dozen of them. Cockroaches. Just like damn cockroaches. Still, he took out almost half of them before he felt the sting of something hitting his arm.

Expecting to see blood, when he looked down, he saw something else instead.

Already it was affecting him. Lightheaded, he swayed and went down on his knees.

"Axel?"

Beth's panicked voice sounded so very far away.

"Sss-rry," he slurred as more strength leeched from his body and he slumped all the way onto the ground.

The last thing he saw as the world around him began to fade was Beth's body as she slumped down beside him.

Sorry, wisp, I'm so damn sorry for failing you.

April 19th
    6:03 A.M.

. . .

Why did her head hurt so bad?

For a long moment, Beth couldn't remember anything. She didn't know where she was, how she'd gotten there, or what had happened.

Panic began to seep into her mind.

Did she have amnesia again?

Had she finally gotten all her memories back only for them to vanish like a wisp of smoke?

Wisp.

Axel's nickname for her.

Axel, her husband. The man who had saved her life in more ways than one. He'd taught her how to love, helped her to heal, and been there for her every step of the way through her recovery.

Her memories weren't gone. She remembered her childhood, she remembered being sold to Russian oligarch Leonid Baranov. She remembered the pain and humiliation he had put her through before she was rescued by a Delta Force team. She remembered Axel and all of the other men on his team. She remembered the five years of heaven she had lived with them before she was kidnapped. She remembered being forced by Baranov to fight and kill his men if she wanted to survive. She remembered having amnesia when she escaped and got back home.

And she remembered finally getting her memories back when Axel had been blown up and she'd almost lost him.

She remembered everything up until she and her husband were running for their lives through the woods and were outnumbered by men on ATVs.

No amnesia.

Obviously, she'd been knocked out, or shot, or something and while she was unconscious, she had been brought to some place. A place that *felt* exactly like the one she had been held in for eight long months.

There was a sterile feel to it, and a faint hint of antiseptic in the air. It was like a hospital only it lacked all the usual hospital busyness.

Open your eyes, Beth.

The order she gave herself was ignored.

She didn't want to open her eyes and see herself back in a small white cell with a bed shoved into the corner, a shower head embedded in the wall, a toilet and a sink, and a small table and chair. She didn't want to be back in the place she had already escaped once before, but knew that escaping again wouldn't just be unlikely it would be impossible.

Okay, start with something easy then. Are you hurt anyplace?

Taking mental inventory of her body, she felt a little battered and bruised. There were a few stinging places on her face and her arms, but there was nothing that suggested she had been badly injured. Even the ache in her head wasn't like she had been hit and knocked out, it was more like there was a heaviness, like concrete wrapped in fuzzy material had been stashed in there.

If she hadn't been shot, and she hadn't been hit over the head, then how had she been brought here?

Focus, Beth. What's the last thing you remember? Be exact, specific. It's important.

Forcing herself to take a deep, cleansing breath, she walked through the last things she remembered. Being in the back of the van, the guys killing the guards, herself running away because she was scared of getting them killed. Axel had come after her, found her, made love to her, then they'd run when a vehicle had found them. They'd swum through a river, Axel had blown up a car, then they'd run again until more men had found them.

Her husband had killed several of them before he'd just dropped.

She'd been terrified he'd been shot and was dying right before her eyes or already dead.

Something sharp had pierced her arm, and she thought she'd been hit, too.

Only it wasn't a bullet, there had been no blood, her head had immediately gotten fuzzy, and she'd lost control of her limbs.

"Drugged," she muttered aloud. She and Axel had both been drugged, and while they were unconscious, they'd been brought here, wherever there was. Or at least she had. "Axel?"

There was no answer, and Beth now wasn't afraid to open her eyes, she was desperate to. They popped open and she sat up, too quickly, it turned out because a wave of dizziness almost pulled her under again.

Fighting against it, she shoved to her feet and did indeed find herself back in a small white cell. Concrete walls, floor, and ceiling all painted white. Bed in the corner. A showerhead embedded in the wall. Toilet and sink. Table and chairs. It was like she had traveled back in time, and was right back where she had been just over a year ago.

What scared her the most was there was no sign of Axel.

Where was he?

Since the walls of her cell were concrete, she couldn't see through them, but if this place really was either where she had been held before or a replica of it, then she knew there were other cells there. She'd seen them as she was walked down to the room called the arena, and then when she was brought back here after a stay in the infirmary. Just because she had killed the men she was pitted against didn't mean she had escaped unharmed.

Was that where Axel was right now?

Was he in the cell next to hers?

Maybe he just hadn't woken up yet and that was why he hadn't answered her.

Still unsteady on her legs, she stumbled to the front of her cell and curled her hands around the metal bars. Beth pressed her face to them, trying to look through as far as she could, but all she could see was the concrete wall on the other side of the corridor that led past the row of white cells to the door at the end.

"Axel?" she called again, hearing the panic in her voice. "Are you there? Axel! Wake up. Please. If you're there I need you to wake up. I need you to be there," she added.

What was she going to do if Axel wasn't there?

Surviving another round of this hell just wasn't an option. There was only so much a person could take before they broke. While Beth considered herself to be a strong person, she hadn't really ever had any other choice, she wasn't invincible. Already, her mind had fractured to protect her from this reality once before, what would happen to her if she had to live through it again?

If Axel was already dead, would she even bother trying to fight?

Before she'd fought because she had to, she had to get home to the man she loved, but without Axel there was nothing to fight for. She'd rather be dead than live in a world without her husband.

"Axel, please," she begged. Tears streamed down her cheeks and she didn't try to stop them. Her heart was breaking into a million pieces, terror was a living, breathing thing inside her. It was trying, and close to succeeding, in consuming her from the inside out.

Please be here, Axel.

Please just still be unconscious.

Don't be hurt.

Don't be dead.

The silent pleas only made her cry harder, and with the drugs still lingering in her system, she swayed and sunk to the floor. Pulling her knees to her chest, Beth wrapped her arms around them, then buried her face and began to sob.

Huge, body-wracking sobs.

Her husband could be dead.

She couldn't go on without him.

That was the only thought that ran through her mind as she huddled there and wept. It wasn't until she had been crying for what felt like hours but was probably more like minutes, that she realized something.

Both of them had been drugged. If they wanted Axel dead, they would have shot him with a bullet, not a tranquilizer dart.

Her husband was alive. Even if he wasn't unconscious in one of the cells, he was there somewhere, or at the least, he was alive somewhere else.

If Axel was alive then she had no choice but to fight.

You can do this.

Could she?

Maybe.

But she wasn't giving up.

Not yet, anyway.

Slowly, she wiped away the last remnants of her tears and grabbed the bars for support as she dragged herself to her feet. If there was one thing Beth knew about herself, it was that she wasn't a quitter. She hadn't taken the easy way out and ended her life when she was a kid, and she hadn't allowed Leonid Baranov to break her. When he'd made her fight of her life, she'd done it, and if she had to she'd do it again. She wasn't letting him break ...

Her thoughts trailed away as another memory popped into her mind.

The force of it and its ramifications slammed into her with such force that she stumbled away from the bars until she reached the bed, then dropped down onto it.

How had she not remembered?

It changed everything, and it explained a lot of unanswered questions.

It also decreased the chances that either she or Axel were going to walk out of this place alive.

CHAPTER
Sixteen

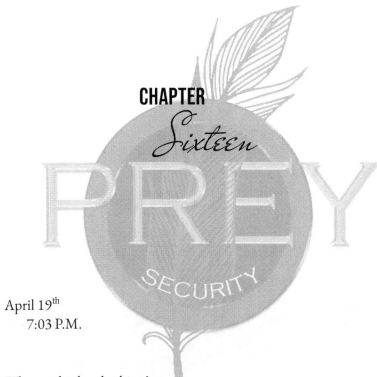

April 19th
   7:03 P.M.

Why was his head aching?

It took a split second for Axe's brain to come online, and once it did, his heart dropped and the heavy weight of failure clung to him.

Beth.

Moments after he'd been shot with a tranquilizer dart and dropped, leaving her vulnerable and unprotected, Beth had dropped down beside him. If he was alive then he believed that she was, too.

He had to believe that.

There was no other choice.

If he allowed himself to think, even for a second, that his wife was already dead then he would lose any control he might have.

Ignoring the lingering pain and stuffiness from the drugs, Axel went to shove to his feet only to find that he was unable to move.

Opening his eyes, he looked down his body to see that he was laid out on what looked like a hospital gurney. His ankles were cuffed to the bottom of the gurney, and his wrists were cuffed to the sides. He was

April 19th

still dressed in the same clothes he'd put on the morning they set out to see if Beth could backtrack to the place where she had been held. Was that today? Yesterday? Longer than that?

There was an IV in his arm connected to a bag hanging above his head so it was possible he had been drugged and kept out of it for days.

Beth.

Where was his wife?

A quick scan of the room showed that he was in an infirmary. There were three more empty gurneys on the other side of the room. And as he tilted his head sideways on the pillow, looking to his left, he saw another empty gurney. But when he turned to the right, he saw a person on that gurney.

That person was too big to be Beth, so he was about to dismiss it and start figuring a way to get off this gurney and out of there so he could go find his wife, when something about the other man caught his attention.

The man was lying flat on his back same as Axe was, and there was an IV running into his arm. Only unlike Axe, the other man was buck naked, and there was a thin tube running to a small bag attached to the side of the gurney that was filled with a yellowy liquid that looked a lot like urine.

Catheter?

Why would they need to put a catheter in the man? How long had he been kept there?

What the hell was going on in this place?

And where was his wife?

Sick of Baranov and his twisted games, Axe lifted his head as far off the pillow as he could and yelled at the top of his lungs. "Beth?"

There was no point in playing possum and pretending to be unconscious, he could see the cameras on the ceiling. Whoever was watching them would already have seen him moving, and while he could get out of the restraints, he wasn't going to get a chance if they were watching him, they'd be there before he could get himself free. As Axe saw it there was no benefit to pretending to be unconscious so he was going to focus on what was most important.

Finding his wife.

"Don't bother, you won't see her until they're ready."

The voice came from the man on the other gurney. It was a cultured voice, and one that was heavily tinted with Russian.

No.

It couldn't be.

Could it?

But that would be ... impossible.

Turning his head back toward the other gurney, Axe saw that the man was now looking at him, and his suspicions were confirmed.

What did this mean?

Leonid Baranov was restrained on the gurney beside him, and from the looks of the man's gaunt face and paper pale skin he had been there for some time. Baranov had gone missing right around the same time as Beth had been abducted. Of course, it wasn't like the man could go about living a normal life when so many countries had him on their most wanted list, but there were usually sightings of him at least every month or so. With his vast resources Baranov was constantly on the move, it was how he'd managed to evade capture for so long. But there were also bounties on his head, which meant some people were prepared to face the oligarch's potential wrath and call in a tip that he had been spotted.

Those tips had ceased twenty months ago when Beth had disappeared.

Was this why?

But then who had been responsible for Beth's abduction? And why?

"What's going on, Baranov?" he growled.

The man gave him a somewhat petulantly sullen look which was ridiculous given he was cuffed to a gurney, naked, with a catheter and an IV in him. Did he really think that keeping quiet was going to help him out of this situation?

"What is going on, Baranov?" Axe repeated, allowing every ounce of hatred he felt for this man who had been responsible for such a large part of Beth's suffering ring through in his voice.

"He's not very chatty, is he?" a third voice asked. This one was female, and Axe could have sworn that he recognized it.

But why would the voice belong to Sarah Sanders?

While they had theorized that Sarah had been kidnapped by Baranov when they found her daughter's blood in the kitchen of the house Sarah was supposed to be living in under her new identity, he hadn't expected to find that Baranov wasn't responsible for her abduction.

When he turned his head toward the infirmary door, he found the woman standing there. She was dressed casually in jeans and a T-shirt, her hair was piled on top of her head in a messy bun, and she had on a touch of makeup. Sarah looked healthy, relaxed, and happy. She wasn't being held here against her will.

"What the hell is going on here?" he bellowed, making Baranov flinch, but Sarah's smile grow.

"It didn't have to be this way you know," she said as she crossed the room to stand between their two gurneys. "We never intended for you to be hurt. We knew you were allies of sorts, but then you just wouldn't let it go and we had no choice."

"What the hell are you talking about, Sarah? This man kidnapped and tortured you. What is he doing here?"

The look the woman sent Baranov had to be the most bloodthirsty expression Axe had ever seen on a human being's face. "What's he doing here?" she said as she went to the counter running behind the gurneys and picked up a vial and a syringe. "He's here because he kidnapped and tortured me. He's here paying his penance. Isn't that right, Leonid?"

Tracking the syringe, the oligarch's skin somehow managed to pale several more shades until it was just this side of belonging to a man who wasn't dead. "Please, no," he said hoarsely.

"No? How many times did I beg you not to hurt me?" Sarah asked, there was pleasure in her tone, and Axe knew that whatever was in that syringe was going to inflict on Baranov the kind of pain he had inflicted on others.

Axe couldn't find it in him to care.

"Look, Sarah, I get it. You hate him. I hate him, too. The man is a vile, despicable excuse for a human being. I don't care that you want to get your revenge. Have at it. I'd love to get in a couple of well-placed hits myself. All I care about is Beth. Is she here?"

"She's here," Sarah answered as she injected the contents of the syringe into the IV.

Baranov thrashed in the bed as though that was going to stop the inevitable. Which of course, it didn't. Axe knew the second the drug hit Baranov's bloodstream because a howl of pain that was more animal than human echoed through the room.

Setting the syringe down, Sarah smiled as she watched Baranov scream and thrash in the bed. Whatever was in the drug was powerful enough that even without having experienced it Axe could already tell that death was preferable.

Honestly, Baranov deserved what he got, and Axe didn't have an ounce of sympathy for the man's screams of agony. Instead, he focused on Sarah. "Where's Beth?"

"You'll see her soon."

Not soon enough. "Is she okay? Did you hurt her?" Former victim or not, if Sarah had laid a single hand on Beth nothing would save the woman from his wrath.

"I never hurt her. Not once in all the months she spent with us," Sarah replied, never taking her eyes off the howling Baranov.

Obviously, their definitions of hurting someone were vastly different. Beth had been hurt while she was held prisoner by Sarah, both physically and psychologically. She'd been forced to do things that had caused her mind to shut down in an attempt to protect itself. Whatever reasons—valid ones at that—Sarah had for hurting Baranov, there shouldn't be any for hurting Beth who was a fellow victim.

What could she possibly have to gain from further tormenting Beth?

"I don't understand, Sarah," he said, frustration coursing through him.

"I know."

"I want to know what the hell you have planned and why I'm here."

"And you will."

"When?" he growled.

Finally, she tore her gaze away from her tormentor long enough to look at him. "As soon as they get here."

~

April 19th
    7:38 A.M.

"You," Beth said, shoving to her feet when a man appeared outside her cell. "This was all you and Sarah. I thought ... I thought it was Baranov again ... but it wasn't."

A part of her knew she shouldn't be speaking up to this man. He might not be Leonid Baranov, but he was a sick, twisted monster who fed off other people's pain.

Who had fed off *her* pain.

Tomas Butcher and Sarah Sanders were the ones who had kidnapped her twenty months ago. Who had locked her up in a small white cell like this. Who had forced her to kill people for their own amusement.

She hated him.

Hated him.

Sarah, too.

While she expected nothing less of a man who would work for someone like Leonid Baranov than to bestow pain and suffering on everyone he came into contact with, she didn't expect it from Sarah. The woman had been a victim just like she had been. They had both been subjected to Baranov's vicious torture. Why would Sarah want to make Beth suffer all over again?

They had both survived, they had both been given a second chance at life. While Beth had embraced her future and found happiness, love, and peace with Axel and Bravo Team, it seemed like Sarah had turned to the dark side.

But why?

She didn't understand.

"Baranov is barely smart enough to tie his own shoelaces without supervision," Tomas snorted as he unlocked the cell door and beckoned to her.

Ignoring him might give her a molecule of fleeting pleasure, but it wasn't actually going to achieve anything more than irritating Tomas. And an angry Tomas was not something she wanted to deal with.

So, even though her body and mind rebelled at the idea of getting close to Tomas, of leaving the relative safety of her cell, she stood and walked toward him. Beth did her best not to let her fear show, she kept her back straight, her steps even, and met and held Tomas' gaze.

There was grudging respect in the light brown eyes that looked back at her, but his grip was hard and unyielding when he grabbed her arm and began to drag her down the hallway. Once they left the corridor, Beth could see that this place wasn't exactly identical to what she remembered, so wherever they were it wasn't back at the compound she and Bravo Team had identified. It must be one of the other facilities Tomas owned.

They crossed through one corridor after another until she felt all turned around. She'd have to do better next time if she was going to figure out the lay of the land and look for weaknesses she could exploit when she attempted to escape.

Because that was absolutely her plan.

Find Axel, and then the two of them would find a way out.

That plan died in her mind when she was shoved into a room that was eerily similar to the arena where she had been forced to fight for her life half a dozen times. It wasn't the big open space surrounded by chairs though, that had fear raging to life inside her.

It was the sight of her husband strapped onto a gurney.

Tomas released his hold on her, and she didn't bother to ask for permission, she just ran to Axel's side and threw her arms around him as best as she could with him tied down on his back.

"Are you okay?" he asked roughly, and she could see his hands bunching into fists before she buried her face against his neck.

"They didn't hurt me," she assured him. "Are you okay?"

"Didn't hurt me," he gave the same assurance she had offered.

"Tomas—"

"And Sarah," he inserted.

"Did this," she finished, lifting her head. "You know?"

"When Sarah showed up in the infirmary and she wasn't restrained in any way, I realized she was involved. Since we know that Tomas was the father of Sarah's daughter—her *murdered* daughter—then I figured the two of them were in on it together."

"I don't understand why," Beth said helplessly. Not that it would change anything to have answers, but at least she would know why she had been made to suffer so horribly. "I didn't remember at first that they were involved. It never occurred to me. I remembered that Baranov was here watching me, but I think ... I think he was cuffed to a gurney like you are right now."

"He was. He is."

When Axel nodded his head at something behind her, Beth turned to see Sarah wheeling Leonid Baranov into the arena. At the sight of her tormentor, Beth felt all the blood drain from her head. Once again, she was back in that tiny cage with a rusty metal collar around her neck waiting for this monster to come and inflict more horrors on her.

"It's okay, wisp. You got this. You're stronger than him," Axel murmured softly enough that his words were only for her benefit.

They helped enough that she was able to shove off the worst of the fear and meet Baranov's beady black eyes. "You look terrible," she told him, then looked to Sarah. "I assume I have you to thank for that at least."

"It was a pleasure," Sarah said cheerfully.

"I'm sure it was," Beth muttered not really sure why exactly Sarah was doing all of this.

"I've had my fun and now it's time for you to have yours," Sarah announced.

Glancing at Axel, Beth found he looked just as confused as she felt. It made zero sense that Tomas and Sarah would have gone to all the trouble of kidnapping her and then keeping her close to the Bravo Team compound. Even less sense that they had obviously been at that facility for years and knew it was right by Bravo Team, and yet had made zero attempts to take out the team. Which they could have done at any time.

Drop a bomb on them.

Raid the place and shoot it up.

They had the numbers on their side, yet they hadn't made a single move until she had found her way back to the facility they'd kept her locked in for eight months.

"What does that mean, Sarah? Explain yourself now, I'm getting tired of this nonsense," Axel snapped.

"I'm sorry, my wife does have a flare for the dramatic, but sometimes she forgets that not everyone can traverse her train of thought," Tomas said as he moved to stand beside Sarah, slipping an arm around her waist. "Do you want to tell them, darling, or do you want me to explain it?"

"I don't want to talk at all," Sarah huffed like a recalcitrant preschooler.

It was obvious that somewhere along the way, either during her time as Baranov's prisoner or after, the woman had lost her mind. Understandable given the trauma she had lived through. But why was she so intent on inflicting that same trauma on other innocent victims?

They had suffered at Baranov's hands together, and Beth felt betrayed to know that her fellow victim had made her a victim all over again by kidnapping her and making her kill people.

Tomas chuckled indulgently and nodded. "Very well. We'll play our little game first and then we can explain to our guests what you decided you needed to do to heal." Looking over his shoulder, the man gave a nod at some of his men, and the next thing Beth knew, she was being dragged away from Axel.

Even though she knew kicking and screaming and fighting them wasn't going to be helpful, in fact, it might make them angry enough that they would hurt her, she couldn't seem to help herself. She didn't want to do this alone, she didn't want to be made to kill someone or be killed. She didn't want to be anywhere but with Axel.

One of the men backhanded her, making her head snap to the side, and she heard Axel growl low and dangerous.

Not that anyone seemed to care. She was dragged into the middle of the arena and dropped unceremoniously. Then the men went to Baranov and began untying him.

That was who they wanted her to kill?

Of course, after everything he had done to her, she wanted him dead. She had even dreamed about hurting him the same way he had hurt her. But in the end, she didn't really want to take another life, not even Leonid Baranov's.

"I think you remember the game?" Tomas asked with a wicked smirk. "Winner takes all, nobody leaves the ring until only one is left standing. Oh, and, Beth. We thought it would be fun to add a little additional incentive, not that I think you need it, you want him dead as much as Sarah and I do. But if he kills you then Sarah will kill your husband."

Her terrified eyes moved from Tomas to Sarah and lastly to Axel.

She didn't want to do this, but she had to.

If she didn't, Axel would die.

While she wanted them to be together forever, not like this. Not in death.

"You can do it, Beth," Axel said confidently, latching his gaze onto hers. "I believe in you."

That was all well and good, but she wasn't the same woman she had been twenty months ago when she had first been kidnapped. Back then, she had trained with Tank every day, running self-defense drills. She worked out in the gym with Axel all the time, sometimes just the two of them and sometimes with the rest of the guys. Her body had been stronger, fitter, and better trained.

But she'd lived the last year with zero memories.

No running drills.

No time in the range.

No working out in the gym.

How was she supposed to take on a man twice her size and win?

"As usual, we have given you a little advantage," Tomas told her as Baranov was dragged out of the gurney, his naked body pulled over and dumped in the ring along with her.

"Advantage?" she asked, confused.

"You didn't really think you could beat all those men on your own, did you, dear?" Sarah asked condescendingly. "We always gave you an advantage because we *wanted* you to win. All the men you fought were loyal to Baranov so they were no use to us. A dose of a drug that causes unimaginable pain to burn through your body was always administered shortly before a fight. We didn't want them at their best. So as impressive as your skills are, you still wouldn't have walked away alive from a single one of those men."

Right now, staring into the dead eyes of a man who had done unspeakable things to her, Beth didn't care about any of that.

"Think about every time he hurt you, wisp. Picture it, feel it, live it, let it fuel you. Let your anger at everything he stole from you save you now," Axel's voice coached.

"On that note, let the games begin," Tomas called out.

Baranov didn't waste any time, he just sprung at her.

Although she tried to dodge out of the way, she was too slow, and a fist slammed into her stomach shoving the air from her lungs.

Beth gagged and fell to her knees, trying desperately to suck in more oxygen.

Another fist caught her in the side of the head, and she saw stars. But she wasn't going to let this man get the best of her. Staying low, she struck out at his knees, managing to take him down, then pounced, getting in a couple of good blows to his head before he was able to shove her off him.

Trying to remember what she'd been taught, Beth rolled and came up on her feet. She dodged a fist, and then another before being a split second too slow to avoid the third. It slammed into her shoulder, and she felt the joint pop out of place.

Axel's roar of fury reminded her of the stakes, but she was too slow again when Baranov grabbed her and spun her around, pinning her against his chest.

"No one beats me, not even you," he snarled in her ear as one of his big hands grabbed her breast, his fingers finding her nipple through her shirt and pinching it painfully.

Just like that, all those feelings of fear, and anger, and helplessness that she had felt when he held her prisoner came rushing back.

Instead of trying to get out of his grip, she reached behind her, grabbed onto his flaccid penis, and yanked as hard as she could.

His howl of pain was like music to her ears, and Beth refused to let go of it as he released her and began to try to bat her away. She held on, imagining not just him and what he had done to her, but her father, her uncles, her brothers, her cousins, and squeezed for all she was worth.

Baranov's howls of pain intensified, and she made sure to dig her nails in as well, anything to cause him pain and take him down.

Once he was on his knees, she finally released him and started delivering blow after blow to his neck. At first, he tried to fight her off, probably got in a couple of blows of his own but she was beyond feeling right now. Beyond anything other than killing the man who had caused her so much pain because if she didn't her husband would die.

It took her a while to realize that Baranov was no longer fighting back.

A while longer to process that it was over.

That she had won.

She had killed him.

But even with her personal bogeyman dead, neither she nor her husband were any safer than they had been before.

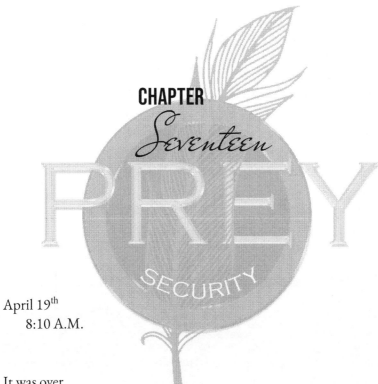

CHAPTER
Seventeen

April 19th
    8:10 A.M.

It was over.

Ironically, it was also seven years to the minute since Sarah had been snatched from her car as she stopped at a red light while driving home from work late one night.

Leonid Baranov was dead, and it felt wonderful.

So wonderful Sarah didn't even care that she hadn't been the one to end his life.

Without even thinking about what she was doing, she ran to the woman who had just ended Baranov's worthless life and flung her arms around her. Beth was stiff in her hold, and she was sure the woman had cried out in pain, but right now she didn't care. She just needed to hold her fellow victim because of everyone left alive, only the two of them knew just how dark and depraved Leonid Baranov truly was.

"Thank you, thank you, thank you," she wept over and over again as she held onto Beth.

After a long moment, one of the woman's arms moved to wrap

around Sarah's shoulders in a loose hug. "It's over now, he can't hurt either of us again, or anyone else," Beth whispered.

"I ... wanted to kill him myself but ... I couldn't. Hurting was one thing, but killing him ... I'm not as strong as you are."

That was the absolute truth.

While she did not like Beth Lindon, who had somehow managed to do what nobody else had and actually survived Baranov's brutality, she had to admire the other woman's strength. Of course, at the time when they had both been prisoners, she hadn't known the extent of suffering the woman had lived through, she now knew all about poor Beth's horrific past.

No wonder the woman could survive the devil, she'd grown up in hell.

"I didn't want to kill him either, Sarah. Not really. I wanted him dead, but I don't want to be surrounded by violence anymore. I just want peace," Beth said softly. "Please, you can understand that, can't you? I did what you wanted, I killed him, please can you just let me and Axel go now?"

There was a part of her that wanted to, she didn't want anyone on Axel's team dead, after all, they had saved her life. But letting them go wasn't possible.

"I can't," she said simply, standing and brushing at her wet cheeks. Sarah crossed to her husband, and grabbed his shoulders, pulling Tomas down so she could press her lips to his. "Thank you for letting me have my revenge."

"Of course, darling," Tomas said, his tongue trailing across her bottom lip. "Anything for my girl."

"You two can make out later, Beth needs medical attention," Axe said, his voice hard.

Tearing her gaze away from Tomas, she looked over to see Beth on her knees beside Baranov's dead body. The woman was hunched in on herself as though in pain, and she cradled one of her arms against her chest in a protective manner that Sarah had already seen Beth do before.

"We'll have her taken to the infirmary to be patched up. We're not monsters you know, Mr. Lindon," Tomas told him.

"I'm going with her," Axe said in a voice that brokered no argument.

"Yes, of course," Tomas agreed.

"Both of you are coming, too. I want answers and I'm done waiting for them," Axe continued like he was the one in charge.

Before she could snap at him, Tomas' hands smoothed down her arms. "Yes, of course. Both Sarah and I are happy to explain, aren't we, darling?"

"I guess," Sarah huffed. What she really wanted to do was take Baranov's body and cut it into tiny pieces, then smash them all up until there was nothing left of him but dust.

Tomas nodded at some of his men, and two of them went to grab Beth. Another two went to Axe's gurney and began to wheel it back to the infirmary. Baranov's body remained where it was, Sarah knew Tomas wouldn't have it moved until she decided what she wanted to do with it. She changed her mind more often than she changed her clothes.

"Beth, honey, look at me," Axe said in a soft, soothing voice once they were all in the infirmary.

With eyes clouded by shock, Beth's gaze moved slowly to meet her husband's.

"You did amazing, wisp. I'm so proud of you. Your strength is limitless and every day you make me love you more," Axe told his wife.

A small smile curled Beth's lips up. "Love you, too," she whispered.

Axe never took his eyes off his wife while one of Tomas' doctors attended to Beth. He relocated her dislocated shoulder, he cleaned and stitched a gash on her cheekbone, and he prodded at her ribs and declared them bruised but not broken. It wasn't until Beth was seated on a gurney beside him, holding his hand, clean and medicated, that Axe's hard eyes turned to her and Tomas.

"How long have you been together?" he demanded.

"Tomas wanted me from the beginning, but Baranov doesn't share his toys," Sarah said bitterly.

She could never understand why Tomas hadn't made a move to take down his boss and stop the man from hurting her. Whenever she brought it up, Tomas always told her that he hadn't been able to make his move until the timing was perfect.

Why did it have to be perfect when she was being tortured every single day?

Wasn't that more important?

Tomas said it wasn't, that if things weren't perfect, he wouldn't win and she would have to remain Baranov's toy forever. It wasn't that Sarah thought her husband was lying to her, but she just didn't understand his reservations. Tomas was bigger, stronger, and smarter than Baranov. Without Tomas, the man would have been arrested a dozen times over. Tomas was the one who paid off cops and witnesses or had them killed if they couldn't be bought. He was the only reason Baranov was as feared as he was. Baranov was but the puppet, it was Tomas who was the puppeteer.

"Tomas is the reason I was still alive. Baranov wanted to kill me, but Tomas told him that if he did then he would kill him," Sarah explained.

"Baranov was afraid of you?" Axe asked Tomas. "I thought he wasn't afraid of anyone."

"I wouldn't say afraid was the right word," Tomas replied. "More like he knew he was reliant on me if he wished to remain out of prison. I was the one who took care of all his problems for him. Yes, he could have had me killed and found someone else to do my job, but I was the one with the reputation. So, we worked out an agreement. He got to keep his toy but had to keep her alive."

"So, after we rescued Sarah you two were free to be together," Axe said.

"We were," she agreed, smiling at her husband.

"It was you who had Baranov's male victim killed," Axe said.

Sarah shrugged. She'd liked Dennis, but business was business. "Not by choice. He wouldn't let it go. I begged him to move on, to stop worrying about Baranov, but I couldn't tell him that Tomas and I had a plan to destroy the man and take over his empire. When he wouldn't let it go, we had to act. He realized that Tomas and I were involved, and he was going to tell you. Killing him was the only option."

"You killed your own daughter," Axe said in disgust. "How could you do that?"

"The child was neither planned nor wanted," Tomas said dismissively. "She might have been a useful tool in keeping our cover on Sarah's farm, but when it was time to move on we had to get rid of her. When Beth was able to escape, we had bigger concerns than an unwanted brat. When we realized Beth did not remember that it was Sarah and I who were responsible for her disappearance and you all believed it was Baranov there was no need to do anything further about the problem unless her memories returned."

"I don't understand why you even took Beth," Axe said. "She was no threat to you. And I don't understand why you didn't kill me and my team when you knew where we were all along."

"Killing you would not have furthered our goal," Tomas replied. "We were on the same side, Baranov was an enemy to us both. As for taking Beth, it was a strategical decision and one that was necessary to destroy Baranov. Beth was the only toy he'd ever had that could not be broken, he was fascinated with her. Watching her kill the soldiers who were most loyal to him, watching how indestructible she was, how perfect, but knowing he could never have her was the most delicious form of torture for a man like Baranov."

At least that was part of the reason.

Not all of it as far as Sarah was concerned.

She had her own reasons, just ones she hadn't shared with her husband.

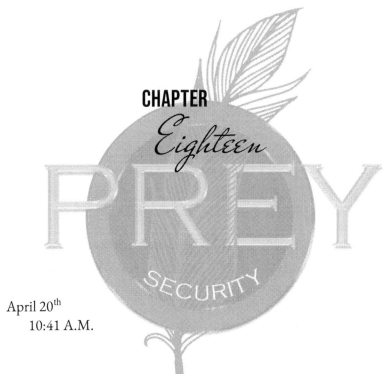

CHAPTER

Eighteen

April 20th
   10:41 A.M.

To say Axe was frustrated would be the understatement of the century.

He was so far beyond annoyed he couldn't even see it anymore.

Every time he got himself out of one of the cuffs a guard would walk calmly into the infirmary and replace it. No words, no rebuke, no warning not to try it again, no taunting that he didn't have a hope of getting himself out of there let alone getting himself and Beth out.

It was driving him insane.

How Baranov had survived over a year and a half of being restrained like this was beyond him. This helplessness was killing him. Beth was there somewhere, he wanted to get to her, wanted to get her the hell out of this place and away from these crazy people.

Well, Tomas wasn't really crazy unless you called being so hungry for money and power there wasn't anything you wouldn't do, but Sarah Sanders was absolutely insane. Somewhere along the way, the woman's mind had just checked out on her. To believe in any way that Tomas loved her it had to have.

The man had stood by and allowed her to be abused, doing nothing to stop it even though if he really wanted to, he probably could have. Sure, he had kept Sarah alive, and that might count for something, but he certainly hadn't done it for Sarah's benefit.

From what he could tell, Sarah seemed to genuinely believe she was in love with Tomas, but there had been a flicker of something in her eyes when he talked about killing their daughter that told him there were still bits of humanity left inside her. Something sketchy about the way Sarah behaved around Beth had Axe on edge. Something in the way the other woman looked at his wife that he didn't like.

Hence, he was losing his mind trapped there.

"Good morning," Sarah singsonged as she strolled into the infirmary. She had a big smile on her face and a bounce in her step that told him she was excited about something. What, he had no idea, but he was sure whatever it was he wouldn't share that excitement. "Did you get any sleep?"

"We're not friends, Sarah, and I'm not your guest," he reminded her calmly.

The woman pouted. "You did save my life."

"And you ruined mine when you stole my wife."

Another pout, and there was anger in her eyes at the mention of Beth. "Tomas said I'm supposed to give you the drug, but I don't want to. You might be mad at me, but you did save my life and I don't want to cause you pain."

Yay for him.

But the drug was given to men to make them slower and weaker, a more even match for someone smaller than them.

Fear reared its ugly head inside him.

Did this mean what he thought it meant?

"You know you could stay here with us for a long time," Sarah said, sidling up to him. One of her hands traced the lines of his biceps through his long-sleeved T-shirt. The hand dipped lower, tracing across his abs, stopping at the waistband of his pants. "I told Tomas to let me take your clothes off so they didn't get all yucky like this. I didn't want you to be uncomfortable, but I think Tomas was a little jealous, you do have a great body." Sarah gave a little giggle that was part amused, and part pure insanity.

"I don't care about being comfortable or not, Sarah," he told her.

"I know, but I care. Here, let me help." As much as he hated it, he could do nothing as Sarah unzipped his pants and struggled to pull them down his legs when he refused to help her in any way. It wasn't until she got to the cuffs on his ankles that she seemed to realize the pants weren't coming off. Not that it deterred her, she simply found some scissors and proceeded to cut off his pants, his shirt, and his underwear, leaving him naked.

The way her eyes traveled his body made Axe feel like a piece of meat, and while he was in no way comparing this to the horrors Beth had endured, it did give him a tiny bit of insight into what she had been through.

"Much better," Sarah said, nodding appreciatively at her work. "And after this morning, we can get you properly settled here as a long-term guest." Her hand reached out and grabbed his length, stroking it with an almost puzzled look on her face. "Tomas doesn't like for me to touch him. When we're in bed he likes me to just lie there and let him use me however he wants."

Axe didn't doubt it. The man might not be as much of a pervert as his boss had been, but Tomas Butcher was every bit as evil. Whatever the man felt for Sarah it wasn't love. Not real love. Obsession perhaps, lust definitely, but not love. Because if he loved her, he wouldn't have allowed her to keep on being abused by Baranov.

"I like to touch though," Sarah continued, although she seemed to be more thinking aloud than actually speaking to him. "It makes me feel more involved, like a participant and not a doll. I liked to touch Baranov. He hated it. I used to make him hard and then stop, not letting him come. Then I'd wait until he went limp and start all over." A bright smile lit her face as she released him and stepped back. "It was fun."

The trauma Sarah had been through had warped her mind in ways that could probably never be fixed, and honestly, he didn't have the time nor the concern to worry about it right now.

Get Beth.

Get out.

That was all he cared about.

"Well, we better go," Sarah said, circling the gurney until she was standing up by the top of his head. "Tomas is waiting."

It didn't take a shrink to figure out why Sarah had latched onto Tomas Butcher so tightly. He was the reason she was still alive. According to Baranov, she was already broken and therefore of no further use to him since she could no longer provide him with any amusement. If it hadn't been for Tomas' intervention she would have been killed, her body dumped along with all the others.

As unlikely as it was he would be able to convince her to turn at this point, he had to try. The chances of him and Beth escaping were slim, and he was going to work every possible advantage he could.

"Sarah, it's not too late you know," he told her, forcing a gentleness into his tone he certainly wasn't feeling.

"Not too late for what?" she asked, rolling him out of the infirmary.

"To end this. To go home. Baranov is dead, he's not a threat to you anymore. You can go home to your family."

"My family?"

"Yeah, you remember them? Your mom and dad just celebrated their thirtieth wedding anniversary. Your big sister has two little girls now, Sarah is four, and Sarabi is two. Your little sister will be getting married in the fall. You can go home to them, Sarah. Be part of their lives again. Be surrounded by people who truly care about you."

When they'd rescued the women from Baranov's place, Sarah's family had been given the option of going into hiding with her, but they had refused, saying it wouldn't be fair to their other daughters to uproot their lives and disappear.

If they had made a different choice would things have turned out differently?

Axe would like to say he hoped so, but the reality was Tomas had already gotten his hooks into Sarah long before she was rescued.

"How do you know about my family?" Sarah asked, a hint of bitterness in her voice.

"We keep in touch via a secure email system Panther set up. They regret not going with you, Sarah." That was the truth. Shortly after Sarah had been given her new identity and settled in a new place, her parents had wished they'd chosen to go with her. Unfortunately, by then it was too late.

Sarah froze. "They do?"

"Of course they do. You're their daughter and they love you. They miss you. They panicked at first, but they would go back and do it over if they could."

He was getting through to her, Axe could tell that he was, but then Tomas went and ruined everything.

"Hurry up, Sarah, we're waiting," Butcher's voice called out.

"Doesn't matter," Sarah muttered, walking again, rolling his gurney along with her. "It's too late. Too late to go back. Too late for a lot of things. You have a game, and this time your opponent isn't going to be given an advantage."

~

April 20th
    10:48 A.M.

"Good morning, doll," Tomas said cheerfully as he appeared outside her cell.

For the life of her Beth couldn't come up with any sort of bravado-induced snappy comeback.

One thing her life had taught her at a young age was that people preyed on the weak. If you could muster an air of strength, people believed it. Didn't mean they didn't hurt you, but there was some kind of subconscious respect there.

If they turned you into a cowering, crying mess then it was already over.

You had already lost.

Only right now, she couldn't seem to summon any energy to play the game.

Having Axel here changed everything. *Everything.*

It was so much easier when you were trapped in hell all alone with no one else's survival but your own to worry about. Sure, she'd had a couple of female cousins who had suffered the same things she had as a child, but they hadn't always been around, the men usually kept them separated. She had cared about them, protected them when she could, but it wasn't like this. Same when she was Leonid Baranov's prisoner. There had been Sarah, and three other girls had died during the time she had been there. While they had all been kept in cages in the basement, often they had in gags, and there were always threats of what would happen if they were caught talking.

Knowing her husband was there, the person she loved most in the world, a man she would do anything for, killed something inside her.

With nothing other than trepidation in her steps, she moved to the now open cage door. Her clothes had been stripped off her when she was returned to the cell yesterday, and as she stood naked before him, Tomas gave her a lingering once over.

Beth knew it wasn't the bruises littering her torso or the way the arm of the shoulder she had dislocated was tucked against her stomach that had drawn his attention.

She knew the look of a hungry predator when she saw one.

The gaze raking over her reeked of sexuality.

Well, his anyway, she was repulsed by the idea of him touching her.

"You know, I never really got why Leonid was so obsessed with you. It was only when you killed six of his men that I finally got the appeal. Granted, I gave you an advantage because I wanted those men dead, but your technique was still amazing, your tenacity admirable. You are a true fighter, my dear." Tomas took a step closer, one of his hands trailing a lazy line from her lips, down her chest, pausing to painfully squeeze first one breast and then the other before settling between her legs. "It's a shame I never got to sample you. Still, if you win today's battle perhaps I will."

After dragging a finger across her dry center, he grabbed the wrist of her dislocated arm and began to pull her along after him, knowing full well—*enjoying* full well—the pain he was causing her.

When she was dragged into the arena and saw who was there waiting for her, Beth froze.

Every cell in her body rebelled against what she was seeing.

"No." The word was out of her mouth before she even realized she had spoken. Beth didn't care about the punishment for being disobedi-ent, speaking out of turn, for refusing what would shortly be a direct order.

She wasn't doing it.

Simple as that.

"You don't have a choice," Sarah singsonged in her annoying way. It was hard to have sympathy for the woman even though it was clear her mind had splintered due to her ordeal.

"I always have a choice, and I choose no," Beth said, a feeling of calm settling over her. There was no way on Earth she was going to fight her husband and kill him. That meant she would be the loser and her life would be over. Surprisingly, she felt no fear over that.

Not that she wanted her husband to have to live with her death on his shoulders, but if he refused to participate then what could Tomas and Sarah do?

They couldn't force the two of them to duel to the death.

"Wisp, you can't." Axel's voice was tortured and the look on his face was pure devastation in his voice.

"I'm not going to kill you," she said, and as far as she was concerned it was as simple as that.

There was no doubt in her mind that whether Sarah and Tomas had drugged Axel or not, she wouldn't win. Those other men had been trained, but they didn't have the skills that Axel did. She would never beat him, and she had no intention of trying.

"You have to," Axel said, sounding tortured.

"I won't."

"Beth—"

"Axel," she said, cutting him off, "how can you ask me to kill you?"

"How can you ask *me* to kill *you*?" Axel shot back.

She couldn't.

She wouldn't.

All she knew was that she was not going to murder her husband. Beth was so tired of being used as a pawn for other people's amusement, in other people's games.

No more.

It ended here and now.

"If both of you forfeit then you both lose, you'll both die," Tomas said simply.

"Beth, you have to do this," Axel said, not bothering to hide that he was begging. "You don't have a choice. The guys are coming, you know that. Prey will find us. If you kill me then you have a chance at being alive when they find us."

"I don't want to be alive without you," she said calmly. Actually, the level of calm she felt right now was unnerving. It was like her ability to feel had died the second she realized Tomas expected her to fight her husband and kill him. Now she was just numb inside.

"Please, wisp. I've failed you already. This whole last year I didn't give you what you needed. Then I let you get abducted, twice. I won't fail you again." Now there was a thread of something in his voice she didn't like. "If I kill myself, then that still counts as a win for Beth, right?" he asked Tomas.

"Axel, no!" All her emotions suddenly came rushing back in a flood, almost taking her to her knees. In fact, if Tomas wasn't still holding onto her, she likely would have crumpled to the ground.

"You want a winner, I'll give you one," Axel continued as though she hadn't spoken.

"No! You can't do that to me," she screamed. What was he thinking?

When he looked at her his expression was hard, unyielding. "I won't let you die, Beth. Whatever it takes I'll keep you alive."

Maybe—and that was still a big maybe—she'd be alive, but she wouldn't really live. Not without her husband.

"So, do we have a deal?" Axel asked Tomas.

"You kill yourself slowly, painfully, and agree Beth has to watch the show, and we have a deal," Tomas agreed.

Axel winced, and she knew it wasn't at a painful death, it was for her having to watch it. Still, there was no waver in his voice when he spoke. "Deal."

"Please don't do this, Axel," she begged. "I don't want to live without you, I'd rather be dead. Just let them kill us both. Don't make me live without you. If you do this, I'm afraid that I'll ... hate you," she whispered the admission, but knew from his wince that he had heard it.

Before he could speak, the entire world seemed to erupt into gunfire.

"Beth, get down!" Axel screamed.

Fear for him, because he was still tied to a gurney unable to protect himself, was at the forefront of her mind as she dropped to the floor.

Covering her head with her arms, she couldn't see what was happening, but she could hear shouting and more shots being fired. There seemed to be dozens of people in the room when only moments before there had been just the four of them.

When someone suddenly grabbed her, she began to fight, kicking and scratching at the arms that tried to take her.

Her eyes were open, but it was impossible to see, there was smoke everywhere, and she'd spent enough time around military men to know that they'd set off the smoke grenades when they raided the place.

When Prey raided the place.

They were there, had to be. Who else would suddenly be shooting up Tomas Butcher's secret hideout?

It couldn't be one of the Prey guys trying to grab her, they would have identified themselves, and made sure she knew she was safe.

Whoever it was didn't want to save her, they wanted to hurt her.

Gunfire continued to rage around her, and she managed to get what she was sure was a good kick to the stomach of her would-be attacker. Free, she began to crawl in the direction she thought would lead her to a quiet corner of the room where she could wait out the fight, but the smoke made her feel all turned around, and really, she had no idea which way she was going.

Suddenly, pain exploded in the back of her head, and the world around her shimmered away into nothingness.

CHAPTER Nineteen

April 20th
   11:04 A.M.

While he was extremely glad the cavalry had arrived, it sucked to be stuck on this stupid gurney.

Axe wanted off it, and he wanted a weapon in his hand.

More than that, he wanted his wife where he could see her, where he knew that she was safe.

Unlike him, she wasn't a sitting duck, he was sure someone from Prey had located her and she was already safely tucked away somewhere. But it wasn't the same thing as knowing he was with her, he was protecting her.

Not that he doubted anyone on his team or anyone else from Prey. Axe knew they would protect Beth as though she were their own, but he still wanted her in his arms.

It wasn't just for her benefit, or just her safety that he needed to be with her, it was equally for his own sanity. Seeing the pure determination in her face as she refused to partake in a duel had damn near broken him.

She wasn't going to do it.

That had been evident.

Beth had reached a place where she was prepared to accept death rather than let anyone else control her, and it was terrifying. He'd known that the only way to keep her alive long enough to give his team a chance to find her was to take the choice out of her hands.

Not an easy thing to do when she'd told him she would hate him for it.

But at least she'd be alive to hate him.

If it had come down to it, he would have happily sacrificed his life for hers, and he wouldn't have regretted having to hurt her to do it. Not that he ever wanted to hurt his wife, but they were talking life and death here and he'd be damned if he killed his wife to keep himself alive.

What had Beth expected him to do when faced with an ultimatum like the one they'd been given?

Just let her die?

Unacceptable.

A bullet whizzed past his head close enough that he could feel it. With this smoke everywhere, it was almost impossible to see more than an inch or so in front of your face.

Throwing all his strength into it, he managed to free his right hand, he'd already gotten his feet free shortly after the shooting started. With no one to stop him this time, he made quick work of freeing his remaining hand and rolled sideways. Taking the gurney with him as a shield he had no choice but to stay there. With no weapon and the smoke still filling the room—although it was quickly dissipating—he was more liability than he was help.

Finally, the room fell silent.

Most of the smoke had cleared and he was able to make out multiple figures dressed all in black. He didn't have to be able to see their faces to know they were Prey.

Their timing couldn't have been more perfect. If they'd been just a couple of minutes later raiding the facility, he would have already ended his own life to save Beth's. Just because it was a sacrifice he would be willing to make it wasn't like he wanted to die.

The opposite.

What he wanted was a future with his wife free from having to look over their shoulders. He wanted Beth to be able to do whatever she wanted with her life, go to college, get a job, or start her own business. With the money from his trust fund that he'd never spent and invested wisely over the years, nothing was off the table. When she was ready, he'd love to have a family of their own. Whatever they did, he just wanted them to be happy and wanted his wife to be happy. She deserved it more than any other person he knew.

"Needed a hand I see," Tank said, appearing before him, grinning.

"Took you guys long enough to get here," he shot back, shoving to his feet, and shaking out his cramped muscles. Hours of lying on that gurney had driven him insane. Not that he felt sorry for the man, but he had no idea how Leonid Baranov had lasted over a year and a half chained up like that.

"Hey, we came as fast as we could. *You're* the one who got himself kidnapped," Rock teased.

Since there was no snappy comeback he could think up—he absolutely *had* allowed himself to get kidnapped by making sloppy decisions —he glowered instead. But it quickly morphed into a smile. "You guys have perfect timing."

"Course we do," Scorpion agreed. "Now put some clothes on."

Taking the pants and T-shirt his friend held out, he quickly began putting them on. "It wasn't Baranov," Axe told his team.

"Leonid Baranov wasn't here?" Eagle asked, appearing behind Bravo Team dressed in full gear. Knowing that Eagle himself had come to help take down the infamous serial killer because of Baranov's connection to not just Prey Security but also to him and mostly to Beth, should hopefully remind her just how very loved she was. While her own family might be the stuff of nightmares, her Prey family would walk through fire for her.

"Oh, he was here all right," he replied. "But he was here as a prisoner. Tomas Butcher decided to stage a takeover. He's had Baranov here this whole time, that's why there have been no sightings of him since Beth was taken. Butcher then pitted Baranov's loyal men against Beth, made her fight them to the death." They already knew that part since

Beth had remembered that she'd been made to kill or be killed, but he filled in the missing pieces Beth had never even known about.

"Damn," Eagle muttered, and every single man around him looked like they would love to rip Butcher to pieces with their bare hands.

"Butcher has some drug that induces pain, he gave it to the men to even things up, to give Beth an edge since they wanted her to kill them anyway," he explained.

"So, Baranov was here?" Panther asked.

"Yeah, he was here. They made Beth kill him," Axe answered.

"So little Bethie got to take down the notorious killer, good for her," Trick said.

"Wait, you said *they*. Who's they?" Eagle asked.

"Butcher and Sarah Sanders. They're partners, in on this together."

"Sarah isn't a victim?" Tank asked.

"Nope. Not even close. Woman has completely lost her mind. She thinks she's in love with Butcher because, apparently, he wanted to keep her alive after Baranov finished playing with her. Don't know why Butcher cared about her, but they're married, and he killed their daughter because he viewed the kid as an inconvenience."

"I get Sarah losing her mind, but why take Beth? She was a fellow victim, hurting her seems cruel, even for someone who had snapped after going through a traumatic ordeal," Rock said.

"Think they wanted to torture Baranov, showing him how unbreakable his favorite doll was while reminding him he'd never get to play with her again. I don't know, and honestly, I don't even care. Who has Beth?" he asked. Since he wasn't wearing comms like everyone else, he didn't know which of the four dozen or so Prey operatives who had come to rescue him and Beth had taken her someplace safe.

Eagle frowned for a moment then spoke into his comms. "Who has Beth?"

The growing look of concern on his boss' face had fear springing to life inside him. Had something happened to Beth? Had she been shot? Hurt somehow? Just because she had been standing when Butcher dragged her into the room didn't mean she hadn't been injured when all hell broke loose. Or maybe she was hysterical after once again being kidnapped and tortured, goodness knows, nobody could blame her for it.

"What's wrong?" Axe demanded. The need to see his wife, hold her, kiss her, assure himself they were both alive, was too strong to ignore. He felt like if he didn't have her in his arms soon, he was going to spontaneously combust.

"Nobody has eyes on Beth," Eagle told him gently.

"What?" he growled. Nobody had Beth? Then where was she? "She was in here when you guys came bursting in. Butcher and Sarah wanted the two of us to fight to the death. I know they intended for me to kill Beth because Sarah said she wasn't going to drug me first. Beth refused and no way was I going to kill my wife, so I made a deal with Butcher that I'd kill myself so I could buy time for you guys to find Beth."

There was no need to explain further, Axe knew there wasn't a man in this room who wouldn't make the exact same choice.

"Beth?" he called out, rushing around the room in search of his wife, while the others also began to look for her. "Beth? Where are you? Answer me, wisp."

Only there was no answer.

They searched the whole room and found no sign of her.

"Where's Sarah?" he asked, already beginning to search the room filled with Butcher's now dead guards.

"Anyone got eyes on Sarah Sanders?" Eagle asked into his comms.

There must have been a round of negatives because his boss shook his head at him, and the fear inside him raged to new heights.

"I think Sarah must have taken Beth," Axe said slowly. Why did he feel like his wife in the hands of fellow victim Sarah Sanders was worse than her in the hands of either Tomas Butcher or Leonid Baranov?

April 20th
    12:21 P.M.

What was piercing through her skull like an arrow?

Groggy as she was, it took a while for Beth to figure out it was sunlight.

Far too bright against her closed lids, she scrunched her eyes tighter shut in an attempt to block it out only to wince as the pain inside her head intensified.

Something kicked at her hip, and she groaned as pain flared not only through the joint but through her entire body.

The shoulder that had been dislocated when she fought against Leonid Baranov was pure agony, the pain from her bruised ribs screamed at her, and there was an assortment of what felt like new bumps and bruises littered across her already abused body.

What had happened to her?

And when had she gotten outside?

Wasn't she in the facility where Tomas Butcher and Sarah Sanders had taken her and Axel?

She remembered waking up in the little white cell, she remembered killing Baranov, she remembered being separated from her husband and the absolute terror that induced, and she remembered ...

After that, things got a little fuzzy.

Another kick, this time to her stomach, made her groan as a sickening wave of nausea rushed through her system. Beth only just managed to turn her head before she threw up, thankfully missing vomiting all over herself.

"Eww!"

The furious voice was important. The answer to why she was here. To what had happened to her.

When a wave of darkness threatened to pull her under, Beth fought against it. Even if she wasn't quite sure where she was or what was happening, she knew instinctively that she needed to stay awake.

She wasn't safe.

Was in danger once again.

Story of her life.

"You threw up on me!" the voice shrieked.

A familiar voice.

Her mind struggled to place it, then ... it clicked.

Sarah.

The voice belonged to Sarah.

Memories trickled back in. She had been taken to the arena, Axel had been there. Tomas had declared she had to fight her husband to the death, but she had refused. Axel had made a stupid bargain to kill himself to spare her life and she'd told him she hated him.

Were those going to be the final words she ever spoke to the man she loved?

Regret swamped her, but she couldn't go back, couldn't do it over, couldn't apologize and tell him she'd only said that out of fear.

The only thing she could do was stay alive.

Fight.

Same thing she always did.

Gunfire had broken out before Axel could follow through on the deal and end his own life. Someone had grabbed her, tried to drag her somewhere but it had been hard to see who it was through the smoke.

Then she remembered agony tearing through her skull before blackness stole her.

It must have been Sarah who had knocked her out. Since they were outside now, she assumed the reason she felt like there were dozens of new bumps all over her body was because the woman had dragged her out there.

But where was there?

And how close was it to the place Prey had just raided?

"You're not tough and strong, you're disgusting," Sarah snapped, throwing in a few more kicks for good measure.

Pain could either be her enemy or her friend right now. Beth could allow it to overwhelm her and shove her into unconsciousness leaving her vulnerable to a woman who was no longer in her right mind and completely unpredictable. Or she could use it to focus, keep her mind sharp, remind herself that she was still alive and as long as she had breath in her she was going to fight for herself and her future.

You can't give up.

Not now.

Not when Baranov is dead.

The freedom you want is within your grasp, all you have to do is stay alive long enough to grab hold of it.

The pep talk was enough for her to summon the strength to pry her eyes open. The too-bright sunshine felt like a thousand knives stabbing into her brain, but she pushed away the worst of the pain and used the rest to make her mind sharp. Sarah might be the most unpredictable opponent she had ever faced, but she wasn't the scariest. Not even close.

Prey had found them, and Sarah was a similar size to Beth, and given that she had been deadweight she doubted the other woman could have dragged her all that far away. The others were somewhere close by, and as soon as Axel realized she was missing, he would go all out to find her.

All she had to do was stay alive until then.

There were trees surrounding them, they were clearly in the woods, but she and Axel had both been unconscious when they had been brought to the place where Tomas and Sarah had held them captive, so she had no idea how far away from home they were. She was lying flat on her back and the sky above was a clear, bright blue. Not only was it bright but the sun on her skin brought warmth as well. It felt warmer than it should have for New York State at this time of year, so she suspected they had been brought further south.

Blinking to try to clear her somewhat blurry vision, Beth saw Sarah standing above her. There was blood on the other woman's T-shirt, and she wasn't sure if it was hers or Sarah's. Hair disheveled, face streaked with dirt and sweat, puffing and panting, the woman was a mess.

But what freaked her out the most was Sarah's eyes.

They were wild.

There was a detachment to reality there that chilled her to the bones despite the warmth of the sun's rays.

Was there any chance Beth could get through to her?

Convince her not to do whatever it was she had planned?

"I always told Tomas you weren't as perfect as he and Baranov seemed to think you were. One little bump on the head and you're throwing up everywhere," Sarah snarled.

There was true hatred in the woman's tone. It seemed like Sarah had decided they were adversaries for some reason. That wasn't how Beth saw things at all. They were on the same side. They had both survived Baranov's sick and twisted games. They were both lucky to be alive, they had both been given a second chance at life, and for the life of her, Beth couldn't understand why Sarah had squandered it.

Of course, she understood trauma and recognized that Sarah's mind had fractured much the same way her own had shut down, blocking everything out and giving her amnesia. But why did Sarah seem so intent on hurting her? She hadn't done a single thing to the other woman.

"Never said I was perfect," Beth croaked. Maybe if she could show Sarah that she had struggled to cope after being rescued, the woman would understand they were the same. There was no need for Sarah to punish her for some perceived sins on Beth's part.

"No, of course not," Sarah mocked. With her hands on her hips and a pout on her face, she looked more petulant toddler than anything else. But a fully grown adult petulant toddler, and a dangerous one at that. "You only shoved it in my face every time you failed to break when Baranov was hurting you. Nothing would break you. *Nothing.* I watched as he whipped you, strangled you, drowned you, burned you, cut you, hit you, raped you, and you never once bowed under his torture."

That might be true, but it certainly wasn't because she was perfect.

It was just because she had already learned how to shove pain away, how to blank her mind, how to cling to her sanity when everything else urged her to give it up and fall apart. She had survived too much from childhood to allow one sick monster to break her.

But she wasn't perfect.

Not even close.

"I see through you, you know," Sarah continued, obviously not requiring a response. "I see that you're not as strong as you pretend to be. Inside you're broken, every bit as broken as I am."

"Didn't say I wasn't," Beth told her. No one knew better than her how many cracked and shattered pieces she had. It was only because of Axel's love and support, and the unwavering acceptance of his friends that she had been able to take all those cracked and shattered pieces and somehow stick them together.

Continuing as though Beth hadn't spoken, Sarah said, "It won't save you. Pretending to be perfect isn't going to save you from the same fate as them."

At that, she nodded to the side and automatically Beth turned her head in the same direction, then immediately wished she hadn't.

Beside them was a large hole.

Inside the hole were bodies.

Lots of bodies.

Lots of *dead* bodies.

A mass grave.

"Your future isn't sunshine and rainbows. It isn't happiness and love. It's this." With that, Sarah kicked her again, this time hard enough to shove her sideways and Beth went tumbling down to join the pile of dead bodies, of which she would soon be one.

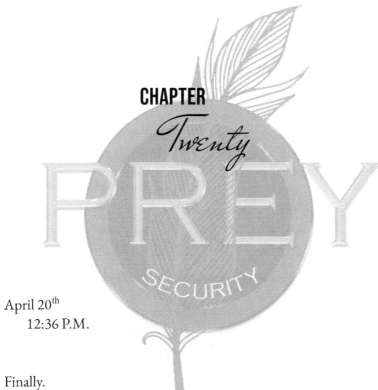

CHAPTER

Twenty

April 20th
    12:36 P.M.

Finally.

Beth Lindon was going to die.

Sarah had certainly waited long enough for this moment.

Standing there above the mass grave, knowing that she was about to bury her nemesis alive was the most wonderful feeling in the world.

She hadn't felt this good in ...

Years.

Not since before she was kidnapped and sold to Leonid Baranov.

Back then, she'd been just a normal girl, not particularly beautiful, but not really ugly either. Just plain. Story of her life. She wasn't the gorgeous, intelligent one like her big sister, and she wasn't the cute, sweet one like her little sister. Sarah had suffered from a major bout of middle-sister-itis.

The forgotten one.

The one stuck in between the lights of the family.

She wasn't going places like her big sister who was so smart she could do anything she wanted. Having modeled as a little girl, her big sister had decided to become a lawyer. But not *just* a lawyer. Nope her sister was too wonderful for that. She was going to be a lawyer who worked specifically with abused women to help them escape the clutches of their husbands, get custody of the kids, and support from their abusers. She was a hero.

She wasn't going to the same place as her little sister either. While not as pretty and not quite as smart as their oldest sister, the baby of the family was just so cute and sweet that she sucked you right in. While having only just graduated high school at the time Sarah was twenty and abducted, her little sister already knew she wanted to work for a charity when she finished college. She wanted to help kids who had been abused and neglected, or who had grown up in the foster system.

How could you stand out when surrounded on either side by such selflessness?

Ordinary.

Completely plain and ordinary.

That was what Sarah was.

No wonder her parents wouldn't leave behind her sisters, or have them uproot their lives, just because Sarah had been abducted, tortured, and then rescued.

Didn't matter that she had needed a support system while she struggled to rebuild not just her life but herself.

Guess her sisters' charity didn't extend to their own blood.

The only person who had been there for her after she was rescued was Tomas. He'd waited until she was swept off alone into witness protection, taken from the city and shoved in a tiny country town, the complete opposite of the life she'd lived before, then he'd come for her.

It didn't matter what anyone else said, he had been there for her. He had shared with her his plans to destroy Baranov, make him pay for everything he had done to Sarah and the others. Well, not that either of them cared all that much about the others. But Baranov had to pay for what he had done to her.

He had to.

Simple as that.

And since Tomas was the only one who seemed willing to let her help him bring the man down, of course she had said yes. After all, if it wasn't for him interceding on her behalf, then Baranov would have killed her like all the others.

All the others except the woman staring up at her with horrified eyes.

Perfect Beth.

Perfect Beth who had survived a childhood that would have shattered any normal person.

Perfect Beth who hadn't succumb to Baranov's torturous games and managed to remain alive since she wouldn't give the monster the one thing he craved.

Perfect Beth who should have been all alone in the world after being rescued, but had instead wound up with an entire team of people—strangers—who had been there for her.

Perfect Beth who had built herself a family full of warriors prepared to die for her.

Perfect Beth who had married a strong, kind, caring, uber-wealthy man.

Perfect Beth who had everything while Sarah had nothing and no one but a lonely farm in the middle of nowhere and Tomas.

"I hate you, perfect Beth," she shouted down into the hole.

"I'm not perfect, Sarah," Beth said, trying to clamber to her feet. The hole wasn't particularly deep, around ten feet, even short as she was Beth would be able to climb out easily enough by piling up a couple of bodies so she could throw an arm over the edge and pull herself up and out.

Not going to happen.

She'd waited too long for this to allow anything to mess it up.

"Your little band of merry soldiers aren't going to show up to save you this time," she told Beth.

If the idiots at Prey hadn't raided the facility moments before Axe was going to kill himself, Beth would already be dead. She wasn't going to allow Tomas to let Axe go through with that plan. It was Beth she wanted dead, not the leader of Bravo Team.

This time it wasn't going to be anyone else's call but her own.

"Your fate is in my hands now, Beth, and I can assure you that unlike everyone else I'm not falling for your perfect persona."

"I'm not perfect," Beth said again, sounding annoyed as she tried to reach up to the top of the hole, coming up much too short.

"Trust me, I know, I believe that even if everyone else doesn't. This time, Tomas isn't there to keep you alive because he enjoyed taunting Baranov. This time you don't get to go back to your happy little life because Tomas doesn't want to draw attention to himself. Attention has been drawn, Prey found where we were hiding in plain sight. Your hero husband won't be riding in on his white horse, and neither will anyone else from Prey. This. Is. It. The day you finally die."

With a smile of triumph, Sarah ran over to the bulldozer and climbed up onto it. It was time to fill in the mass grave where they had been throwing the bodies of the people who competed in Tomas' games. While he might have different interests than his former boss, Baranov wasn't the only one who liked to play God with people's lives. He just wasn't as hands on about it. He found homeless people and runaways, offered them a job, then brought them to one of their four facilities and pitted them against one another. Winner lived to see another day, loser was disposed of in a mass grave.

"Please, Sarah, you don't have to do this," Beth's voice called out.

"I know I don't *have* to, but I *want* to." Didn't the woman get that? Sarah wanted her dead, she was sick of hearing about perfect Beth. With the woman finally out of her hair, maybe she really could move on with her life.

It had been six years since she and Beth and another woman had been rescued from the depths of hell known as Leonid Baranov's house of horrors, but it felt like it had only been six minutes. The terror was still as raw as it had been back then, nightmares still haunted her sleep, she couldn't stomach small, enclosed spaces, she was still prone to burst into tears at the sight of the scars littering her skin.

In short, Sarah was still a mess, and she was sick of it.

"We can get you help," Beth continued. "Maybe being back with your family will—"

"My *family* didn't care about me. They abandoned me," she shouted. "I was left all alone with nothing while you got everything. You had a whole team of people there for you, you don't even know what it's like to be all alone in the world."

"You're wrong. I do know what it's like. *I'll* be there for you, Sarah."

The offer only enraged her further. "Of course, perfect Beth thinks she can do everything, even saving me, her would be murderer. Her *will* be murderer," Sarah corrected. Because this was happening and it was happening now.

It was time to take back control of her life. For the first twenty years, she had lived in the shadows of her two perfect sisters, lost to their greatness. Then she had been used and abused by a monster. In the aftermath of that ordeal, she had once again been lost to the greatness of another survivor, been forced to live in her shadow for the last six years.

No more living in the shadows.

No more being lost to the perceived greatness of another.

Leonid Baranov was dead.

Tomas was dead.

When she was finished there, maybe Sarah would track down her family and kill them all one by one until they were forced to see her.

And now perfect Beth was going to die.

Turning on the bulldozer's engine, she began to push the first load of dirt into the ten-by-ten hole that would very soon become perfect Beth's tomb.

CHAPTER
Twenty~One

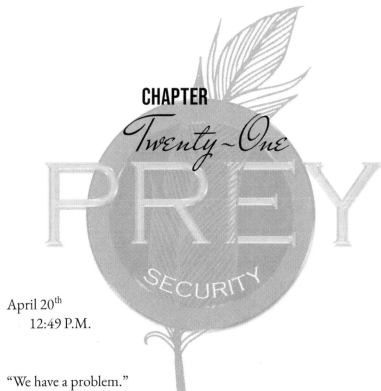

April 20th
  12:49 P.M.

"We have a problem."

At Eagle's words, everyone stopped what they were doing to look over at the man who commanded authority just by being in the room. While Axe only had mild interest in whatever his boss was going to say, he along with the others waited attentively for news.

He was just praying the news was a lead on Beth.

Knowing Sarah was likely the one who had taken her didn't mean they knew where they had gone.

Right now, the where was the most important thing.

Having been checked out by Rock, he'd been cleared and now had a weapon in his hand. He felt better being armed even if the room was littered with dead bodies. Dead bodies that had now been all lined up as Prey worked on identifying each one of them.

Well, everyone else was working on that. All Axe could do was pace and worry about Beth.

"Tomas Butcher isn't amongst the bodies," Eagle answered, grimly. "And there's no sign of Baranov's body."

There was a chance that Tomas had somehow slipped away, maybe was even responsible for Sarah and Beth's disappearance, but he had seen Beth kill Leonid Baranov with his own eyes.

"Baranov is dead," he said firmly. "Beth killed him. I watched her do it. There was a moment there when I thought I was going to watch my wife get murdered right before my eyes. But Beth is too strong for that. She fought back and destroyed that sick monster. Trust me, it was a sight to behold."

"Not doubting you, Axe," Eagle said just as firmly, making eye contact to reinforce his words. "Your woman is amazing, an inspiration to all of us, her resilience and perseverance are legendary at Prey. If I could bottle it, I'd make a fortune."

"You already have a fortune," Ivory Morales, a member of Prey's infamous all-women Artemis Team sassed.

The expression on Eagle's face was tender as he looked over at the young woman. Eagle had rescued Ivory and her three sisters from a man who had abducted them as babies and kept them on a remote Alaskan compound where he trained them to be his own personal army. As much as Prey was a family and Eagle looked out for everyone, he had a soft spot for Ivory and her sisters. "More of a fortune then. Look, Axe, I'm not doubting you, I'm saying that the body has been moved. Let's assume Tomas and Sarah are going to run, you said Sarah seemed jealous of Beth, it makes sense they might not want to leave her alive."

Of course, he knew there was a chance Beth might already be dead, but the thought of her body dumped alongside Baranov's made him feel ill.

No way was she being tied for eternity in her final resting place to Leonid Baranov, the man who had caused her so much pain and suffering.

"Have you got a hit on her yet?" he asked Panther. Axe would forever be grateful that he had tagged Beth with a tracker before they went hiking through the woods in search of where she had been held prisoner. At the time, he hadn't thought anything was going to go wrong, but he'd rather be safe than sorry.

It would have saved their lives when they were taken by Tomas Butcher, and it had saved their lives today. Apparently, there had been some sort of blocker in place at the facility that had slowed Panther and the rest of the Prey tech geniuses down, but in the end, they had found him and Beth and he refused to believe the tracker wouldn't lead them to his wife now.

"The blocker is still in place down here," Panther replied. "We just used the last known location we had and went old school from there to find this place."

"Got something," a voice called out. Everyone's attention moved to Steel, the leader of Prey's most shadowy unit. More rumors were running around Prey about Delta Team than anything else. While Axe had met the men several times and worked the occasional op with them, he couldn't say he knew any of them well at all. Not even close.

If the rumors had even a grain of truth in them, he could see why.

"What?" he asked.

"Secret door here," Steel told them.

That got his attention.

Hurrying over to where Steel was standing, his team with him, Axe barely noticed his own team following him.

"How did you find it?" he asked when he saw the section of wall sitting partially open. As far as secret doors went this one had to be about the top of the line. He'd been in this room a couple of times, he'd done a visual sweep looking for weakness and all possible exit and entry points. Not once had he noticed this door.

Steel exchanged glances with one of his men but both simply shrugged in response. Exactly why these guys were so mysterious. They rarely spoke, they didn't give anything away, they had skills that topped anything Axe had seen before, and yet he was wary of believing the rumors because he knew how easy it was to spread them. Coming from such a wealthy family, his teenage years had been filled with rumors being spread about him, who he dated and what he did in secret. It was all crazy and he'd hated it so he made a point of only believing things he knew to be true.

"Let's go," Axe said, already brushing past the Delta Team guys to get through the door. This had to be where Tomas and Sarah had taken Beth because it was the only entry point Prey didn't use. They had a pretty good start, but they couldn't have left the compound area yet because if they had, Panther would have been able to pick up Beth's tracker again.

The hallway through the secret door was quiet, sloping down a little as it obviously went deeper unground than the rest of the facility. The corridor was sparsely lit with dim globes hanging from the ceiling at approximately ten-foot intervals. There wasn't a single sound emanating from anywhere in front of them, and as they slowly descended through the tunnels the sounds from behind them began to fade.

"Got something here," Dragon, a member of Delta Team announced, stopping suddenly beside something on the floor.

"Is that blood?" Axe asked, heart in his throat as he bent to see what the other man was looking at.

Dragon merely nodded, then stood and began to walk further down the hallway. Everyone else followed him as he seemed to be on a trail, sporadically spotting more droplets of blood when Axe was positive no one else would have seen them in this light without the use of luminol.

When they came to a point where the tunnel took three separate turns, Axe didn't hesitate to follow Dragon down the one he had chosen. The man was like a bloodhound, and since he didn't have anything better to offer right now he was absolutely going to stick with the man who seemed to know what he was doing.

They had just started to rise again, likely having bypassed under the facility and now ready to come back up and to the outside, when they spotted it.

A figure lying on the ground about twenty yards in front of them.

A body.

From the way it was lying at an awkward angle, a dead body.

Beth's?

Before anyone could stop him, Axe was running toward it.

Training meant nothing at this moment when his wife might be lying there dead.

It wasn't until he'd closed more than half the distance that he realized the figure was too big to be Beth, and that it wasn't naked like she had been the last time he'd seen her.

"Not her," he said, sagging to his knees several yards away from the body. "Not Beth."

The words were more for his own benefit than anyone else's.

She wasn't dead, that meant he still had time to find her.

"It's Tomas Butcher, and someone stabbed him in the throat," Trick said.

"Beth?" Scorpion asked.

"No," Dragon said simply, like he had been here to watch the events unfold. "It's her blood I've been tracking." He offered no explanation for how he knew that, and all of Bravo Team knew better than to ask. Delta Team wouldn't be offering any answers.

"Then it had to be Sarah," Rock said.

"But why would she kill Butcher when you said she was in love with the man, married him, credited him with keeping her alive when Baranov would have killed her?" Tank asked.

"Because Butcher wanted to keep Beth alive and Sarah didn't," Axe said softly, sure in his gut that he was right. "Sarah wants Beth dead, and she eliminated the only thing standing in her way."

∼

April 20th
　1:17 P.M.

A scream fell from her lips as she was pushed backward.

No.

It couldn't end like this.

Beth seemed to fall in slow motion, landing with a bone-jarring thud back in the mass grave filled with bodies.

She cried out as her battered body landed awkwardly causing pain to scream along each of her limbs.

So close.

She had been so close to making it out.

She had managed to climb out of the pit, not an easy feat with a dislocated shoulder that had been relocated only to then be dislocated all over again as she was dragged along the ground while she was unconscious. But before she'd been able to make a run for it, Sarah had driven the bulldozer directly at her.

The force of it and the huge pile of dirt it pushed along with it, shoving into her, had been too much. Although she'd done her best to dart out of the way or do the impossible and somehow keep her balance even though she was being pushed backward, right toward the hole she had only just managed to escape, there was no hope for her.

The landing had been brutal, but the wave of dirt that fell with her was almost worse.

It rained down on her like a summer storm. Dirt got in her eyes, her nose, her ears, her mouth, but worse, it landed all over her body like a heavy weight she didn't really have the strength to dislodge.

Especially when that one load of dirt wasn't all that came.

More and more of it rained down.

It just kept coming.

And coming.

And coming.

The more she tried to shove it away the more it covered her, pinning her body down until her struggles became weaker and weaker, until they were nothing more than small, ineffectual tremors.

Buried alive.

Even though reality was telling her differently, Beth's brain didn't seem to comprehend that this was how her life was going to end.

It just ... couldn't.

Not after everything she had been through.

Not after everything she had survived.

How could she die in a mass grave filled with the bodies of the innocent, and she suspected the not-quite-so-innocent, covered by a thick blanket of dirt?

It seemed so unfair.

Yet when had life ever been fair for her?

Never.

Well, that wasn't quite true.

Life had been more than fair when it had given her Axel. Any other man would have just shipped her off to a hospital and left her to fend for herself. Sure, maybe she would be thought of every now and then. The poor girl with no family to take her in after such a horrible ordeal, but soon she would become just another successful op.

But that wasn't what Axel had done. He'd made sure that he built her a support system. He was patient with her as she navigated an entire world that was completely foreign to her. For the first time in her life, she had been shown kindness and compassion. Had been treated like a human being with equal rights, with needs and desires, with her own thoughts and interests. A real person, not just a slave to be used as others saw fit.

Now, as she lay there, slowly being buried alive by pile after pile of dirt, Beth found her biggest regret was what would be her final words to her husband.

They would haunt her as she took her dying breath.

Hate.

Despite Sarah's insistence that Beth was perfect, that couldn't be further from the truth. She had hated a lot of people in her life. Her parents for allowing her to be abused and participating in that abuse. Her uncles and cousins for treating her like she was less than human, and enjoying torturing her. Leonid Baranov for buying her like she was a piece of meat and not a person. Tomas Butcher for playing God with her life and using her as a way to punish Baranov. She even hated Sarah herself for going over to the dark side, from victim to perpetrator.

But never once had she hated Axel.

She loved him so much it hurt.

Hurt worse than the dislocated shoulder, the bruised ribs, and the assorted bruises and cuts. Her chest literally ached with the fear that Axel wouldn't know those words had been spoken out of fear that she would have to watch her husband die and be left alone all over again.

Axel wouldn't believe she hated him. Would he?

Surely, he had to know that he was her everything. How many times had they said that to one another?

My man.
My woman.
My heart.
My life.

How badly Beth wished she could have one more moment with Axel to tell him how sorry she was for saying something that wasn't true. She knew he was trying to protect her the only way he could in what was a situation with limited options. Sure, she was angry that he would rather leave her alone than allow her the freedom death would have brought, but she didn't hate him.

"Don't hate you, Axel," she whispered into the growing darkness.

Already the thin layer of dirt covering her was enough to block out any warmth from the sun along with most of its light.

Ironically, Beth had always loved the earth. As a child, when she wasn't doing chores or being raped or beaten she was often outside in the garden. Tending to the vegetable gardens was the only chore she actually enjoyed. It had always been quiet out in the gardens, alone with the plants, there had been no one watching her, no one ready to yell abuse, no one just waiting to slap her or hit her.

Just her and nature.

Planting things, tending to them, and watching them grow, it had given her a sense of purpose, like she was worth more than being the family punching bag. She did that, her, alone, grew the food her family ate.

After Axel and his team had rescued her and invited her to live with them at the compound they were building, she'd made a vegetable garden there, too. She'd wanted to contribute, not be a complete burden, but it had wound up having the same therapeutic value the garden at her family's farm had. It gave her time to just be, without expectations, judgment, or fear of being hurt.

Now the thing she used to find peace was slowly suffocating the life out of her.

Sarah drove a bulldozer like she'd been doing so all her life, and it moved so much quicker than her damaged body could.

Although she had tried her best to survive, this time it wasn't enough. Her attempt at getting out of the hole had been thwarted, and now the dirt covering her was more than she could move on her own. Since nobody was there to help her, she had no choice but to be resigned to her fate.

The peace that had filled her earlier when she had refused to participate in the duel against her husband was gone. It had just ... disappeared.

It was easy to be brave about death when it was on her terms. But now, once again, she was being controlled by someone else, having their will forced on her. That made all the difference.

Beth didn't want to die there.

Not now.

Not alone.

Not while Axel thought she hated him.

The weight of the dirt as it continued to rain down on her was enough now that it hurt. As effectively as it was going to cut off her ability to breathe, it was also slowly crushing her. Each individual grain was tiny, immaterial, insubstantial. But together they were powerful, strong, unbeatable.

No longer could she do more than suck in a few small mouthfuls of air. Her body was held immobile, the pressure of the weight of the dirt against her bruised ribs caused agony to spread throughout her body. When she'd fallen earlier, she'd landed awkwardly, and her dislocated shoulder screamed in pain along with her ribs.

With her eyes closed and the dirt quickly covering her face, Beth was encased in darkness. A darkness so complete it permeated her very soul.

Death.

She was staring death in the face.

It waited in the darkness ready to finally claim her. It had waited a long time, but that wait was now almost over.

Mouth and nose completely covered in a thick layer of dirt, Beth could no longer find any air. No air meant no oxygen, no oxygen meant she slipped further away from this earth, from her husband.

Drawing the last little bit of air left into her lungs, Beth held her breath. It wouldn't buy her enough time to survive, but enough to send a silent wish up into the universe.

It owed her after the crummy life it had given her, and she prayed it delivered.

Please, Axel, know that I love you, that I never hated you, not even for a single second. Know that I fought to stay with you and that I'm sorry I failed. You gave me everything. Peace, happiness, joy, love. I wish I didn't have to leave you, but I don't have a choice. I love you, now and forever, whether I'm alive or dead, nothing can ever change that.

CHAPTER

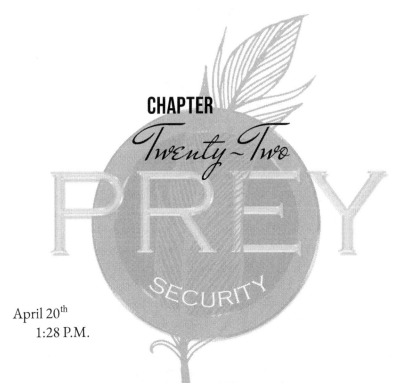

Twenty-Two

April 20th
1:28 P.M.

Pretending he wasn't panicking would be pointless.

Axe wasn't just panicking, he was pretty close to completely losing it.

Hiding it seemed pointless because he already knew without a shadow of a doubt that if any one of the eleven other men with him was in his position, they would be close to losing it, too. The Delta Team guys might all be single as far as he was aware, but he knew every man on his team was completely and utterly in love with the women they planned to spend the rest of their lives with.

If those women—hell, *when* those women had been in danger—needed them and they weren't there it would kill any one of them.

That was love.

It was hurting worse when it was the person you loved in trouble than when it was yourself.

All of a sudden Blade straightened, cocked his head, and looked further off down the corridor.

Without a word, he looked at his team, nodded once, and took off running.

"We gotta go," Steel said and not one to doubt Delta Team and their somewhat unbelievable talents, Axe took off after Blade.

They ran for what had to be a good half a mile before he heard it.

The sound of heavy machinery.

A bulldozer?

Why would someone be using a bulldozer?

Were they going to come out from the underground tunnel to find they were right next to a farm? Or a building site?

That didn't seem logical. Tomas had stayed under the radar for so long by being careful. Sure, it was a risk to be so close to Bravo Team's compound, but a calculated one since he knew nobody would be looking for him there.

Light filtered in, and Blade shoved through a partially open door only seconds before Axe. There was no farm out there, and no building site either. But there was a bulldozer, and it was being driven by Sarah.

There was no sign of Beth.

Frantically, he gave another visual sweep of the area, praying he was missing something and that Beth was tied up somewhere nearby.

But she wasn't.

There was just Sarah using a bulldozer to push dirt into what appeared to have been a large hole.

Why would the woman be doing that?

She'd made it out without anyone realizing she was gone. She could have been in the clear. So why had she decided to hang around and fill in a hole? And where was Beth?

Apparently catching sight of them as the rest of Bravo and Delta Teams came running out of the tunnel, Sarah gave what could only be described as a manic laugh. "You're too late. Perfect Beth is gone forever."

The hole.

The dirt.

It clicked

A grave.

From the size of it a mass grave.

Sarah had stayed because she didn't really care about getting away. She wasn't thinking calmly or rationally. She had a goal, and it wasn't to evade capture. It was why she'd killed Tomas, he was going to prevent her from getting what she really wanted.

"Perfect Beth got everything I should have had. Everyone cared about her and no one cared about me. Well, now she's dead and there's nothing you can do about it," Sarah squealed in delight.

Red rage filled his vision.

This woman might have once upon a time been a victim, but now she had killed an innocent woman.

His woman.

Before he had a chance to aim his weapon and pull the trigger, ending Sarah Sanders' life, someone else did it for him.

Dragon looked over at him. The man's unusual violet eyes locked onto his. "Beth's not dead," he said.

There was confidence in Dragon's voice, and Axe didn't waste time asking him how he could possibly know that. He simply turned to scan the mostly filled hole. There was no way to know where exactly Beth had been when Sarah began filling in the hole. Tracks circled the space, so it was obvious Sarah had been driving around for a while moving the dirt. Even with twelve of them, excavating the hole would take far too long.

Beth didn't have that kind of time.

Even if she was alive now, she couldn't last long buried under all this dirt.

All of a sudden, Lion sprung forward, bounding down the couple of feet into the hole and zeroing in on one specific area. "Here."

The one word spurred them all into action, and moments later, they were all down on their hands and knees shoving dirt aside in a desperate attempt to get to Beth. It didn't matter that the Delta Team guys had only met Beth a handful of times over the last six years, they were side by side with Bravo Team, the tension emanating from them the same as from his own team.

Despite the rumors surrounding these men, they were more than just killing machines, they were real men with big hearts.

"Got something," Steel called out, shoving away a little more dirt and holding up a pale hand.

Beth's hand. Even if he hadn't known it anywhere the simple gold wedding band and the engagement ring with the diamond Beth had always claimed was too big would have given it away.

"It's her," Axe said, shifting positions so he could take his wife's hand in his.

While he held her hand the others dug around it, slowly uncovering Beth. As they worked, he talked.

"Hey, wisp. It's me, it's Axel, I'm right here. I don't know if you can hear me, but if you can you hold on, okay? I know you're so tired of having to fight all the time, and I wish you weren't in a position where you have to do it again, but I need you to be strong one last time for me. I swear to you, wisp, that if you fight for me this last time, I will make sure you never have to again. I will protect you, keep you safe, and never let anyone hurt you. I promise you, Beth, so just fight for me, okay? Please, wisp, fight. I can't lose you. I can't. I need you, honey, more than you ever needed me."

"Got her head," Tank announced, brushing away enough dirt that her face became visible.

"I've got a pulse, but she's not breathing," Rock announced as he pressed two fingertips to Beth's dirt-streaked neck.

"We have to get her out," he said desperately.

Doubling down, it took the guys a couple of minutes to free Beth's body from the mound of dirt enough that they could lift her out. As soon as she was free, Axe shifted so he could gather his wife's limp body into his arms.

No one asked him to give her up so he could climb the couple of feet out of the hole, a few hands just rested on his back, steadying him as he carried Beth out of what would have been her grave.

Immediately dropping to his knees, he laid Beth out on the dirt-streaked grass and knelt beside her. While he grasped her chin, opening her mouth and using his fingers to scoop out the dirt that clogged her airways, Rock cleared her nose, and Delta Team's medic Voodoo poured water over Beth's eyes, using his sleeve to clear away the dirt that caked onto her eyelashes.

As soon as her airways were clear, Axe hunched over her. One hand pinched her nose closed, the other tilted her head back and her chin down, then he covered her mouth with his own and breathed into her.

One breath.

Then a second.

Pausing, he leaned over so his cheek was above her mouth.

There was no puff of air on his skin, and her chest didn't rise and fall as she took a breath.

"Still got a pulse, try again," Rock instructed.

Covering her mouth again, he did two more breaths before pausing to see if Beth would take a breath on her own.

She didn't.

"Pulse is getting weaker," Rock said.

"Come on, wisp," Axe pleaded. "Don't leave me, Beth. Come on, take a breath for me. You fought just as strong as you always do, now all you have to do is take one breath. After that first one the second will be so much easier, and the third easier still."

Another breath and another, and he stopped to check if she was breathing on her own, but she wasn't. Rock's head shake indicated her pulse was still getting weaker.

She was going to die.

Fade away.

Right in front of him.

Seconds.

They'd been too late getting to her by seconds.

If he'd asked for Beth sooner, noticed Sarah was gone quicker, ran faster down the tunnels, dug the dirt away from her more rapidly, he wouldn't be losing her.

Beside him, Voodoo nudged his shoulder. "Let me try."

It was on the tip of his tongue to refuse. If Beth was dying, he wanted her to at least go cradled in the arms of the man who loved her more than life itself.

But he'd heard some crazy stories about the lives Voodoo had saved.

So, he nodded and shifted slightly, reaching out to grasp one of Beth's hands.

Voodoo took the place he had vacated, and pinched Beth's nose closed, then pressed his lips to hers and breathed a huge breath into her. Somehow the second breath seemed to be even larger, and then they all heard it.

A sharp intake of air.

From Beth.

Voodoo didn't hesitate to move out of the way so Axe could be back at his wife's side. One hand palmed the back of her head, the other cradled her cheek. "Come on, wisp, just like that. Good girl, take another breath for me, honey."

Beth inhaled again.

And again.

And again.

A collective sigh of relief went up. Somehow Voodoo had performed another of his miracles, quite literally bringing Beth back from the brink of death.

Beth began to stir as consciousness returned along with her ability to breathe on her own.

"Don't open your eyes, wisp," he instructed, "they're still all dirty. Don't try to move, don't do anything, just rest and breathe, we'll get you to the hospital as soon as we can."

"Ambulance on the way," Thunder informed him.

"Hear that, wisp? An ambulance is coming. All you have to do until then is just rest and breathe."

Axe shifted so he was sitting and pulled his wife into his lap. She was still limp, but her chest continued to rise and fall, and Rock smiled when he pressed fingers to her neck to check her pulse.

Ignoring his command for her to rest, Beth whispered something so softly he couldn't make out the words. Whatever it was seemed important to her though, because a trembling hand raised to grab at his shoulder.

Leaning down he held his ear against her lips.

"Never hated you," came the softly murmured words. "Love you."

Tears began to stream down his cheeks. That's what she was worried about right now? That he might think she'd meant it when she said she'd hate him for choosing her life over his own?

"I know that, wisp," he assured her. "I knew you didn't mean it, knew you could never hate me. I love you, too. More than anything in the world. My sweet, strong, beautiful wife. My life."

~

April 21st
        3:38 A.M.

Dirt.
        Everywhere.
        In her eyes
        Her mouth.
        Up her nose.
        It pressed down on every inch of her body rendering her immobile.
        Trapped.
        Suffocating.
        Couldn't breathe.
        Dying.
        Axel.
        Hate.
        Love.
        Beth was going to die with her husband thinking she hated him.
        No.
        Had to fight.
        Only she couldn't.
        If you couldn't move then you couldn't fight.
        If you couldn't fight then you died.
        "I'm sorry, Axel," she murmured.
        "Beth, wake up. Now!"
        Weighted down as they were, her lungs could no longer inflate with air.
        "Beth! Come on, wisp, wake up for me."
        "Sorry, Axel."
        "Wake now!"

Her body was suddenly yanked out of the dirt that was slowly smothering the life out of her and her eyes snapped open.

No dirt.

No brown.

Only white.

Hospital.

Not in the mass grave surrounded by dead bodies, slowly being buried alive.

Safe.

Rescued.

Axel had come for her again.

Saved her life again.

And now he had to watch her fall apart all over again.

Bursting into noisy sobs, she tried to tell him how sorry she was. For everything. The horrible words she'd said, putting them both in danger by running away instead of staying with her husband and his team, for not being strong enough to survive, for not being strong enough to be okay now.

When Axel dragged her into his arms, holding her in an embrace that was one millimeter shy of crushing, her tears only grew louder and messier.

"I'm sorry," she sobbed. "This is all my fault. I should have trusted you to help me when I had amnesia, maybe if I had, I would have gotten my memories back earlier and you wouldn't have had to make a deal to take your own life for mine. And I shouldn't have run away when I was scared of losing you. I just keep making bad choices. You almost died because of me. I can't ever forgive myself for that. I wish I could take it all back, but most of all I wish I could take back that I said I hated you. I don't hate you. I don't. I love you. I love you so much."

Panic was swamping her, and Beth grabbed at her husband trying to pull Axel closer, wishing she could merge their souls together so he would know how badly she regretted those horrible words she'd thrown at him.

Somewhere nearby other voices spoke, but she couldn't make out what they were saying.

Didn't care what they were saying.

All she cared about was making sure her husband knew how much she loved him.

It was hard to see through the tears blurring her eyes, and the sound of her weeping pretty much drowned out anything else.

The feel of her husband's hands on her, stroking her back, smoothing locks of hair off her wet cheeks, stroking her skin, caressing it, those touches were the only thing keeping her grounded when her whirlwind of emotions wanted to pick her up, toss her around, then slam her back down.

Soft kisses rained down on her face. Forehead, temples, cheeks, the tip of her nose, even her chin. When firm lips pressed against hers, kissing her until her crying had no choice but to cease, Beth felt the worst of her panic begin to fade.

"I love you, Beth. Always. Forever. I'm not angry with you for struggling to deal with amnesia. You literally weren't yourself. You didn't remember me or know how much I loved you. You had nothing solid to hold onto. I don't blame you for running when you were scared, you were trying to do what you thought was best even if you were wrong. Of course I wish things were different, but that doesn't mean I blame you, am angry with you, or thought for one second you meant it when you said you hated me."

"I wish I could take it back," she whimpered. "I want to take it back."

There was so much tenderness in his eyes, his touch as he swept a hand across her cheek, and in his voice when he spoke that it started a fresh wave of tears. "I know you do, honey. But you don't have to worry about it. I never believed it for a second. You hear me? Not a single second."

How badly she wanted to believe that was true.

But doubt was smothering her just as the dirt had done hours ago.

"I love you," she said, trying to infuse the depths of emotion behind those few small words.

"Wisp, I love you too." Along with the sincerity in his voice and his expression, there was a heavy dose of pain.

She was hurting him.

Again.

Because her stupid emotions were getting the best of her.

Just like they'd done when she escaped from Tomas and Sarah the first time. This time her mind might not have shut down on her to protect her, but she was still hurting her husband, the man she would do anything for, who she loved more than life itself.

"I love you," she said again. How many times would she have to say those words before she finally believed she had undone the damage of saying the opposite?

Would that ever happen?

Or would those words, spoken in fear, haunt her for the rest of her life?

"I love you," Beth repeated as Axel shifted on the bed so they weren't kneeling facing one another but he was settled against the pillows with her draped across his chest.

"I love you, too, Beth. Nothing has changed. Not a single thing."

Maybe not for him, but for her everything had changed.

She'd said words she couldn't take back and couldn't seem to let it go no matter how many times Axel assured her he had never believed them and still loved her.

"What's going to convince you that I love you more today than I did the day I met you?" Axel asked, his large hand smoothing her hair over and over, his touch slowly soothing her.

"I don't know," she whispered, wishing she was strong enough to pull herself back together. "I wish I could marry you all over again."

"Then that's what we'll do."

That surprised a laugh out of her. "We're already married, don't think you can marry someone again unless you get divorced first, and no way am I letting you divorce me just so we can have another ceremony. I'll be okay." Somehow, Beth still managed to believe that. It defied logic after everything she had been through but still, she felt deep down inside that with Axel's love and her Prey family around her, she would find her way back.

"We'll renew our vows."

"Renew our vows?"

"Sure, why not? It's the closest we can get to marrying again, and it will remind you that I have never for one second regretted falling in love with you and making you my wife. We'll do something special. Magical. With Baranov dead, the targets on my back and the rest of my team are gone. We don't have to keep to the shadows anymore. We'll go somewhere, a castle maybe, one that's half in ruins, to show you that when you think you're broken down, beaten down, that things will never improve, beauty can grow from those ruins."

Axel was sounding more excited by his idea by the second, and like it was contagious, Beth could also feel a spark of excitement flicker to life inside her.

"We busted up Tank and Tillie's wedding again," Axel continued, "we'll take them with us, they can say their vows for the first time while we repeat them. Hell, we'll take the whole team. Rock and Ariel are engaged anyway, Scorpion wants to marry Jessica before the baby comes, and Panther wants to do the same with Elle. And we all know Trick was just waiting for the perfect time to propose to Stephanie, if he would just hurry up and realize there is no such thing as the perfect time, that every second is precious then they can join in. We'll marry as a team, show the world that Bravo Team is stronger together, that we're a family that nothing and no one can break up."

"I ... like the idea," Beth said, her lips curling into the first smile she'd had since being dug out of the mass grave that was supposed to become her own grave.

"Then it's done. But I don't want to wait long. I can't wait to shout from the rooftops that you're my wife, that of all the men in the world you chose me to love forever."

"May Day," she said immediately. "May first, halfway between the spring equinox and summer solstice, because our relationship is still sweet and fresh like spring, but we're heading into the best years of our marriage, the summer."

"Perfect."

"You're perfect." Beth dropped a kiss to her husband's lips. "My man."

"My woman."

"My heart."

"My life."

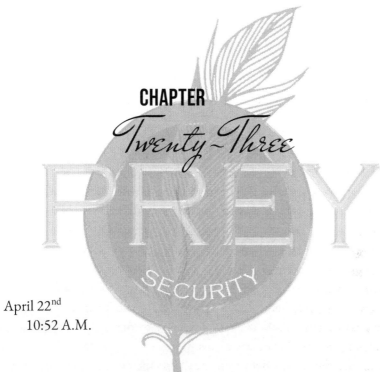

CHAPTER
Twenty~Three

April 22nd
    10:52 A.M.

The last forty-eight hours had been hard.

Not harder than the hours proceeding them when he and Beth had been at the mercy of Tomas Butcher and Sarah Sanders, but for Axe, watching his wife struggle emotionally was every bit as hard as watching her literally fight for her life.

It wasn't that he had expected Beth to regain consciousness after almost being buried alive and act like nothing had happened. His wife was strong, but nobody was *that* strong. The reactions she was having, the nightmares, the panic attacks, the random meltdowns into a sobbing mess, and her constant need to reiterate that she was sorry for saying she hated him and telling him how much she loved him, were all perfectly normal.

His faith in his wife wasn't shaken. There were now more physical scars littering her body, and many more psychological ones, but Axe knew she would once again rise from the ashes.

Beth was too strong not to.

He wasn't the only one intent on showing her that she wasn't alone. All the Bravo Team guys and their soon-to-be wives—all of them had agreed to the joint wedding in Scotland—had been around. The Oswald siblings and their families had been, too. Alpha Team and Artemis Team had been there, the retired SEALs who ran the west coast offices as well. And he had seen more of Delta Team in the last twenty-four hours than in all the years they had worked for Prey.

No one was going to let Beth think for one moment that she was still all alone in the world. Just because her biological family hadn't loved her or cared about her didn't mean she had no family. In fact, she had the biggest, toughest, most loyal and caring family a person could ask for, not just at her back, but at her sides and in front of her, too. Surrounding her in a bubble of love and support.

Now she had been discharged from the hospital, and they were about to arrive back home. On top of almost dying, Beth had been diagnosed with a concussion from the head injury Sarah had inflicted when she'd knocked Beth out, her dislocated shoulder had been dislocated all over again, likely by being dragged through the tunnels, and she had two cracked ribs. Then there was the irritation to her eyes, nose, mouth, and throat from the dirt, and the risk of infection from dirt getting into her open head wound. Pumped full of antibiotics and painkillers, his wife was as excited to get home as he was to get her there.

"I thought I would never get to see this place again," Beth whispered as he opened the gates to the compound and drove through them, closing them behind them.

"There was a moment when I was sure neither of us were to come home," he admitted. Axe knew that what his wife needed right now was not for him to pretend he wasn't every bit as affected by their ordeal as she was, it was for him to be open.

Once already they had made the mistake of not just telling one another what they needed, and he had no intention of repeating it.

From here on out, openness was going to be the most important ingredient in their marriage.

Reaching over to take his hand, Beth squeezed his fingers tightly. "I know you've told me a hundred times already I don't have to keep telling you how sorry I am that I said I hated you, but I need to tell you again that I love you."

While Beth had been sleeping earlier, he'd talked with Piper Hamilton-Eden, Prey's on-staff psychiatrist. She had told him to let Beth apologize as many times as she felt she needed to, not to try to stop her from expressing herself, and to just keep doing what he'd been doing and assure her that he had never believed she hated him. It seemed like simple advice, and while, of course, he wanted to hear that his wife loved him, he hated that she kept saying it because she was afraid if she didn't, he might not believe it.

Turning their hands over so hers rested on his, he shot her a smile as he drove down the driveway. "I'm never going to want my wife to stop telling me she loves me, and I'm never going to stop telling you how much I love you."

"You were willing to die for me, I know how much you love me," Beth murmured as a stray tear snuck out and rolled down her pale cheek.

"And you were willing to live for me. You fought. Again. For your life and for mine. You killed Baranov to keep me alive, and you fought as hard as you could not to leave me."

"I will always fight for you, for us," Beth said solemnly.

"Ditto."

Her cute little nose scrunched up. "Ditto is a weird word."

Axe laughed at that, and it felt so good to laugh, to feel the freedom of knowing his wife was no longer being hunted, to have her hand in his, to smell her sweet scent filling the car. If she wasn't injured and they both weren't ravished by exhaustion he'd take her inside, carry her up to bed, and show her with his body as well as his words how much he loved and adored her.

"Home sweet home," he said as he pulled up outside the cabin.

"Is this still going to be our home?" Beth asked. "You guys built this place because of Leonid Baranov painting targets on your backs. Now he's dead, you don't have to hide out on a remote compound anymore."

"Do you want to leave?"

"No." The word was uttered immediately and emphatically. "I love living here. I love the peace and quiet, I love the beauty and tranquility of nature, and I love having our family all around us. I want to stay right here, but if you want to move then I want to be wherever you are."

"I want to stay right here. I talked with the guys and offered to help them set up somewhere else if they wanted to move. Every single one of them, and their women, said that while the compound might have been built to keep everyone safe, it's home, and none of them could imagine living anywhere else. This will always be Bravo Team's home."

Beth relaxed back into her seat, obviously having been worried about it. "Perfect. I love this place, it's the first home I ever had and I want to live here until the day I die. Die a very old woman," she added.

"You ready to head inside?" he asked, turning off the engine.

"Yep. Can't wait to be free of the never-ending hustle and bustle of the hospital. All I want to do is curl up in your arms, light a fire in the fireplace even though it's much too warm, curl up under a blanket, drink hot chocolate, watch the flames, feel your arms around me, and just enjoy being alive. Being free."

"Then that's what we'll do."

Undoing his seatbelt, Axe got out of the car, rounded it, and opened Beth's door. She was waiting for him, and when he captured her chin between his thumb and forefinger and tilted her face up so he could kiss her, she kissed him back with the same sense of love, peace, and freedom that he felt.

They were no longer being hunted.

Their enemy was dead.

The rest of their lives were free to be lived however they pleased.

Wanting his wife close, Axe scooped her into his arms, bumping the car door closed with his hip so he could carry Beth into their home. A home he hoped one day soon might be filled with the sound of childish giggles and little feet. They had never talked in detail about starting their own family, but he knew it was what both of them wanted, they had just been waiting for the time to be right.

Somehow, he managed to unlock the cabin door without having to set Beth down, and the moment he flung it open a chorus of voices called out.

"Welcome home!"

Both he and Beth startled at the sound. Some special forces soldier he was, he hadn't been giving their surroundings the least drop of attention, it was all for the wife he held in his arms. Their cabin was filled, standing room only, by every member of Prey and their families. Even Athena Team who rarely went into the field were there, and Charlie Team who hadn't been able to help with taking Tomas Butcher down since they had been on a more personal op.

Plates of food covered every available surface, balloons filled with helium made the ceiling invisible, children giggled and darted about through the maze of adults, and everyone was smiling and laughing. It was chaotic but it was perfect.

It was family.

But it wasn't what Beth had wanted.

She'd wanted peace and quiet, not loud and crazy, and whatever his wife wanted she got.

"Want me to tell them to leave?" he whispered in her ear as the crowd of people surged toward them.

"Not on your life," Beth whispered back. "This is much better. This is family. This is love."

Axe couldn't agree more.

∼

May 1st
    8:29 P.M.

Magic.

Beth couldn't think of a more perfect word to describe this day.

Somehow, Axel and the rest of the guys had managed to pull this whole thing off in just a matter of days.

Not even two weeks had passed since Leonid Baranov, Tomas Butcher, and Sarah Sanders had been killed, and she and Bravo Team had been freed of the shackles that had bound them for six long years. Axel had declared that he and the other guys were going to arrange everything, all she and the other women had to do was organize their dresses, hair, and makeup.

At first, she had been a little skeptical that six alpha warriors could pull off a wedding, but she shouldn't have been. No one could have done a better job. Axel's money had certainly got everything done, he hadn't cared what the cost was, he wanted this day to be perfect for her and his friends.

And it was.

Reminiscent of Ross' wedding to Emily in Friends—her all-time favorite TV show—instead of an old church, they were in the ruins of what was once a castle. There were enough remaining stones to show the beauty and splendor of the building when it had been in operation. There was a rawness to the landscape. Unlike in her favorite TV show, they weren't in the middle of one of the biggest cities in the world, surrounding them were wide open spaces, grassy heather moors, and in the distance, a line of trees leading to a forest.

There was freedom here as well as beauty.

Add in the setting of the sun as all six brides had walked down the aisle, and now the lingering dusk light melded with the thousands of flickering candles to create the most gorgeous glow. Beth had no idea how the candles were all staying lit in the soft wafts of wind, but she'd seen people darting about relighting them so she suspected that Axel and the guys had assigned certain people the job of keeping them lit.

Sticking with the May Day theme, garlands of flowers were everywhere, and a stunning Maypole stood behind where the minister was officiating.

All the other couples had gone first, Beth had insisted on that since they were all getting married for the first time while she and Axel were renewing their vows. Rock and Ariel had gone first since they had known each other the longest, then the others had decided to go in order of when they had met. Tank and Tillie had been second, followed by Scorpion and Jessica, both of whom couldn't seem to stop touching her small baby bump. Next up had been Trick and Stephanie, and then Panther and Elle, with Andy and Ruthie standing by their sides had joined their little family together.

Now it was her and Axel's turn.

All eyes were on them, and Beth would have felt self-conscious if she wasn't so excited and nervous to remarry the man of her dreams.

Because her husband had insisted, she wasn't wearing the same simple white dress she had when they had first married. Axel wanted her to pick out the dress of her dreams and feel like the princess she was to him. Although she'd been a little reluctant at first, she'd fallen in love with the prettiest dress she'd ever laid eyes on.

Beads and lace on the bodice, ruffles of silk cascading down from the satin bow at her waist, hair piled on top of her head in an intricate mass of curls dotted with small diamonds, with a diamond shaped into a heart at the base of her throat, and matching diamond earrings, Beth *did* feel like a princess standing here in front of everybody she loved.

All of Prey was there, from the youngest to the oldest, no team had been sent into the field, they were all there to help Bravo Team celebrate this very special day.

Standing before the minister, her hands cradled in Axel's, the twinkling lights all around them, family there to support them, she couldn't be happier. This couldn't be more perfect, but what made it the most perfect of all was the man smiling down at her with so much love in his eyes she felt it.

Actually, felt it like a physical caress.

Caressing her body, her heart, her mind, and her soul.

Touching her down deep in places that had been so badly damaged they shouldn't ever be able to heal.

But heal they did.

Because of this man.

"Axel and Beth have prepared their own vows to speak to one another this evening," the minister announced to the gathered throng.

Focusing all his attention on her, Axel began to speak. "I grew up privileged. Everything I wanted, I got. At least material things. My whole future could have been mapped out for me. Working long hours in an office, safe, protected, in charge of a vast empire. It would have been so easy, I could have lived in the lap of luxury and never had to worry about a single thing. But something was missing. Purpose. I had no purpose there. I wasn't making a difference. So, I walked away from that life believing there was more I was supposed to do with my life. That I was supposed to make a difference somehow."

The hands holding hers, with thumbs brushing softly across the inside of her wrists, were mesmerizing, and she waited with bated breath to see what he was going to say next.

"I thought the difference I was supposed to make was big. I thought I was supposed to save the world, save thousands of lives, kill dozens of terrorists, but I was wrong. As soon as I laid eyes on you, I knew. My purpose wasn't big, it was small. It wasn't a thousand people I was supposed to save, it was one. It wasn't a dozen terrorists I was supposed to kill it was one man who hurt the woman I love. You were mine from that very first second, I knew it. I didn't understand it, but I knew and trusted in that feeling. Never once have I regretted trusting those instincts."

When he reached out and touched the pad of a thumb to her cheek Beth was surprised to find she was crying.

Happy tears though.

"My love for you has grown as I've seen you face your fears, learn so much about yourself and the world, and be so very brave. That's what I love the most about you. Yes, I love your beauty, I love your big, caring heart, I love your strength, strength that would put any warrior to shame. Because you are a warrior. The very definition of the word. Your bravery knows no bounds. It hasn't been an easy journey, but you have gotten up every day and faced that journey even when most would have just given up. And that is why I could never love anyone more than I love my sweet, beautiful, strong, brave Beth. My wife, my heart, my soul, my life. My everything."

If she'd had any doubts about Axel still being able to love her when she'd said such horrible words to him, they evaporated.

Like a wisp of smoke.

Just ... gone.

When the minister looked at her and nodded, Beth drew in a breath and spoke, not to their family watching them, but to this man, who loved her so very much. "Lucky. I feel lucky. I know it's crazy, what I've lived through has been horrific, and maybe I should mark myself the unluckiest person alive, but I haven't, I don't. Any team could have been there that day to rescue me from that house of horrors, but it wasn't. It was you. In that instant, my life changed. I didn't know love existed, I'd never seen it before. All I knew was that there was something different about you."

How very glad she was that she had trusted in her own feelings.

"I was scared to trust you because all I knew of men was that they hurt you. But you were so gentle with me, you taught me what gentleness was. You taught me tenderness, you taught me trust, you taught me faith, and you taught me love. I would be lost without you. But I'm not without you and I'm not lost. I can never be lost again because our souls are tied together. Once, all I knew was loneliness, now all I know is family. You, your team who adopted me and treated me like I was one of their own from the beginning, the wonderful women they've fallen in love with, and everyone at Prey. I used to think family was a terrible word, one laced with pain and suffering, now it's the most precious word in the universe. You, Axel Lindon, didn't just give me yourself and your love, you gave me a family, a place to belong, and one day soon I hope we can have our very own little family. I love you. Forever. Without reservation and conditions. You're mine and I'm yours."

"With those beautiful words I now pronounce you all over again husband and wife," the minister announced.

Taking the ring, with a simple gold bow on it, Axel slipped it onto the ring finger on her right hand. The bow symbolized that they were tied together forever, and she would cherish wearing it.

"Now you may kiss your bride."

At the minister's words, Axel gently dipped her back and pressed his mouth to hers, sealing their renewal of vows with a kiss.

Cheers and clapping sounded from the gathered Prey crowd, and as they walked hand in hand through the castle ruins, they were surrounded by so much love it made her heart swell. Everyone hugged her, offering their congratulations and joy, and by the time they reached the doors to the castle, she realized she no longer felt an instinctive need to stiffen and pull away when someone touched her.

Family.

Love.

The darkness of her past could no longer touch her through the light shined upon her by the people who had become her family.

As long as she had Axel by her side she would never be alone again.

CHAPTER
Twenty~Four

May 1st
   2:09 A.M.

As much as he didn't want the magic to end, Axe also couldn't wait to get his wife alone.

Not that he had any intention of hurrying her.

The smile on her face was everything, and the peace in her eyes was even better. He would bet anything that she wouldn't be apologizing again for saying she hated him. Although he was looking forward to hearing her tell him that she loved him, that he could listen to all day, every day, and never get bored of hearing it.

Beth was giggling as she and Cooper Charleston, team leader for Prey's Charlie Team, came over to where he was standing in a quiet corner, enjoying the magical atmosphere of the castle ruins, and the joy on everyone's faces as they danced well into the night. The kids had mostly fallen asleep and were curled up on chairs dotted throughout the ruins, but none of the adults seemed ready to call it a night yet.

Guess he'd have to wait a little longer to get his wife to the hotel and naked in the bed.

"Coop has to go, something important came up," Beth told him as she took the hand he held out as she approached.

Maybe it was weird considering it was their renewal of vows, but Beth had spent more time dancing with everyone else than she had with him, and it didn't bother him in the least. Other than the Charlie Team and Delta Team guys, everyone else was happily married, and the men on those teams were like brothers. This was Beth's family, always would be even if for some reason they weren't married, and he wanted her to enjoy her day with the people who loved her.

Besides, the smile on her face and the pure, unadulterated joy as she was spun around the makeshift dancefloor would have made it worth it even if he hadn't liked the idea of her dancing with other men.

"Thought maybe you'd like to take your wife for a spin," Cooper said. Although the man's smile was genuine, something in his gaze told Axe this wasn't just something that had popped up. Given what he knew about Charlie Team—which was comprised almost exclusively of biological brothers—he could guess what the something was and knew it was more important than hanging around at a wedding party.

When he saw that the other Charlie Team guys had also said their goodbyes and were waiting near the door for Cooper, he met the other man's gaze. "Good luck. Hope you finally find the answers you need."

Nodding in acknowledgment, Cooper leaned down to kiss Beth's cheek. "I'm glad to see you so happy, you deserve it more than any other person I know. Enjoy the rest of your night, sweetheart."

"Want to dance, wisp?" he asked when they were alone.

"Well, maybe just once, then what I really want is you, alone, naked, and in bed," she whispered, then giggled.

Axe groaned. "Honey, you can't say things like that to me while we're surrounded by our family."

She just giggled again. "I think everybody here knows that we're going to be having sex later. Pretty sure even the already married couples are going to be heading straight to their hotels and getting naked and into bed."

Couldn't argue with that.

Love was definitely in the air tonight.

Guiding his wife onto the dance floor, he tucked her against him, and they began to sway to the music.

"You know who's a *really* good dancer?" Beth asked.

"Who?"

"Thunder. You'd never guess to look at him."

He couldn't argue with that either. The Delta Team man was huge and looked like he'd be much better at stomping and clomping than dancing.

"If you didn't know them, those guys would be scary," Beth said. "I wish I knew a way to help them."

"Think they have to figure out their own path," he said. There were so many rumors about those guys it was hard to know what was truth and what was fiction, but if even a small percentage of it was true, those men had reason to be angry. Their lives had been played with and he hoped they were eventually able to get the justice they deserved.

Dancing with his wife was the perfect ending to a perfect wedding, candles still flickered, the sweet scent of flowers hung in the air, soft voices chattered, and the moon and a sky full of diamonds shined down on them.

Perfect as it was, Axe was ready for alone time with the woman he loved.

"Ready to get out of here?" he asked.

"Thought you'd never ask."

It took them a solid thirty minutes to say goodbye to everybody and thank them for dropping everything to fly across the world for a wedding, and another hour to drive to the five-star hotel he'd chosen.

The suite was huge, and Beth's gasp as they entered it reminded him that she hadn't grown up in his world. Not just in his wealthy, privileged world, but not even in a regular person's world. She'd stayed in his old place with him after being discharged from the hospital following her initial rescue, but then she'd lived only at the compound. With the targets on their backs, and Beth's need to feel safe, they'd never ventured far from it. This was her first time traveling—excluding being sold to Leonid Baranov and taken out of the country—and her first stay in a five-star hotel.

While he fully intended to drag their honeymoon out, taking her all over the United Kingdom and Europe before they headed back home, tonight he didn't want to play tourist, he just wanted to make sweet love to his beautiful wife.

As soon as he locked the hotel suite door, he had her in his arms. "You are absolutely stunning in this dress, you look like a sexy angel dropped down from heaven, but I still can't wait to get you out of it," he whispered as his lips trailed a line of kisses up the column of Beth's neck.

She shivered, and a breathy sigh escaped as she tilted her head to give him better access. "Mmm, naked sounds good."

Carrying her through to the bedroom as he continued to nuzzle her neck, when they got in there, Axe set his wife on her feet and then moved to stand behind her. Inch by inch he eased the zipper down, exposing soft, creamy skin. There were old scars there, thin white lines that were easily visible, and as much as he wished he could erase them, erase all the pain she had suffered, they were a testament to her strength and bravery.

They were part of what made her the woman he had fallen in love with.

When the zip was undone, he eased the material over her hips and let it fall to her feet in puffs of silk and chiffon. She wasn't wearing a bra, just a scrap of lace covering the part of her he couldn't wait to touch, and taste, and bury himself in.

"So beautiful," he murmured. His hands spanned her waist, and he lifted her out of the pile of wedding dress, setting her down before him. With the heart diamond at the base of her neck, the diamonds scattered throughout her hair, the white heels that made her legs look like they went for miles, and the delicate lace thong, she was the sexiest bride that had ever existed.

"Hurry up, Axel, I need you to touch me," Beth whimpered as he raked his gaze over her.

"Not as much as I need to touch you," he told her as he guided her backward and onto the bed. Once he had her laid out before him like a delicious snack he couldn't wait to devour, he climbed onto the bed and nudged her legs apart so he could settle between them. "You know there's something I've always wanted to try."

"What?" Beth asked, looking up at him through heavy-lidded eyes.

"This." Grabbing the scrap of lace, he gave a hard tug and ripped the thin material from her body, making Beth give a breathy laugh.

"That was way too sexy," she told him. "But not sexier than seeing your head between my legs."

"Not sexier than this either." Touching the lightest of kisses to her opening, he then swept his tongue across her center and blew a soft breath. The puff of air against her wet flesh made her shudder, and he liked knowing he could affect his wife in the smallest of ways, with the barest of touches.

Later, he'd take his time and draw out her pleasure, but not this time.

This time, he was burning to feel his wife come around him, share that journey with her as they would share every journey from here on out.

Coating his fingers in her wetness, Axe slipped it inside her as his mouth closed around her bud. While he worked her bundle of nerves with his mouth and his tongue, and his fingers stroked deep inside her, Beth's hands came down to clutch at his head, tangling in his hair as he feasted on her.

He could feel the orgasm building inside her as his fingers grazed the spot inside her that Beth had at one point been convinced didn't exist, he could feel her internal muscles begin to quiver.

Her head fell back on her pillow, the fingers in his hair tightened their grip, her breathing grew faster, more ragged, and then his name fell from her lips as pleasure exploded inside her. Not for a second did he let up, thrusting his fingers, sucking hard, flicking her bud with his tongue through her pleasure, dragging it out for as long as he could.

"Axel," she murmured as he shoved off his clothes.

"Yeah, wisp?"

"I made you a doctor's appointment for when we get back home."

Caught off-guard, he froze with one leg in the air, mid-removing his pants. "For the reason I think?"

A sweet giggle tumbled from her lips. "If you think it's for reversing a vasectomy then yes."

"You're ready for a baby?"

"I am. Are you?"

"Yeah, I'm ready. You're sure?" he asked as he quickly took off the last of his clothing.

"Never been more sure of anything in the world. I love you, I love our family, and I'm ready to start our own little family with you."

Kneeling on the bed, Axe ran a hand over Beth's smooth, flat stomach. "I can't wait to see this rounded with our baby growing inside you."

Stretching out above his wife, he kissed her as he slid inside her. She was hot, tight, wet, and perfect, and he quickly set a steady rhythm. One hand balanced his weight so he didn't crush her, his other touched her where their bodies joined, starting a fresh wave of pleasure inside her.

His own pleasure was quickly mounting.

It grew bigger and bigger until it was too big to contain.

The second Beth's internal muscles clamped around him as her orgasm hit, Axe let go and allowed his own to consume him.

"My man," she whispered against his lips.

"My woman."

"My heart."

"My life."

His everything.

Will Cooper Charleston find the answers he needs to finally clear his mother's name in Egypt or will this be another dead end? Find out in the first book in the action packed and emotionally charged Prey Security: Charlie Team series!

Deceptive Lies (Prey Security: Charlie Team #1)

Also by Jane Blythe

Detective Parker Bell Series

A SECRET TO THE GRAVE

WINTER WONDERLAND

DEAD OR ALIVE

LITTLE GIRL LOST

FORGOTTEN

Count to Ten Series

ONE

TWO

THREE

FOUR

FIVE

SIX

BURNING SECRETS

SEVEN

EIGHT

NINE

TEN

Broken Gems Series

CRACKED SAPPHIRE

CRUSHED RUBY

FRACTURED DIAMOND

SHATTERED AMETHYST

SPLINTERED EMERALD

SALVAGING MARIGOLD

River's End Rescues Series

COCKY SAVIOR

SOME REGRETS ARE FOREVER

SOME FEARS CAN CONTROL YOU

SOME LIES WILL HAUNT YOU

SOME QUESTIONS HAVE NO ANSWERS

SOME TRUTH CAN BE DISTORTED

SOME TRUST CAN BE REBUILT

SOME MISTAKES ARE UNFORGIVABLE

Candella Sisters' Heroes Series

LITTLE DOLLS

LITTLE HEARTS

LITTLE BALLERINA

Storybook Murders Series

NURSERY RHYME KILLER

FAIRYTALE KILLER

FABLE KILLER

Saving SEALs Series

Prey Security Series

Prey Security: Alpha Team Series

Prey Security: Artemis Team Series

IVORY'S FIGHT

PEARL'S FIGHT

LACEY'S FIGHT

OPAL'S FIGHT

Prey Security: Bravo Team Series

VICIOUS SCARS

RUTHLESS SCARS

BRUTAL SCARS

CRUEL SCARS

BURIED SCARS

WICKED SCARS

Prey Security: Athena Team Series

FIGHTING FOR SCARLETT

FIGHTING FOR LUCY

FIGHTING FOR CASSIDY

Prey Security: Charlie Team Series

DECEPTIVE LIES

Christmas Romantic Suspense Series

CHRISTMAS HOSTAGE

CHRISTMAS CAPTIVE

CHRISTMAS VICTIM

YULETIDE PROTECTOR

YULETIDE GUARD

About the Author

USA Today bestselling author Jane Blythe writes action-packed romantic suspense and military romance featuring protective heroes and heroines who are survivors. One of Jane's most popular series includes Prey Security, part of Susan Stoker's OPERATION ALPHA world! Writing in that world alongside authors such as Janie Crouch and Riley Edwards has been a blast, and she looks forward to bringing more books to this genre, both within and outside of Stoker's world. When Jane isn't binge-reading she's counting down to Christmas and adding to her 250+ teddy bear collection!

To connect and keep up to date please visit any of the following

Made in the USA
Monee, IL
13 August 2024

63811335R00139